Christmas in Castleby

J.M. Simpson

Also by J.M. Simpson, available on Amazon.

The Castleby Series
Sea State
Sea Change
Sea Shaken
Sea Haven
Sea Rift

Twitter @JMSimpsonauthor
Instagram @JMSimpsonauthor

Copyright ©J.M. Simpson 2024

The right of J.M. Simpson to be identified as the author of the work has been asserted by her in accordance with the Copyright, Designs and Patents Act 1988. All rights reserved. No part of this publication may be reproduced, stored, or transmitted, into any retrieval system, in any form, or by any means (electronic, mechanical, photocopying, recording or otherwise) without the prior written permission of the publisher. Any person who does any unauthorised act in relation to this publication may be liable to criminal prosecution and civil claims for damages.

This is a work of fiction. Any references to real people, living or dead, real events, businesses, organisations and localities are intended only to give the fiction a sense of reality and authenticity. All names, characters, places, and incidents are either the product of the author's imagination or are used fictitiously, and their resemblance, if any, to real-life counterparts is entirely coincidental.

This book was written in its entirety by a human and has no artificial intelligence content.

Cover design copyright ©J.M Simpson 2024

ISBN: 9798339556039

Imprint: Independently published.

CHAPTER 1

He stood on the motorway bridge, the cars below him whizzing by in a blur of white and red lights. The sound deafening, like a loud roaring buzz. A bizarre soundtrack of the chorus of Slade's 'Merry Xmas Everybody' played in his mind on constant repeat. He was tired; so very tired. Drowsily, he scanned the traffic. Searching. Fear settled in; he knew what was going to happen. He'd seen this a thousand times. He felt his heart thumping. Felt the dread he always felt. He had to warn them; had to tell them. Then he saw it. The car he'd been searching for. Frantically, he waved his arms in huge movements trying to attract the driver's attention. He screamed to warn them. Yelled until his throat was hoarse. But no words came. He felt helplessness and despair. He felt tears on his face. He heard knocking. Louder. Too loud. Drowning out the noise. WAKE UP!

Forty-year-old Griffin Jones awoke with a start, drawing in a deep breath. The knocking continued. *What the bloody hell was that?*

He realised it was someone banging on his car window. He blinked, trying to focus. The knocking got louder.

'Hello?' An annoyed female voice. 'You can't park there. There's a delivery coming.'

Griffin opened an eye. Shit. He was in his car. He'd fallen asleep. He'd arrived in Castleby in the early hours, starving hungry. He'd driven down from Newcastle in driving rain and almost zero visibility and when he'd arrived, all he'd wanted was a hot drink and some food. He remembered Maggie's cafe always used to be open early, so he'd driven there to wait and had clearly fallen asleep. He'd not been able to face going to his mother's house. It had been shut up for years, and he had no idea what sort of state it was in.

'Hello?' The window was tapped again. Griffin blinked rapidly to try and wake himself up.

'OK, OK, I'm going,' he called. 'Sorry.'

He buzzed the window down, peering out, blinking in the harsh light.

'Sorry, I'm going.'

'As I live and breathe. Griffin Jones is that you?'

Griffin focused on the person with the voice. '*Maggie*? Jesus, are you *still* here?'

'They'll carry me out in a box. Now get out here and give a girl a hug.'

'I'd hardly call you a girl, Maggie,' he said mildly. He climbed out of the car, eyeing her in one of her tight T-shirts that proclaimed Maggie's Beach Cafe had the best grub in town.

'Oh, stop it,' she tittered, enveloping him into a perfume and hairspray infused hug. It had been a while since Griffin had received a hug from anyone, and he found himself strangely tearful. He hugged her back tightly.

She drew back and inspected him.

'Still absolutely bloody drop-dead gorgeous. You home for good my love?'

Griffin blinked back the tears. 'I'm not sure where that is any more, to be honest,' he croaked.

'I was sorry to hear about your mum,' Maggie said.

'Thanks.'

'You were away? It was quick though.'

'What I heard.'

'Couldn't get back?'

'Not even if I'd tried.'

She tutted. 'This can't be the first time you've been back here since she went?'

'Just got in last night.'

'Why were you asleep in your car?'

Griffin sighed heavily. He looked over Maggie's shoulder towards the beach.

'I got here about four. Couldn't face going to Mum's house straight away. I knew you opened early, so I figured I'd have some food and then think about going when it was light.'

Maggie pursed her lips and patted his arm.

'I'm not open yet, but I'll always make an exception for old friends.'

Unable to speak for a moment, Griffin was surprised by the tide of emotion he felt seeing Maggie's familiar face and the kindness she displayed.

'That'll be great, Mags,' he managed. 'Thanks.'

Griffin sat at the table and Maggie placed a large mug of tea down in front of him. He looked around the cafe noting the Christmas decorations and the brightly decorated tree by the door. The radio played carols softly in the background and he experienced a warm nostalgic feeling of Christmas.

Griffin scrubbed his hands through his dark blonde hair, which was in dire need of a cut, and regarded Maggie with troubled deep brown eyes.

'Do you think she suffered?' he asked, wrapping his hands around the mug, drawing warmth from it. He'd got cold overnight in the car, as a heavy frost had settled.

Maggie shrugged. 'I don't know, my love. But she was in here one day, happy and chatty, having her usual tea and Welsh cake, and the next morning I heard she'd passed. So, I'm guessing it was pretty quick and unexpected.'

'They said a massive heart attack.' Griffin sipped the hot nectar. No one made tea like Maggie. 'I only heard about it a couple of days after she'd gone. Apparently, she didn't want a funeral or anything.'

'I heard that. She always mentioned you,' Maggie said, squeezing his arm. 'Her war hero.'

'Hardly.' Griffin snorted. 'I was a chef on a Royal Navy warship for ten years. Hardly war hero stuff.'

'It is to the hungry lads who just want to get back to the boat to eat and sleep. They always feel better with a full belly,' Maggie said quietly. 'Are you out of the navy now?'

'Yup. Been working in Newcastle, but the hotel just went bust. I figured I would look for some seasonal work here over Christmas and live at Mum's before I decide what to do.'

Maggie nodded. 'Is the house in a bit of a state?'

'No idea. Expect so, it's been empty so long. It's why I need to look at it on a full stomach.'

'Very wise,' Maggie said, patting his hand. 'I'll keep an ear out for anyone who wants a chef.'

John, Maggie's chef, came over with an enormous plate for Griffin and placed it down in front of him.

'Thanks, mate,' Griff said, rubbing his hands. 'Looks amazing.'

'Can I have a word, Mags?' John asked, gesturing towards the kitchen.

Maggie followed him out and Griffin focused on eating. Maggie returned a few moments later.

'Griffin.'

'What?'

'Fancy filling in here today and tomorrow? Cash in hand?'

'What?' Griffin stared at her, knife and fork poised in the air.

'John's brother's just rung. His mother's had a fall and John needs to go and sort her out. I need a chef for a few days; a week at most, he reckons. She's fine, but he needs to make an appearance and sort stuff out.'

Griffin looked around the cafe and then at the menu. Christ, he could do this with his eyes shut.

'Happy to help out a friend, Mags,' he said. 'Anything's better than going to Mum's.'

'That's settled then,' she said happily. 'Eat up, dear, then I'll show you the ropes.'

§ § §

Tess Dutton shivered and burrowed deeper into her thick jumper as she waited in line. Her phone buzzed twice, finally picking up a signal. She dragged it out of her pocket and opened the first of the two texts.

Whereabouts are you? X

The text from her sister was succinct. Smiling, she replied.

Hour away. Coffee needed! She attached a yawning emoji.

OK. Drive safe. Love ya.

Tess replied with a heart emoji. She opened the next message. It was from *him*. She sighed in irritation.

I miss you. When are you coming back?

Tutting, she didn't bother to reply.

'Latte for Tess?' a barista shouted.

Tess took her large latte in its brightly coloured disposable Christmas cup and navigated her way out of the cafe at the motorway services. She hurried to her car and settled herself back behind the wheel, cranking up the heating to stop herself shivering. She was freezing, despite her massive jumper and thick socks. The forecast had been threatening 'wintry showers'.

Tess peered at the sky as she pulled out of the car park. She had about an hour to go until she got there. Taking a much-needed glug of hot coffee, she selected an upbeat Christmas playlist and drove off, singing loudly and tunelessly to WHAM's 'Last Christmas'.

After an entire bottle of wine on a nearly empty stomach (except for a tube of Pringles), Tess had made a drunken promise to her sister, Lorraine, over Zoom a few weeks ago. She'd promised to help out at her restaurant, The Fat Gannet, in the coastal town of Castleby, for the Christmas period. Lorraine was exhausted. She needed someone she could depend on, who knew the ropes, as she was almost fully booked up to Christmas.

Shortly before Lorraine had cajoled her to come and help, Tess had left the career she had been in for nearly twenty years. She was a nurse in emergency medicine, and although she had always loved her job, the fall out of her general and mental health since the Covid pandemic had taken a significant toll. She couldn't cope with the pressure, and the push of responsibility onto the nurses was just too much. Her nerves were frayed and her anxiety at work was off the charts.

Her sister had pounced when she found out Tess had finally left her job. Tess knew the restaurant business inside out since most of her holidays had been spent at the restaurant. Tess loved her sister. It had just been the both of them for nearly ten years now, and she was increasingly concerned that Lorraine worked too hard and that she might be losing her love for the restaurant.

Tess was thirty-eight and single. She'd been in a three-year relationship with a doctor she worked with until four months ago. Then, out of the blue, he'd ended it cruelly, citing a myriad of reasons, which focused mainly on his views of Tess's shortcomings. A month prior to being dumped, Tess's bestie and flatmate, had moved out of the flat one day, with no warning, explanation or note. She had, since then, refused to have any contact with Tess whatsoever, despite Tess's efforts to connect.

Tess had found herself grieving deeply over her break-up with Vincent; she had loved him with a passion and struggled to understand his reasons for ending their relationship. She was also grieving for a lost friendship. She had no real idea what the hell she was supposed to have done to warrant being ghosted in such a way and found the two combined heartbreaks difficult to cope with.

Once word was out that they were no longer together, Tess heard from various colleagues that Vincent was quite the Lothario at work. Apparently, he had many encounters with willing participants in places ranging from the on-call rooms to the store cupboards.

To ease her pain, Tess had tried to move on and get back into the dating scene; half-heartedly embarking on a series of slightly disastrous attempts at dating. These attempts had ended after one particular night, when her date took a lengthy Facetime call from his ex-girlfriend, and asked Tess to wave hello and blow kisses to his shared cat. Following that night, Tess decided she was done with dating.

Her new 'single' situation was not being helped by Vincent. He was texting her regularly, saying that he missed her and wanted to come round and see her.

She yearned for him and missed him terribly, but she hadn't yet given in to his pleas. However she felt, she refused to be his booty call, but he was nothing if not persistent. The texts nearly always came late at night or very early in the morning.

Tess slowed down as she navigated the pretty high street in Castleby. She enjoyed the rush of nostalgia she always felt. To her, this was like coming home; mainly because Lorraine had lived there for over twenty years. She noticed the town had started with the Christmas decorations and she wondered if Lorraine had decorated the restaurant yet. It was the beginning of December and that meant going all out on Christmas decorations. Shopfronts sparkled with tinsel and fairy lights. The pavement glistened with a heavy overnight frost which hadn't yet melted away.

The large Christmas tree, decorated prettily, stood at the top of the high street, by the church. The lights were always switched on by Santa, when he rode up the high street on a beach buggy, on Santa Saturday.

Tess knew the restaurant was busy going forwards; there were already loads of Christmas bookings. From previous experience, she knew they'd be flat out, right up until they closed the doors on Christmas Day at 6 p.m.

Putting on her hazard lights, she pulled in as close to the restaurant as she could get. She figured she'd unload there, before moving her car.

Lorraine's flat was situated above the restaurant, so Tess tooted loudly and hopped out, admiring the Christmas wreath with bright red ribbon on her door. Knocking loudly, she moved to open the boot of her car.

After five minutes of hammering on the door, she was frustrated.

'For the love of bloody God,' she said crossly, as she hammered on the door again. 'Lorraine! Where the bloody hell are you?'

Swearing under her breath, she dug about in the centre console of her car until she found her key to Lorraine's flat. She tried the key, but the door wouldn't open. Putting her shoulder against it, she tried to force it, but it would only budge slightly. She heard a faint bark and wondered where it was coming from.

'Why the bloody hell won't this open?' she said, exasperated.

'You're making an *awful* lot of noise for a burglar,' a voice said behind her.

Whirling around, she faced a giant of a man who had bright blue eyes, a tanned, handsome face and an amused expression. By his side sat a large Alsatian.

Tess rolled her eyes and laughed. 'Busted. Mind you, I reckon there would be richer pickings over the road. I've been inside here, and there's nothing worth nicking.'

'Is the door stuck?' he enquired.

'Feels like there's something stopping it,' she said.

'And you are?' he ventured. 'I don't want to help you get in, only for you to turn the joint over. I'll never live it down.'

'Are you Foxy?' Tess asked. 'I think my sister's told me about you.'

'The tall, handsome, extremely charming guy?' He grinned.

'No, the new owner of the climbing centre.' She pointed to his fleece, with the 'Endure' logo emblazoned across it.

He inclined his head. 'Ahh, so I now deduce you must be Tess, Lorraine's sister? She said you were coming to help out. Slave labour is how she put it.'

'Charming! Yes, here to help out. Obviously, she said all the other stuff, you know… tall, etc.' Tess laughed.

'Obviously.' He rubbed his hands. 'Want a hand? Too cold to be standing about for long.'

'Please.'

He approached the door and pushed, then frowned and pushed again gently. Squeezing his head through the gap, he managed to peer behind the door. He let it go abruptly and turned to her.

'Call an ambulance,' he said.

'What?'

'Lorraine. She's behind the door. Must have fallen down the stairs.'

'Oh Christ. I need to get to her. I'm a trauma nurse.'

While she dialled the emergency services, Foxy managed to push the door open enough for her to slip through. She clicked into professional mode, checking Lorraine's vitals and keeping a running dialogue with the ambulance control centre.

Tess was worried but tried to hold it together. Her sister was everything to her. Her only family. Lorraine was pale but breathing well. Tess thought she'd probably broken a leg, looking at the weird angle her foot was at, plus she had a huge bump on her head.

Foxy stuck his head around the door. 'I think I need to move your car; people are struggling to get past, and the ambulance won't be able to get through.'

'Thanks,' she said gratefully and passed him the keys.

'How is she?' he asked.

'Unconscious. I think her leg is broken. Her foot's wrapped in the cord for the hoover.'

'Do you think she's been there long?'

Tess shook her head. 'No. She texted me an hour ago. She's got a nasty bump to her head too.'

'Do you want to move her?'

'No. We'll let the paramedics do it.'

Tearfully, Tess stood by and watched the paramedics work on her sister, then load her into the back of the ambulance. Foxy returned from moving her car and stood at a respectful distance. As Tess climbed in, Foxy handed her the car keys.

'What about Frank?' he asked.

She blinked. 'Who's Frank?'

'Lorraine's dog. Frank. He's in the flat, I can hear him.'

'I didn't even know about him, to be honest,' she admitted. 'She kept telling me she had a surprise for me, so perhaps it was that she'd got a dog!'

'I'll take him for a bit. It'll make Solo feel big and important,' he said, gesturing to the Alsatian, who was sat by his side again.

She smiled, handing him Lorraine's house keys.

'You know, for a stranger, you're pretty helpful.'

'I learnt we all muck in around here. Come and find me when you're back. I've put your car by Endure. If it's shut, I'll be in the flat upstairs.'

'Thanks for your help!' she called, as the paramedic slammed the door shut.

CHAPTER 2

Tess climbed out of the taxi and looked at the outside of Endure, the climbing centre. It was a large Victorian building which sat next to the castle walls, which were lit brightly. She saw people high on the outside wall, attached to various ropes and brightly coloured handholds, which dotted the wall.

Spotting her car tucked in neatly next to a large Land Rover Defender, she approached the main door. She saw Foxy opening it for an attractive red-headed woman. She watched, slightly embarrassed, as they hugged, and he gave her a light kiss. He glanced up as the woman left and saw Tess.

'Oh hey!' he said. 'How's Lorraine?'

'Broken leg, bad concussion,' Tess supplied, grimacing.

'Oh crap,' Foxy said. 'The nightmare before Christmas!'

'You said it. Not sure how I'll cope.'

'We'll all muck in.'

She gave a half-laugh. 'You say that now… Look, thanks for sorting the car out.'

'And Frank.'

'Yes. I've yet to meet Frank.'

'I'll grab him.'

'How long has she had him?'

'Erm… probably a few months. He's a rescue from Suzy,' he said, disappearing inside.

'Who the hell is Suzy?' she murmured to herself. Foxy returned a moment later followed by his Alsatian and a small pug that trotted happily behind his heels.

When Foxy stopped, the pug stopped.

'That's Frank?' Tess asked doubtfully.

'It is. Here's Lorraine's keys back.'

'Christ. Thanks.'

'Not a dog lover?'

'Never had one. Job didn't really make it fair.'

'I think he largely looks after himself. Likes to sit in the window in the restaurant most of the day watching the world go past. Always seems to be there.'

'Right. Well, I'd better get on.'

'Shout if you need anything.'

'Thanks for looking after the car and stuff.'

'No problem. Hope she's on the mend soon.'

'See you later.'

Tess walked to the car and Frank trotted after her. He gave a small bark as she went to climb into the driver's seat. She glared at him.

'Just so you know, I'm not one of these people who pander to small annoying dogs,' she said firmly. She opened the passenger side door and watched him jump in and sit neatly on the seat. 'I'm not even sure if we're going to get on.'

The pug eyed her warily, then sighed and turned to look out of the window.

Tess and Frank were largely ignoring each other. She had squeezed her car in next to Lorraine's at the rear of the restaurant, and then finished unpacking it. She'd rung the hospital for an update and had managed to chat briefly with Lorraine, who moaned grumpily that she was waiting for an orthopaedic surgeon to consult, and that they weren't doing anything until the swelling had reduced. They'd told her she'd probably be off her feet for a minimum of six weeks.

Tess had been busy. She'd unpacked, sorted out her room and tidied up the flat a bit. There was a pile of paperwork on the table and Tess idly flicked through it. On the top, was a formal letter of resignation from Carl, telling Lorraine his last shift at the restaurant was 30 November. Tess stared at the letter with rising panic. But Carl was the chef! She scrabbled through the paperwork and found a draft advert for a chef for a busy restaurant serving English/European food, with flexible hours and good pay. She stared at it. Christ alive. Now they didn't even have a chef!

She rifled through more of the paperwork and found a scribbled note about the advert going live. Two days ago. She looked at the contact details for people to apply. It was the business email, which thankfully, she knew the password for. Firing up Lorraine's computer, she opened the inbox and saw there were twenty unread emails.

'Phew! Hopefully, there's someone in here who can start soon!' she murmured, as she flicked her eyes over the list.

After talking to a slightly drugged-up Lorraine again, Tess had a shortlist of three. Since time was of the essence, she emailed asking whether the applicants would be prepared to have an online interview later that day if possible, and then, depending on how that went, come into the restaurant to look around and cook something.

Lorraine had said she had already arranged a cover chef from a local agency, starting Thursday, for the rest of the week. So, Tess had a few days to either find a chef or carry on using the agency until she did.

Tess stood in the restaurant and surveyed it with a critical eye. Frank had insisted on following her and he'd jumped up onto a small cushion in the corner of the large window sill and settled down with a sigh, throwing her a mournful look.

She walked through the restaurant, thinking she needed to get the decorations up. Mercifully, Lorraine had closed the restaurant for a few days, so Tess had two days to decorate and try to find a chef to start in a few days. Squaring her shoulders, she went to the storeroom to look for the decorations.

She wrestled a few large boxes off a tall shelf and dragged them out, just as Frank started barking excitedly at something he'd seen out of the window. A few seconds later there was a gentle knocking on the door and Tess saw Foxy outside.

'Hello!' she said, opening the door. 'Was Frank barking at you?'

'Solo more like. They're inseparable. Just wondered how Lorraine was?'

'Come on in,' she said. Frank launched himself off his cushion and snuffled around Solo with open adoration. Tess relayed the latest on Lorraine.

'Coffee?' she asked.

'Go on then. I could go a quick espresso,' Foxy said, rubbing his hands.

Tess headed over to the coffee machine, pleased that she'd had the foresight to switch it on when she arrived. It was ancient, temperamental and needed time to warm up. She felt she could relate.

'Did you know the chef had quit?' she asked Foxy.

'Carl? Yeah, he felt bad. He's got some family issues and had to make a choice. It was either find a different job or find a different wife.'

Tess pulled a face. 'Like that, was it?'

'Yeah. They've got six-month-old triplets. The hours weren't working for them.'

'Christ,' Tess muttered. 'No wonder.'

'Have you got cover?' Foxy asked.

'Lorraine sorted an agency chef to cover short term, but they're expensive! She also put an ad out, but I've got to interview them.'

'Couldn't Linden step up?' Foxy asked, referring to the trainee who worked in the kitchen, doubling as a kitchen porter and assistant chef.

'Linden is fine to make a sandwich and prep, but I don't think he's got the chops for the main stuff. We have to hope that someone fits the bill, but if you know of anyone, let me know.'

'Will do.'

She handed Foxy an espresso, which he downed in one.

'Delicious,' he said. 'Right, I must crack on. Good that Lorraine is out of the woods. Do you need a hand with any of these boxes before I go?' he asked.

'No, it's fine thanks. It's just Christmas decs that need to go up,' she said ruefully.

'Excellent. A lucky escape for me.' He grinned. 'Thanks for the coffee, see you later!'

Frank whined pitifully as Tess closed the door and locked it. He jumped back onto his cushion and stared mournfully after Foxy and Solo. When they were out of sight, he lay down heavily, looking sad.

Tess checked the email and saw responses from all three people she'd emailed. One of them responded rudely saying he'd waited long enough for a response and had taken something else, but the other two were up for an online interview and had both selected acceptable timeframes for later that day. She checked with Lorraine and then sent them each a link and confirmed.

With the help of a Christmas radio station and a large hot chocolate, it took Tess just over an hour to decorate the restaurant. She was pleased with her efforts. She'd found a bundle of warm-toned fairy lights and had strung them artistically around the place. She'd also decorated a small tree she had found propped against the door outside.

All the time, Frank watched her suspiciously, in case she encroached into his area. She set the timer for the fairy lights and decided to go and treat herself to one of Maggie's legendary breakfast rolls and walk Frank on the beach. She needed some fresh air too. She clipped Frank's lead on, shrugged into a warm coat and they set off down the road, towards the cafe.

'Tess, darling!' Maggie screeched, as Tess entered the cafe. She trotted around from behind the counter to envelop her in a large hug. 'Darling. You look wonderful. Now, how is Lorraine? Foxy said she'd taken a tumble.'

'She's broken her leg and has a concussion, so she's still in hospital. I'm here helping out.'

'She said you were coming to help out for Christmas. She said you'd left nursing?' Maggie gave her one of her all-knowing looks.

'Yup,' Tess said quietly.

'Well, whatever we can do to help, we'll all muck in.'

'I'm getting that idea. Thank you,' Tess said gratefully.

'Let me get you a coffee,' Maggie said. 'You eating?'

'Yes, I'd like one of your heart attacks in a roll, please,' Tess said firmly. 'I actually miss those things and dream about them.'

'Coming right up,' Maggie said. 'Go and sit. I'll bring a sausage for Frank too.'

As Tess settled down, her phone pinged. It was Vincent.

Where are you and when are you coming back to work? Please, darling, I miss you so much. I'm sorry.

She stared at the text for a while and then decided to ignore it until she'd thought about it.

'You're being nice to Frank, aren't you?' Lorraine asked, peering at the screen, with a worried expression, trying to look behind Tess.

'He doesn't like me,' Tess said.

Lorraine was sitting in on the Zoom interviews with prospective chefs, so they were catching up before their first interviewee appeared virtually.

'Are you sure you're up to this? You look like crap.'

'Oh, thanks! I'm OK. They've given me painkillers so I'm quite happy. Listen, be nice to Frank, he loves everybody. Especially Solo. Those two are hilarious together.'

'So I've seen! Any news on you?'

Lorraine grimaced. 'Surgery tomorrow and then six weeks off my feet.'

'God. What are you going to do?'

'I was going to tell you later. I'm going to stay with Emma. She's in a bungalow. She said she'd come and pick me up. I think it's easier than trying to navigate the flat's stairs. That's too much of a recipe for disaster if you ask me. I'm afraid Frank will have to stay with you. Em's allergic to dogs. Is that OK?'

Emma was Lorraine's best friend.

'She said you could come for Christmas after you close up if you want,' Lorraine said hopefully.

'I'll think about it. I'll probably collapse in a big heap. Right. You ready? The first guy has dialled in.'

'Let's go!'

Two hours later, they were down to one applicant who was going to come and cook on Sunday afternoon. He wasn't available to start for another week, so Tess and Lorraine agreed to contact the agency chef to extend the contract.

§ § §

Cooking at Maggie's was a breeze for Griffin. He allowed himself to forget everything and get into a rhythm, and he was enjoying it. Maggie was fun to work with and her two waitresses were hard workers, but a good laugh. The day whizzed past and before he knew it, Maggie was standing before him telling him to cook himself some dinner, because they were shutting in ten minutes.

After she'd locked the door and turned the 'Closed' sign around, she made herself a drink and sat opposite him while he ate.

'You going to your mum's place after this?'

He nodded, chewing before he responded. 'I don't have a choice. Need to sleep there.'

She pulled a face. 'How long has it been shut up for?'

'Too long.'

'Want me to come with you?'

He sat back in his chair and rested his cutlery on the side of the plate.

'Now why would you want to do that, Maggie?' he asked gently. 'You need to go home, put your feet up and relax. You've been on your feet all day.'

She waved away his words. 'I can rest when I'm dead. I'll come. You might need help with something.'

'Like what?'

'No idea. Don't look a gift horse in the mouth. Most of you men can't even put a king-size duvet cover on without help. Eat up then we'll get going.'

Griff pulled into the driveway of his mother's house. The streetlight threw light against the dark windows and cast a yellow hue on the tired render of the once-beautiful three-storey Victorian villa. He peered up at the house and saw peeling paintwork, cracked render and general disrepair. He looked sadly at the collection of litter, flyers and leaves piled high in the corners of the front porch.

Maggie pulled in behind him, parked and climbed out. She stood looking at the house, with her hands on her hips.

'Neglected. Needs love,' she announced.

'Don't we all?' Griff muttered.

'Keys?' she asked.

He produced a set of keys and motioned for them to go around the back.

The back garden was a mess: overgrown and wild. His mother had loved her garden and it pained him to see it in this state. He rounded the corner of the house and selected the key for the back door.

Griff took a breath and pushed the door open. He flicked on the kitchen light: nothing happened.

'Fuse box?' Maggie asked in his ear, switching on the torch on her phone.

In the darkness, Griff found the cupboard under the stairs, feeling for the torch that always used to live on the fuse box. Bingo. He switched it on and put the power on. The kitchen light flickered a few times, making small buzzing noises, before it stayed on. He heard a myriad of noises, as if the house was waking up. Small things beeped, hummed and rattled once life force flowed back into their electrical veins.

Griff looked round the kitchen. Although there was a thick layer of dust over the surfaces, it was almost immaculate. He moved into the dining room and saw the furniture covered with sheets, but again, just dust over the exposed surfaces. Moving into the spacious lounge he saw the end of the house his mother had always favoured; it caught the morning sun and was close to the fireplace. There was a cluster of furniture covered with more dust sheets. He knew from years ago, it was probably two chairs huddled around a TV, and bookcases around her, within easy reach.

'It all seems in pretty good nick,' Maggie murmured. 'Who did all this?'

'No idea. But I'm very grateful,' he replied.

Together they headed upstairs and found much of the same. The place was neat and tidy and covered with more sheets. The only thing that worried Griff slightly was the large stain on the ceiling in one of the small bedrooms, and the size of the enormous spider in the bath who appeared to have taken up residence.

He watched as Maggie went back down the stairs and heard her moving around the kitchen and opening cupboard doors. He stood on the upstairs landing and opened the door to the airing cupboard. Stacks of neatly folded linen were piled on the shelves, and the faint scent of lavender tickled his nostrils. In the bottom of the cupboard, duvets and pillows were neatly labelled in clear bags.

'Who the hell did all this?' Griff wondered.

'Griffin?' Maggie called.

He found Maggie in the kitchen.

'I've turned the water and the boiler on,' she said. 'All of the kitchen stuff is here, clean and tidy. Even the fridge smells OK. I found this taped to the fridge.' She handed him an envelope with his name clearly printed on the front.

He took the envelope and glanced at Maggie's expectant face.

'This is Mum's writing,' he said. He lifted the dust sheet covering the table and chairs and sat down heavily with the letter.

'I'll go,' Maggie said. 'Leave you to read it.'

'Stay, Mags,' he said quietly. 'Please.'

He opened the envelope, realising his hands were trembling slightly.

My darling Griffin.

If you're reading this, you've made it home, but I'm not here any more. I am sorry I went before we could say goodbye, but I must tell you how incredibly proud I am of you and the man you have become. I struggle to put into words the depth of my love for you, but rest assured that I loved you with everything I had. My only sadness is that I didn't see you more and that your father died too prematurely to see the wonderful man his son grew into. You would know that the house is yours because the solicitor would have written and said. I wasn't sure how long you would be, so I paid for a firm to come in and deep clean and then put the house to sleep until you could come and wake it up. She needs love and attention, but she is all yours.

The accident was heartbreaking for you, but I was so proud of you and how you took responsibility. I only hope you've made peace with yourself. It wasn't your fault; it was an accident.

Now you're back, perhaps you'll try and make a life here. If you contact the solicitor, he has some money put aside for you to use to get the house back into shape. I think it might need a new roof. Sorry, love. Either way, use it to bring the house back to life and make her sparkle even if you plan to sell her. I'd love you to put down roots here and put your past behind you; but if you feel you can't – then you have my blessing to sell.

Time for you to get sorted. Wake this house up and restore her to the beauty she once was. I will rest easy knowing you are home and where you are supposed to be. I will always love you and watch over you.

Your loving Mum.

Griff exhaled loudly, blinking away tears. Maggie squeezed his arm. He passed her the letter. She read it and placed it gently on the table.

'Bless her,' she said softly. 'What accident is she talking about, Griff?'

He rested his elbows on the table and put his head in his hands, sighing. Finally, he rubbed his face and looked at Maggie, his eyes filled with tears.

'I did something awful, so terrible,' he whispered, struggling to speak. 'I fell asleep at the wheel and killed someone.' Tears ran down his cheeks. 'I went to prison.'

Maggie gasped. 'Oh, your poor boy,' she said and scooted her chair closer to envelop him in a hug.

Griff found himself unable to stop the torrent of emotion that had built up as soon as Maggie surrounded him with one of her hugs. Months of grief poured out and he sobbed into her comforting shoulder. She gently rubbed his back as if she would soothe an upset child.

Finally, he raised a tear-stained face and looked embarrassed.

'Sorry,' he said, taking the tissue she proffered, blowing his nose loudly. 'Wasn't expecting that letter and stuff from Mum… you know.'

Maggie watched him sympathetically. 'Tell me what happened.'

CHAPTER 3

Griff slept incredibly well and woke early, refreshed and feeling slightly less in despair than he had in previous days. It felt good to be home in his childhood house. Comforting.

He showered and decided to walk along the beach to work so he could enjoy some fresh air before he spent the day in the kitchen.

His phone buzzed and he saw a text from his old friend, Mark. Mark had been his neighbour when Griff and his fiancée, Gabby, lived in Portsmouth; the three had become close friends. Griff had always been reassured that Mark looked out for Gabby whenever he was at sea. He was gradually reconnecting with old friends since his release and had plans to meet another friend – who was based in the next town – for a beer in the coming days. Pleased to hear from Mark, Griff responded, and they exchanged a few more texts and then promised to catch up in person soon.

Griff passed a large man with a tattoo, one he recognised from his years in the forces, running along the beach accompanied by an

Alsatian. As he rounded the corner towards Castle Beach, he heard a woman's voice calling out frantically.

'FRANK! COME BACK HERE NOW!'

Griffin carried on walking, noticing with amusement, a pug approaching him, running flat out with a lead trailing behind him.

'FRANK!'

Griff realised the woman calling was trying to catch the pug; he caught her eye.

'CAN YOU TRY AND STOP HIM?'

Griff moved into the path of the small dog, and as he passed by, he stamped firmly on the lead. He bent quickly to pick it up, almost garrotting the small dog, who had carried on running.

The woman reached him, flushed and out of breath. Griff couldn't help but notice how attractive she was.

'Oh my God! Thank you!' she said breathlessly. 'He's such a pain in the bloody arse when he sees Solo.'

'Who's Solo?' Griff asked, passing over the lead.

'Him,' she said, pointing in the distance. 'He is besotted with him. I think I have a gay pug.'

'Ahh. No recall then?' he asked.

She snorted. 'Apparently not. Frank does what he wants when he wants. He's my sister's dog and I've been lumbered looking after him.' She glanced down at Frank. 'He's trying my patience a bit, to be honest.'

'Perhaps he's testing you,' Griff said dryly.

'I'm failing epically if he is.' She laughed. 'Thanks again for rescuing him. He would have kept going.'

'No problem,' Griff said, glancing at his watch. 'Sorry. I'm late for work.'

'OK, thanks then. Have a good day!' she said, still being pulled by an enthusiastic Frank, who had picked up Solo's scent in the distance.

Griff arrived at Maggie's and felt embarrassed at crying all over her the previous evening.

'Morning,' he said sheepishly.

'Morning, my love,' she replied. 'Now listen, I'll have none of you feeling weird about last night. I've had bigger and uglier sobbing on my shoulder over the years, so one more is fine in my book. All forgotten about. OK?'

'OK.'

'And before you ask, your business is your business. I won't be telling anyone anything. Are we straight?'

'Yes, boss.'

She tittered. 'Good. Best get on then!'

Griff disappeared into the kitchen.

'Maggie!' he called after a while, and she appeared around the corner. 'I've got an idea for a breakfast special if you're interested. We've got all these wraps to use up.'

She raised an eyebrow. 'What is it?'

He handed her a plate. 'Try it.'

She bit into it and closed her eyes in delight. 'Oh, that's good. What is it?'

'This is Maggie's breakfast burrito. Scrambled egg, chorizo, spicy baked beans, and grilled halloumi, wrapped in a soft tortilla. We can easily charge what we charge for one of the breakfast burgers.'

'Done. It's going on the blackboard outside now as the special of the day.'

'Don't mind me suggesting?' he ventured.

'Not when it's stuff like that.'

Griff carried on. He was enjoying the atmosphere. The orders were fairly constant, and he was pleased to see the breakfast burrito was popular. He enjoyed hearing the chatter of people and laughter floating through to the kitchen. As he was plating up an order, he heard Maggie tittering away loudly, then calling him.

'Griff?' she called. 'Got a sec?'

'Just a minute,' he called. He emerged from the kitchen, passing a plated order to one of the waitresses.

'What's up?' he asked, approaching Maggie who was standing in the open doorway.

'This customer wanted to speak to you about his breakfast,' she said, a twinkle in her eye.

She moved slightly and Griff saw the large man he had passed on the beach with the Alsatian, who he now knew was called Solo.

'Everything OK?' he ventured, addressing the man.

Foxy held out a hand. 'Name's Foxy. Good to meet you. This, my man, was one of the best things I have had for breakfast for years. Just wanted to say.'

'Glad you liked it. I'm Griffin,' he said, shaking Foxy's hand. 'Most people just stick with Griff.'

'I pretty much always have a heart attack in a roll, but this… man. This was good. Keep the stuff like this coming.'

'I'm only filling in for John for a few days.'

Foxy looked crestfallen. 'Least you can do is leave John the recipe then.'

'Will do.'

Griff heard excited barking and turned to see the pug, Frank, pulling the woman he'd seen on the beach earlier. Solo approached Frank and the two of them ran about in circles and rolled in the sand together.

'I'd say that's love,' Griffin observed.

'It's something,' Foxy replied.

'I need to get back in. Good to meet you.'

Griff nodded at the woman he'd met earlier, as he turned to go back inside. He was followed closely by Maggie.

'If Foxy liked it, then it needs to stay on the menu, I think,' Maggie declared.

'You should check it with John,' Griff said. 'I don't want to step on any toes.'

'Oh, hush up,' Maggie said. 'I'll put what I damn well like on my menu.'

The breakfast rush died down and Griffin took a break. The sun was out which made the chilly air marginally warmer, although it was still so cold Griff could see his breath. He sat on one of the benches with his coffee and turned his face up to the weak winter sun.

He remembered the note from his mother and dug his phone out of his pocket to search for the solicitor's phone number. He found it and placed a call; it went straight to voicemail. Griff left a message, saying he was back and working temporarily for Maggie for a few days. He ended the call and enjoyed the sun a little longer while he pondered his future.

§ § §

Tess made an executive decision and moved some of the tables around in the restaurant. She found once she had started, she couldn't stop. On a whim, she looked up the number for Endure and rang it.

'Endure.' She recognised Foxy's voice.

'Hi, it's Tess, Lorraine's sister.'

'Everything OK?'

'Yeah. Bit cheeky,' she said, 'but I wondered if I plied you with Italian coffee, then you might be able to spare me five minutes to shift a few big bits of furniture.'

'Do I *look* like I'm that easily bribed?' he said mildly.

'Absolutely,' she said with conviction, and he chuckled.

'Give me ten. I need to nip out for a sandwich anyway.'

'How about I make you a sandwich too?'

'Done.'

'See you in a bit.'

Tess bustled about in the kitchen while she waited.

She heard Frank yipping excitedly and knew Solo was near. She walked through the restaurant to see Foxy at the door.

'Hey,' she said.

He stepped inside, and Solo brushed past his legs to greet Frank.

'Coffee?'

'Never say no.'

'What sandwich would you like? I have roast beef, tuna, pastrami?'

'Stop!' He held up a hand. 'You had me at roast beef.'

'Done. Mayo or French mustard?'

'Both.'

'OK.'

She made her way into the kitchen, and he followed.

'I like this layout,' he said, standing in the doorway. 'Works much better.'

'I think so,' she said, slicing beef.

Foxy narrowed his eyes and pointed to a counter. 'I think this would go much better over there too. Give you much more space.'

'Exactly! I reckon, if I got rid of that chiller which we don't really use, it opens up the kitchen a little more, so people can see in. There's enough room here to put in a small counter and a few stools and have it as a chef's table.'

His eyes sparkled. 'I love a chef's table. I used to go to a French restaurant in London where, if you sat at the chef's table, you got all sorts of free bits and pieces.'

'So, you like the idea?'

'Really good.'

She passed him a sandwich and gestured to a table, while she set about making him a coffee.

'How's Lorraine?' he asked, taking a huge bite of his sandwich.

'Out of action completely. Groggy. She's had surgery on her leg and next week she's off it for six weeks at a friend's house.'

'Tough for you.'

'More like a nightmare!'

She passed him an espresso and called the dogs over for a few scraps of meat.

'You got lots of bookings until Christmas?' he asked, munching.

'*And* Christmas Day too,' she said. 'This is why I came up to help. She said she'd be flat out and she's been working way too hard. We've got a few Christmas parties too, where the whole place is booked out.'

He pulled a face. 'Shout if you need help. I'll always muck in, although I'll probably be useless.'

She laughed. 'I think there's a limit to what I can ask of you!'

He finished his sandwich. 'You'd be surprised. Right,' he said, rubbing his hands. 'Thank you. Where's this chiller going?'

'Out the back for now, in the storeroom. There's enough space.'

Together, they moved various things until they were satisfied. Foxy found a screwdriver and took down a panel that partially obscured the kitchen. It opened up the space a little more, like an open square window. He asked her for a tape measure and measured the gap below the open square.

'I think I have just the thing to go there, in the storeroom at Endure. I took it out when I first got there, and I've just remembered it. I'll have a look later.'

'Great! If it's going spare.'

He surveyed the restaurant, hands on hips. 'Looks good. Bagsy the first dinner at the chef's table when it's in.'

'Deal,' she said.

'I'll have a look when I get back and let you know.'

'Appreciate that.'

Tess let Foxy out. She assessed the restaurant and felt pleased with herself. Definitely an improvement.

She set about making a plan for table numbers for the waiting staff and then checked stocks, putting in orders for reopening on Thursday. By 3 p.m. she was on top of everything and had decided on the menu for the forthcoming week. Usually this was done with the chef, but this time she figured she'd do it herself.

She yawned and wondered why her stomach was rumbling, then realised she'd had no lunch. She also realised Frank hadn't been out for ages.

'Let's get some dinner and stretch our legs,' she said, picking up Frank's lead. 'I'm starving.'

Together, they walked down the street towards the beach, with Frank pulling her most of the way. He stopped abruptly to pee and then resumed pulling and panting until they rounded the corner where they could see Endure and Maggie's cafe. He barked and strained harder on the lead to get away.

Tess stumbled on the kerb, twisting her ankle. In an effort not to fall, she let go of the lead and Frank careered down the road towards the climbing centre, barking frantically.

'Frank!' she said, trying to follow and limping slightly. 'FRANK! Ow! Frank!' she cried desperately. She watched as the small dog ran precariously close to an RNLI truck that was driving off the beach.

'FRANK!'

CHAPTER 4

Griff threw the last of the boxes into the recycling and stretched out his back. He was knackered, but pleasantly so. He considered that today had been the first good day for ages. The first day he hadn't felt the crushing weight of grief across his shoulders, enclosing him like a shroud. He still felt the brutal ache of missing the person he'd loved with everything he had, but it was good to be here. Back home. It helped. He liked working for Maggie. The work was easy and the people were nice, but if he had his way he would overhaul the menu. But it wasn't his menu or his kitchen, so he couldn't.

Breathing in the sea air, he promised himself a walk on the beach after work. Glancing at his phone he saw an email from his mother's solicitor and quickly read it. The solicitor was delighted Griff was back and said he would arrange for the funds to be transferred to Griff's account once he had his details. He said he'd call in to Maggie's the following day, with some paperwork for Griff to sign.

As he scanned his other emails, he was vaguely aware of a woman's voice, shouting. He looked up and recognised the woman from earlier with the runaway pug. She was hopping about as if in pain. Then the pug whizzed past him towards the beach, just as one of the RNLI trucks came around the corner.

Griff gave chase and ran towards the beach to try and head the pug off. He tried to step on the lead again but missed it. In desperation, Griff launched himself towards the dog, grabbing him and rolling over on the sand, just in time to stop him being squashed under the wheels of the large truck.

'Gotcha,' Griff said to the stout wriggling pug, who was snuffling in his efforts to get away from Griff's tight hold.

He got to his feet, carefully holding the lead, and brushed himself down.

'Christ alive. Are you hurt?' The woman he recognised from the beach earlier that morning limped over, looking concerned.

'I'm fine,' he said. 'This one was almost flattened by the truck. Is he always running off out of control?'

The minute he said it, he regretted it. Her eyes widened, and her shoulders squared slightly.

'He's not out of control *all the time*.' She bristled.

'Looked like he was trying to win the hundred metres,' Griff replied dryly.

'He's not mine,' she said testily. 'I'm just stuck with him for a bit.'

'Whose is he then?' he asked, brushing sand off himself.

'My sister's,' she said stiffly.

'Does he come back for her or is it just you he runs away from?'

'I've no idea. I didn't even know she had a dog.'

'Close then?' he retorted, irritated by her tone.

'I don't think that's anything to do with you,' she spluttered.

'Well, perhaps *she* can start legging it after him then. That's twice I've caught him for you now.'

The woman inhaled sharply and rolled her eyes. 'Well, sorry it's such a hardship you've had to rescue what is *actually* a very small dog.'

'I never said it was a hardship. I just said, perhaps get your sister to look after him properly, then maybe he won't keep running away from you.'

She bristled again. 'He's not running away from me—'

'Looks like it from where I'm standing. Perhaps get her to help you with recall.'

'While that's the obvious solution,' she said, her words dripping with sarcasm, 'she's laid up in hospital, so I think it'd be a bit difficult.'

Stepping forwards, she snatched the lead off him. 'Sorry it's been such a chore to save a small dog.'

'I didn't say it was a chore. Perhaps just keep a tighter hold on the lead, so there's not a next time,' he said politely, starting to walk away.

'The way I feel about him at the moment, if there is a next time, I'd say don't bother,' she called out to him.

'Perhaps I'll remember that *next time*.'

'What makes you think there will be another time?'

He turned, raising an eyebrow and giving her a look. '*Really* want me to answer that?'

Griffin noticed Maggie coming out of the cafe, looking for him.

'I need to get back to work,' he said.

'Sorry to tear you away on such trivialities,' she said sarcastically.

He walked towards Maggie's, shaking his head in disbelief. How could this woman be *so* argumentative?

'You're welcome by the way,' he called loudly, over his shoulder, as he disappeared around the back of the cafe.

§ § §

Tess watched as the man walked around the back of the cafe.

Who the bloody hell was that? Criticising her and the dog? she fumed. The bloody rudeness of him, suggesting the dog was running away from *her*! She glared down at Frank, who was sat staring forlornly at the beach.

'You are rapidly becoming a complete pain in the arse,' she snapped.

Frank looked up with his huge impassive eyes and sighed heavily, then resumed staring at the beach.

Dragging Frank along, Tess marched along the beach until she was calmer. She rang her sister, who admitted to being bored senseless in her hospital bed.

Tess confessed to moving a few things around in the restaurant and making a couple of tiny changes. Lorraine sounded enthusiastic and insisted Tess send photos of the new layout.

'Are you cross? That I've changed things?' Tess asked.

'Nope. Been meaning to do it myself but haven't had the time or the inclination.'

'Good. I'll send pics when I'm back.'

'How are you getting on with Frank?'

'I'm not. We tolerate each other. He keeps running off, and I've just had some bloke have a go at me about it.'

'Why did he have a go?'

'Frank ran off and he saved him from being squashed under an RNLI truck.'

'Oh God, did you thank him for saving Frank?'

'Err, not as such.'

'Can you go and thank him for me?'

'No. He was rude to me.'

'How was he rude?'

'Well, he—'

'Oh God, did you get all snippy with him?' Lorraine interrupted.

'No,' Tess said defensively, feeling guilty.

'You did, didn't you? Christ, don't come in and start upsetting the locals. They're all lovely.'

'I'm not upsetting the locals…' spluttered Tess.

'I bet you are. You're used to dealing with people in a high-stress environment and your default is to get snippy.'

'I *do not* have a snippy default!'

'Yes you do, and you know it. Go and say sorry to the man.'

'I don't think I need to.'

'You know you do. Look, the doctor's here, I've gotta go. Apologise, then go home and chill out. Have a rest before we reopen tomorrow, you'll need it. Bye. Love ya.'

Tess was left staring at her phone in disbelief. *A snippy default?* She shoved her phone into her pocket and carried on marching up the beach, with Frank trundling behind her.

Thirty minutes later, Tess was standing outside Maggie's cafe, wondering whether she should just ignore what her sister said and go home via the chippy, or whether she should actually go in and apologise. Her phone buzzed in her pocket, and she drew it out to see a text from her sister.

You said sorry yet?

Tess replied. *NO*

Lorraine replied. *DO IT.*

Tess tutted and shoved the phone back in her pocket and eyed the door to the cafe. Her sister's words about not upsetting the locals echoed in her ears and she steeled herself to say sorry.

Taking a breath, she pushed open the door, plastering on a bright smile.

'Tess darling. You OK?' Maggie greeted her. 'How's Lorraine?'

Tess smiled at Maggie. She loved her motherly ways. It always made Tess quite nostalgic to see her.

'She's started moaning and ordering me about, so I'd say she's improving.'

'Give her my love, won't you?'

'Of course.'

'Good, now what can I get you? Kitchen's just closed, but I can do you a drink or a scone or something?'

'Actually, I wanted to have a word with the guy who was outside earlier?' She peered round Maggie's shoulder. 'Tall guy? Brownish hair?'

'Griff? He's over the road, dropping something into Foxy.'

'I'll catch him there then. Thanks, Mags!'

Frank strained at his lead, dragging her across the road, beside himself in excitement at the prospect of seeing Solo. As she pushed the climbing centre door open, her pocket caught on the door handle, and she was dragged backwards with a jolt. She accidentally let go of Frank's lead and he shot off like a bullet, yipping loudly.

'Shit!' Her coat tore as she tried to free the pocket. 'Frank!' she yelled.

'And here we are *again*,' the man from earlier said, approaching her, holding onto Frank's lead. 'Who *knew* this would happen and we would meet again so soon? I mean, what are the *chances* of that?'

Tess tugged at her jacket, looking at him murderously.

Solo was trailing after Frank with a forlorn expression at him being led away.

'Are you stuck?' the man asked mildly. 'On the door handle?'

'No.' Tess was flustered.

'Looks like it,' he said, amused.

'OK, maybe a little,' she said, irritated he'd once again rescued Frank.

'Can I help?' he ventured. 'Those door handles can be relentless.'

'It's fine.' Tess suddenly realised how stupid she must look, being held hostage by a door handle, when all she needed to do was slip her coat off. She unzipped her coat and managed to twist it from the climbing centre door.

'There,' she said. 'All done.' She held out her hand for Frank's lead. 'Thank you for rescuing him *again* and I apologise if I was snippy earlier.'

His lips twitched. '*Snippy?*'

She nodded. 'According to my sister, I have a tendency to be snippy on occasion.'

'Ah,' he said sagely. 'Just a tendency?'

Tess squared her shoulders. 'Apparently so. *Her* words, not mine.'

He folded his arms and leant against the wall. 'And what's your view?'

She frowned. 'What do you mean?'

He chuckled. 'Are you here apologising under duress, or is this genuine? Do you think you were snippy?'

Tess raised her chin defensively. 'Perhaps. Maybe a little,' she ventured.

'Ah well, in that case, apology accepted. Thank you.'

'Just the person I want to see!' Foxy exclaimed, approaching her. 'That counter I was talking about will fit.'

'Oh! Fantastic! Let me give you some money for it!'

'Don't be silly. You can feed me again with another monstrous sandwich and an espresso.'

'Sounds like a fair deal,' she agreed.

Foxy looked between the two of them for a moment.

'Did I interrupt something?'

'She was apologising to me for being snippy,' Griff said, with a twinkle of mischief in his eye.

Tess went red. 'I said, my sister *thought* I *might* have been snippy. I haven't actually admitted to it.'

'Oh, I think you did,' Griff said.

'Oh, I don't think I did,' Tess rebuffed.

Foxy rolled his eyes. 'Anyway! Griff, can you give me a hand with something up the road to Tess's?'

Griff shrugged. 'Sure. What are we carrying?'

'Breakfast bar.'

'I can carry it,' Tess said.

'Nope. It's a lump of oak. Super heavy. Griff won't mind, will you, Griff?'

Griffin inclined his head. 'Happy to help out. Tess was it?'

She nodded. 'Griff was it?' She raised an eyebrow. 'Did your parents not like you?'

'Short for Griffin,' he said. 'As for my parents; I walked on water.' He turned to Foxy. 'Point me in the direction.'

Foxy beckoned. 'Tess, see you at yours?'

'OK.'

'Need me to take the dog?' Griffin asked, deadpan.

'I think I'll be OK,' she said sarcastically.

'Watch out for those door handles. They can attack ruthlessly at any moment.'

'Smart-arse,' Tess muttered under her breath to his retreating back.

'Heard that,' he called. 'I feel another apology coming on.'

Tess stomped up the road, fuming about Griffin. She opened the restaurant door and cleared a few chairs out of the way to give them a clear route. She'd already sourced two bar stools from the local junk shop, which she'd scrubbed, and they looked like new. Pushing the stools aside, she unclipped Frank and pointed to his cushion in the window. He ignored her and trotted around the corner to the storeroom, had a drink of water, and then stalked back past her, to his cushion.

'You and me are going to fall out soon,' she said murderously. Frank turned his back and looked out of the window.

When Frank started yipping, Tess knew the boys were close. They manoeuvred their way into the restaurant, and Foxy led them over to where the breakfast bar would go.

'Perfect!' Tess said, clapping her hands. 'That's going to look amazing!'

'Fits like a glove!' Foxy exclaimed and produced a few brackets and screws from his pocket. 'Can I grab that screwdriver from earlier?'

Tess hurried over to the drawer and handed it over. She glanced at Griffin, who was looking around the restaurant with interest.

'So, this is like a chef's table?' he asked.

'Yeah. Foxy took out a load of stuff for me and helped me move it around so we could open up the kitchen more.'

'I like a chef's table,' Griff said. 'Although by rights they should actually be *in* the kitchen, but as it's quite small here it makes sense.'

'Best place for it, I thought,' Tess said, slightly defensive. 'Plus, it means I can get a few more covers in.'

'Hopefully your chef isn't the shy type,' Griff said. 'I know some chefs who won't even entertain the idea of having someone look into the kitchen during service.'

Tess stared at him in horror. The thought genuinely hadn't occurred to her.

'I'm sure it'll be fine,' she said testily, annoyed he'd pointed it out. *Who the hell did this guy think he was?*

Griffin's eyes widened. 'So, you've not checked with your chef?' He gave a half-laugh. 'Good luck with that one then.' He glanced over at Foxy. 'Are we done, mate? I need to get on?'

'No, I'm good. Thanks very much,' Foxy said, as he finished screwing a bracket to the wall. 'Appreciate it.'

'Yes, thank you very much,' Tess said stiffly, just wishing this obnoxious guy would leave. 'I'm grateful for your help.'

His lips twitched, as if he found her discomfort amusing.

'Now that wasn't too hard was it?'

'I don't know what you mean,' Tess said, raising her chin defensively.

'Being nice, and not being…' he frowned, 'what *was* the word? Snippy, wasn't it?'

Tess shot him a dirty look.

'See you around, Tess.'

'So annoying,' she muttered, as she watched him leave. She turned to Foxy. 'Do you want a coffee or anything? Another sandwich?'

'For once I will decline,' he said, pulling the stools over towards the breakfast bar and pushing them underneath. 'Perfect fit,' he murmured. 'I'm out for dinner later, so I'm saving myself.'

'Anywhere nice?'

'My friend's house. Curry night.'

'Nice.'

Foxy stood back and admired his work. 'Looks great, doesn't it? I love it when we find a use for things that would have just sat about.'

'I'll send some pictures to Lorraine. She'll be really pleased.'

'Say hi from me.' He checked his watch. 'I need to go. See you later!'

'Thanks again!' she called after him, and only just managed to grab Frank at the last minute before he followed them out.

CHAPTER 5

Griffin signed the paperwork with a flourish and presented it back to the solicitor. He remembered him from his younger days, and he hadn't changed much at all, apart from significantly less hair.

'She left very strict instructions,' the solicitor said. 'She'd be pleased you're back.'

'I'm not sure for how long, but I will do the house up and get it shipshape again. I'll do it for her, even if I don't stay.'

The solicitor nodded. 'Best she could hope for.' He explained the value of the funds and when Griff would be in receipt of them. He also suggested a couple of reputable roofers who might be able to give an honest quote for the roof. After an illuminating ten minutes, Griff bade him goodbye and pondered on what needed to be done in the house and what sort of money it would take to do it up. He was busy musing when he saw Maggie standing in front of him, smiling.

'Sorry, Maggie. Daydreaming on your dime,' he said, getting to his feet.

She waved a hand dismissively. 'Stop it. Lots to think about, I suspect. Quick question?'

'Go for it.'

'You OK to stick around until Saturday?'

'Anything for you, Mags.'

'Excellent. Any specials today?'

'Someone over ordered on the sweetcorn, I see, so I'm thinking maybe a sweetcorn fritter stack?'

'Tell me more.'

'Erm, maybe sweetcorn and feta fritter stack, with something like grilled tomato, avocado and salad? Maybe with some green chilli dressing?'

She pursed her lips. 'I like the idea. Put it in a brioche bun instead. People like finger food. They can take it to the beach, even in this weather. A stack is just too bloody fiddly.'

'In a bun it is.'

'Or a wrap. Give people the choice.'

'On it.'

'I'll chuck it on a specials board. Oh, can you knock up some more mince pies when you get a sec, my love? People have got the mince pie and coffee bug now Christmas is approaching!'

As Griff got busy, he realised that he was happy. He'd not felt that way for a while. Crushing grief had kept his senses dulled for what seemed like an eternity, but there was something healing about this place, and being among these people in the place he grew up. Was it just nostalgia? Was it home?

He whistled as he set about making his fritters. His mind wandered back to the accident as he worked, his hands moving methodically, without any real help from his brain. He remembered waking up on the side of the road in the central reservation, opening his eyes and wondering what happened. Then he remembered the horror, and then he remembered the pain. He felt a wave of grief coming; the back of his throat closed, and tears prickled behind his eyelids.

'Griff!'

He jumped. Foxy was standing on the other side of the serving hatch, wearing a pained expression.

'Mate. Set my heart on a breakfast burrito and now there's a sweetcorn thing?' He pulled a face.

'You'll like it,' Griff said. 'Don't worry.'

Foxy viewed him sceptically. 'You think?'

'I know.'

'OK. I'll have one then. Got to keep my strength up.'

Griff laughed. 'I'll run it over if you're busy?'

'Top man.'

Griff had spent some time chatting with Foxy the day before. He was interested to hear Foxy had also been in the forces, although he could pretty much tell that just by looking at him. They had swapped armed forces stories and Griff had liked Foxy immediately for being a genuinely nice bloke. He was also toying with getting back into climbing, as he hadn't done any for years and had missed it.

Foxy left and Griff set about making his order. Maggie appeared.

'Foxy wants a—'

'He's placed his order directly,' Griff said with a smile.

'He's a tinker,' Maggie said fondly. 'Don't know where he puts all that food.'

'In his arms by the looks of it,' Griffin said, rolling his eyes. 'They're the size of my thighs.'

'Well, you do need feeding up a bit,' Maggie said, bustling off.

'A challenge I fully accept!'

The lunch rush waned, and Griff stepped outside to take a break. Foxy was loading climbing gear into his Defender, and he called over to Griff.

'Who knew sweetcorn fritters could be so good?'

'Told ya,' Griff grinned.

'How long you there 'til?'

'Saturday.'

'I want breakfast burritos back on the menu before then!'

'Deal.'

Griff watched as Foxy went back inside the centre. His phone beeped with the arrival of a text; it was from an unknown number. Frowning, he opened it.

I know where you are. Watch your back. Killer. You should be dead in prison. You don't deserve to live.

Griff stared at the message. His mind was reeling. He couldn't think who would send something like this.

The telltale bubbles showing someone was typing popped up and then stopped abruptly. Another text arrived.

Your end is coming. Tick tock, watch that clock. Wait to die.

Griff stared at it, a light sweat breaking out over him. *Who the hell is this?*

His phone pinged again, and he had to drag his eyes down to look at it. He was relieved when he saw it was his friend and old neighbour, Mark, asking if he would be back in Portsmouth at Christmas time.

Griff typed a reply.

I'm back at Mum's place for a bit – needs some sorting out. Next time I've got some decent leave, we'll meet up, yeah? Maybe I'll come back and visit!

Without waiting for a response, he stuffed the phone back into his pocket. He looked around carefully to see if anyone was watching who might have sent the malicious message. He checked the time; he needed to be in the next town by 4.45 p.m. Maggie said he could finish at 4 p.m. to get there on time. He had two hours to go. He looked up the hill and saw a large party of people approaching the cafe, so he ducked back inside.

'Come on, COME ON!' he shouted, as he got stuck behind a caravan in a narrow lane. He watched the time ticking away on his dashboard and roared in frustration. He couldn't be late, not today. Finally, he managed to overtake, driving like he was competing in a rally, to make sure he got to his destination on time. He skidded into a car parking space, and ran for five hundred yards almost flat out, arriving with one minute to spare. He buzzed on the secure door.

'Ello?' A disembodied voice floated out.

'It's Griffin Jones. I have an appointment now.'

Griff was greeted with silence and then a loud buzzer sounded.

'Second floor,' came the voice again.

Griff pushed open the door and ran up the stairs. He was hot and bothered from his rush to get there, sweating profusely, despite the frigid air in the building.

A woman with badly cut, greying hair, and red spectacles peered over a tall counter at him.

'Mr Jones? Don't be late again.'

'But I wasn't late,' he said.

'Argumentative,' she said, making a note.

'I'm not,' stammered Griffin, 'I was just saying—'

'Mr Denton is in the office at the end of the corridor.'

'Right… thank you.'

Griffin turned and walked down the corridor to the end where he knocked on a brown 1970s-style office door with a frosted glass panel at shoulder height.

'Yeah,' a voice called.

Griff pushed open the door and faced his new offender manager. He was a large man, with a pale waxy complexion that suggested a healthy dislike of the outside and a poor diet. He wore a crumpled grey suit, with a thick woollen cardigan underneath. He had a perpetually tired expression. Griff estimated he was in his early sixties.

'Mr Denton,' Griff said, extending a hand politely.

'Peter.' The man shook his hand. 'Griffin Jones. You always cut it this fine?'

'I had forty-five minutes to get here, then I was stuck behind a caravan.'

'I suggest you leave earlier.'

'I was working,' Griff said quietly, not wanting to aggravate the man.

'Right. Tell me what's happening. I've read your file from the bloke up north. Can't hardly make sense out of it, but he said you gave him no trouble. Worked hard. So, why are you here?'

'I do work hard. I like to work. The place I was working went bust, so I moved back home into my mum's house. I got permission to move area.'

'She alive?'

'No. She died. Left me the house. Needs a lot of work.'

'You gonna do it?'

'Some of it. Re-roofing it will be a problem for me. I'll admit defeat on that.'

'I see you're a chef?'

'I am.'

'You said you were working. You didn't inform me.'

'It wasn't planned. I'm helping out a friend. Her usual chef's mum had a fall, so I said I'd help out until Saturday.'

'Where is this?'

'Maggie's Beach Cafe, Castleby.'

Peter's whole face changed; it lit up. 'Oh, I know Maggie. Salt of the bloody earth. Fine figure of a woman.' He winked at Griff. 'Tell me, is she still single?'

Griff stifled a laugh. 'I don't think she is, no,' he said, adopting a rueful expression and thinking Maggie owed him a favour. 'In fact, I know she said she was out with her fella tonight.'

Peter's face fell.

'I'll tell her you remember her fondly though?' Griff suggested.

'Do that. Right. Do you have a sentence plan?' He rifled through the paperwork. 'Ah yes.' He scanned it. 'All seems very sensible. Except we need to change employer now and home address, don't we?'

'Yeah. Once working for Maggie ends, I'm going to be searching for a new job. There are plenty of hotels locally, and I'm sure they'll need some help.'

'Good. Any anger issues?'

'No. I don't have that—'

'Sorry, my mistake, that was the previous client.' He frowned as he read the notes. 'Nasty fellow,' he murmured to himself. 'Don't know why he was ever given probation.'

Griff coughed discretely to remind him he was in the room. Peter looked up in annoyance from what he was reading.

'Oh yes. Sorry. So, no issues with anyone?'

'Err. No. Been keeping myself to myself.'

'Best way. Some people have issues with people on probation. Nine times out of ten it's their problem, not yours. So, nothing you wanna tell me?'

Griff wondered whether to tell him about the text.

'Erm, I got a text today. Don't know who it was from. Unpleasant.'

'Show me.'

Griff showed him the screen of his phone.

'Can you screenshot these and email them to me, so I have a record?' Peter asked, making notes in the file. 'Keep a note if any more come in and send them to me. If they escalate, go and tell the police, then you're covered.'

'Covered for…?'

Peter waved a hand vaguely. 'You know, in case it gets out of hand.'

'Oh.' Griff was confused but didn't want to push it.

Peter consulted his notes. 'Right. So, we'll meet every fortnight, I think. Face to face? But we'll do ten days in this first instance and then take it from there until I know you better.'

'OK. Obviously, I might need to change times, etc., if I find a new job.'

'Yes, well, I'm prepared to be flexible.'

Griff suppressed a smile. 'You could perhaps come to Castleby and kill two birds with one stone; check on me and see Maggie.'

Peter's eyes lit up at the prospect. 'Now that's an idea.' He scrabbled about on his desk and produced a hardback diary. He flicked forwards a few pages.

'How does the fourteenth of December sound? Same time? In Maggie's?'

'Works for me,' Griff said.

'Excellent. Now, any training courses or anything?'

'Nope. I've had access to some counselling, but that's over now. It was good though.'

Peter eyed him. 'Head in a good place?'

'As good as I can expect, I think. I feel more settled.'

'Not going to do anything stupid?' He consulted his notes. 'Not that you did anything stupid before; it was one of those things.'

Griffin inhaled deeply and tried to push away the tears that threatened.

'No, I'm not going to do anything stupid, unless you count refurbishing my mum's house.'

Peter laughed. 'Each to their own and all that. But don't forget, it's not your mum's house, it's your house. *Yours*. She left it to you?'

'She did.'

'Then start thinking of it as yours and not hers. Ownership of things is important. It grounds us; gives us roots and a base.'

'OK.'

'Right. See you in ten days. I don't need to remind you of the rules, do I?'

'No.'

'Good. See you at Maggie's on the fourteenth at 4.45 p.m.'

'Thank you.'

§ § §

Tess's day had been a nightmare. The agency chef was close to useless. It was Linden, the trainee, who was doing most of the cooking, *helped* by the useless agency chef. Despair drove Tess to surreptitiously sneak out and ring the agency to complain. After some negotiation, they agreed to send a different chef on Saturday.

Tess found herself running the restaurant as well as helping in the kitchen to get the food out. At the end of service on Thursday night, the agency chef informed her the environment was too stressful for him and he wouldn't be coming in the next day. Tess almost punched him in the face.

As a last resort, she contacted Carl, the old chef, and asked, as a one-off, if he could cover the Friday for her until the new chef came on Saturday. Mercifully, because Lorraine had always been good to him, plus Tess bribed him with a bonus, he agreed.

Tess locked up. Tired, but desperate for some fresh air, she decided to have a stroll around the town with Frank so they could stretch their legs.

She wandered down towards the harbour, admiring the Christmas lights in the windows and the various wreaths on front doors. Frank snuffled along and she took the path up the hill towards the castle, which passed the top of the huge wall the climbing centre used. She peered over the wall and saw the lights were still on; there were people in there climbing, even this late in the evening. She chuckled to herself as she saw Foxy sat by one of the windows, trying to untangle some Christmas lights.

She breathed in the sea air and rounding the corner, climbed the last steep flight of steps leading to the top of Castle Mount. The area was fairly deserted, apart from a young couple sitting together on a bench, kissing. The streetlights cast a warm glow over them, and she had a momentary pang of loneliness; did she miss her ex? Or did she just want to have someone to walk with and kiss on a night like this?

Wandering across Castle Mount, she looked down at the RNLI station, which was in darkness. She followed the steep path which gradually wound downwards and noticed a lone figure sat on one of the benches, illuminated by the streetlight. She saw the figure lean forwards, elbows resting on knees, their head in their hands. She was close enough to make out the figure's shoulders were shaking, and she heard snatches of wracking sobs. As the person raised their head and wiped their face, she realised with a shock, it was the annoying guy from earlier. What was his name? Griffin? *Is he upset?* The carer in her wanted to go down and see if he was alright; see if there was anything she could do. But she wasn't a nurse any more. She wasn't the person to make it all better any more.

She stepped back slowly, afraid he would see her and think she was spying. She wondered what he was doing out here in the dark and cold. Upset. Then she realised she felt sorry for him. She wondered who or what was making him upset. Quietly, she retreated back the way she had come. Home to a bath and then bed.

CHAPTER 6

Castleby was always heaving on a Saturday, so Tess knew the restaurant would be busy. After the nightmare Thursday, Tess had reduced the menu to breakfast, brunch and light lunch dishes, and simplified the evening menu. She ensured as much of it as possible was prepped while the old chef was in on Friday. She'd had a long chat with Lorraine over breakfast, agreeing a lot of her decisions and plans for the weekend. Lorraine was making good progress and was wracked with guilt that Tess had been lumbered looking after the restaurant alone.

The agency chef had arrived, half an hour late, and had breezed in like he owned the place, speaking to Tess like she was a first-class idiot. He reminded her of a few of the consultants she used to work with at the hospital. Within an hour she decided he was an insufferable twat.

There was a steady stream of customers for breakfast and lunch, and a welcome lull in the afternoon. The agency chef took a break and returned over an hour late for evening service, confessing he was exhausted and had fallen asleep in his car.

In no uncertain terms, Tess told him to buck his ideas up or not to bother coming back. She also said she wouldn't be paying for the half hour he was late in the morning, nor the excessive break he'd taken in the afternoon.

At around eight, a group of men appeared at the door asking for a table for nine. Tess had just cleared one of the larger tables, so she agreed, on the proviso they understood the kitchen was closing at 8.45 p.m. Settling them in, they seemed a pleasant bunch and confessed they were on a booze cruise on a friend's boat. They had decided to stay for the night as they liked the town.

They chose expensive wine and all ordered starters and main courses, some of them choosing the most expensive option. The group was pleasant to Beth, the young waitress, and to Tess's relief, they weren't being too raucous.

Their starters and main courses were consumed without complaint and the group started arguing good-naturedly over pudding and brandy.

Tess took their orders and retreated to the kitchen to help Linden make them as the chef had left at 9.01 p.m., refusing to do any prep for the next day. Linden had stepped up.

'Right then,' Tess said, balancing desserts. 'Chocolate mousse?'

A few hands were raised. Tess scooted around to place the dishes down. As she leant over, one man ran his hand up the back of her leg, and between her legs. She jumped smartly out of the way, smacking his hand away, almost dropping a plate.

She glared at him.

'Don't do that again,' she said tightly. 'This is a restaurant, not a lap dancing club. It's completely inappropriate.' She tried to say it pleasantly because she knew what blokes like this were like; particularly when they had consumed a lot of alcohol.

The man raised his hands and adopted a surprised expression.

'Don't know what you mean!' he said.

'Yes you do,' she said firmly, staring him out. 'Don't do it again.'

'HA! What you up to, Frenchie?' slurred one of the men. 'Up to your old tricks again?'

Tess went back to the kitchen to get the remaining desserts, careful to give him a wide berth.

She took orders for coffee and then set about making them.

'Miss! Oh, Miss!' one of the men called.

She breathed deeply and plastered on a warm smile. 'What's up?' she asked.

'Can we have another few bottles of wine?'

Tess hesitated. 'I can sell them to you to take back to the boat, but I have to close in half an hour.'

'We'll have drunk them in half an hour!' another man shouted.

'Fine,' Tess said and reluctantly selected the wine they wanted. She placed the bottles on the table, carefully avoiding the groper, and then went back to finish the coffees.

Half an hour later, Tess approached the table.

'OK, lads, I need you to settle up, please. I have to close. We've all got homes to go to. I hope you've had a good evening.'

'Excellent!' one of the men said, producing a credit card. 'Put it on here and take a thirty per cent tip too.'

Tess took the card, thrilled at the massive tip. 'Thanks very much. I'll get the machine.'

Tess finished the bill and keyed in the amount to the card machine. She handed it to the man, who efficiently tapped in his number.

Tess saw with relief the transaction had gone through. 'Do you need a receipt?' she asked.

He waved it away, shaking his head. 'Right, lads! Are we all set to get back on board?'

The men stood up, and Tess set about collecting jackets. She was side-tracked when another couple asked to settle their bill.

Tess waved off the men and the couple with relief. She closed the door, turned the sign to 'Closed' and slumped against it. Frank opened an eye from where he slumbered on his cushion.

'We'll go out in a minute,' she chided. 'Don't be looking at me like that.'

She went back to the kitchen and sent Beth and Linden home. Then set about finishing prepping the potatoes and vegetables for the next day.

The sound of Frank's sudden barking startled her.

'What's the matter?' she said, walking back into the restaurant. She gasped in a mix of fear and surprise. The man who had touched her inappropriately was standing there, leaning against a table.

Tess tried not to panic. Quickly, she switched the lights to the restaurant back on, in the hope someone passing would think it was strange and perhaps look in.

'Thought we could have a chat,' he slurred. 'I think we've got some unfinished business.'

'I don't think we have. All I need to do is let you out,' she said shortly, going to walk past him. As she did, he grabbed her wrist and yanked her. Gasping, she managed to twist herself out of his hold. He grabbed her again and pushed her against the wall, holding her there with the length of his body, while he rested his forearm across her neck, forcing pressure on her throat.

'*So*,' he breathed. The scent of his breath was foul. 'Not so gobby now, are you?'

She struggled against him and then realised he was becoming aroused. His eyes were glassy, his breathing heavy.

'You put an idea in my head,' he whispered, licking her ear.

Tess shuddered with revulsion. She tried to push him away, but he increased the pressure on the arm pinning her throat.

'Get off me, otherwise you will be spending the night at the local police station,' she managed through gritted teeth, choking as the pressure on her windpipe increased.

'I can assure you, I won't,' he said. 'You see, me and my solicitor friends are somewhat immune to the law.'

He tried to kiss her. She turned her head away and ended up with his spit all over the side of her face. He fumbled, trying to grope her breasts.

Tess felt a wave of anger build at this sweaty idiot who felt he was entitled to take anything he wanted. She saw red.

'Get off me,' she yelled, managing to stamp on his foot. He cried out in pain, and she shoved him away. He tripped over the leg of a chair and ended up on the floor.

Terrified and desperate to get help, Tess screamed. She went to jump over him, trying to reach the door, as he lay on the floor, but she wasn't quick enough. Her heart was pounding. She knew this was going to end badly if she couldn't get away. Fear coiled in her belly. She hadn't felt this frightened since she was almost attacked by a madman on shift in A&E.

As she tried to jump over him, he grabbed her foot and yanked her towards him, so she fell and sprawled out on the floor. He was surprisingly quick for someone who had consumed so much alcohol. He crawled towards her, his eyes glistening with intent. She scooted back away from him, trying to kick him, but he kept dodging.

'Get away from me!' she screamed. Frank was barking and running along the window seat, scrabbling at the window.

'You know you want it. You all fucking do. You're just a bunch of fucking prick teases,' he said, lunging at her.

'Get off me,' she said, kicking out, as she tried to get away. Her foot caught him on the side of the head, and he stared in surprise.

'You bitch!' he snarled. He grabbed her again and she felt her shirt rip. She fought him, pushing him away and trying to scratch him with her nails.

'BITCH!' He backhanded her across the face.

Tess felt her lip split, and it fuelled her rage even more. She screamed for help again and scrabbled away from him. Finally, she managed to get to the door. Knowing he was behind her, she didn't dare risk a glance; she wrenched open the door and ran out into the road, straight into the path of an oncoming car.

§ § §

Griff had worked his last shift for Maggie; John was returning. She had pressed a large envelope into his hand and thanked him profusely for helping out.

'I wish I could ask you to stay, but you deserve more than a little beach cafe,' she said. 'You're a very talented chef.'

'From your mouth to God's ear,' Griff replied. 'Thank you for everything. Especially, you know, for listening and for the probation thing.'

He had reluctantly told Mags about his offender manager. Maggie had remembered Peter from the old days. She had chuckled when Griff relayed that Peter wanted to meet at her place for their next meeting.

She waved his comment away. 'Don't worry. I'll always vouch for you.'

'Thanks.'

'Now get yourself off. Lots to do in that house.'

'I'm not going home. I'm seeing my mate, Tina. She's just moved to Pembroke, so we're catching up over some grub.'

Maggie beamed broadly. 'Good for you. Have a lovely time.'

'See you around, Mags.'

'See you, my love. And Griff?'

He turned. 'What?'

'Anything you need. I'm always here for you. OK?'

Griff felt his throat close with emotion. 'Thanks, Mags. You're one in a million,' he managed.

'Go and enjoy yourself.'

He touched his head in a mock salute and jogged up the road to get his car.

Griff enjoyed seeing Tina. They'd served together, and she'd been his senior on the ship. They'd always got on well and he had learnt a lot from her. They'd both left the navy around the same time, and she'd gone home to a broken marriage. She had finally admitted to herself and everyone else, that she preferred women, and she was now blissfully happy in a new relationship.

They both missed the navy life in some ways, but not in others. They'd eaten in a local pub, where they'd criticised the food quietly to each other, sniggering over various things. After a quick coffee and a series of embarrassing yawns, he'd dropped Tina off and headed home.

Still yawning widely, he drove back to Castleby on autopilot. As he entered the town he swore; there were flashing lights, large plant machinery in the middle of the road, and a diversion in place. Tutting, he realised he'd have to do a sweep of the town to get to the other end of his road.

Turning to follow the diversion, he drove down the high street, absently thinking it was quiet for a Saturday night. Then reasoned with himself it wasn't the holiday season; it was the beginning of December. He braked lightly as he rounded the corner and out of nowhere a woman ran out on to the road. Blood was smeared across her cheek and her shirt was ripped. He stood on the brakes instantly, helpless, as the car skidded sideways on the frost that had settled and the car hit her, the sound a dull thud.

'FUCK!' He scrambled to get out of the car, running around to the front. The woman was lying in the road, eyes closed, and he realised it was Tess, the snippy woman with the pug. Movement caught his eye. A man with a bloody face staggered in the restaurant doorway. He took one look at Griffin and Tess in the road and lumbered off awkwardly.

Griff was torn between giving chase and staying with Tess.

Frank was barking and butting Tess's shoulder with his little snout, whining.

'Don't move,' Griff said to her, although she didn't look like she was conscious. He rang for an ambulance and explained what had happened. A car behind blasted its horn. Griff walked back up and told the car to turn around and go a different way.

Griff ran back to Tess and knelt next to her. She moved slightly and made a small noise.

'Jesus. Thank God,' he muttered. 'Tess? Tess, can you hear me?'

She stirred and opened an eye. 'Oh God,' she groaned and then her eyes opened wide. 'Oh God! That man…'

'That man what?' Griff said. 'Did he hurt you?'

She focused on Griff. 'What are you doing here?'

'You ran into my car,' he said. 'Tess, did that man hurt you?'

Tears ran from the corners of her eyes.

Griff tried again. 'Tess. Are you OK to stand? Does anything hurt?'

'My head,' she whispered. 'My head hurts.'

'Do your arms and legs hurt?'

'What? No… I… don't think so.'

'Can you stand? I need to get you off the road.'

'I'm on the road?'

Griff felt he ought to lift her off the road. He placed her gently on the pavement and then moved his car, so the others could pass. He rushed back and knelt beside her. She was shivering, so he stripped off his coat and gently tucked it around her shoulders.

'Tess, who was that man?'

Tess was deathly pale, and her eyes were closed.

She opened her eyes and smiled at him.

'You've got a lovely face,' she said drowsily. 'Nice eyes.'

Frank was still pushing her with his snout every now and again, looking mournful. In the distance, Griff heard an ambulance.

'Hang in there. Ambulance is coming.'

'Just going to sleep,' she murmured. 'Just need to sleep.'

'No. Don't go to sleep,' he said. 'Tell me what happened.'

'Man tried to…' She gulped out a sob and then passed out.

The ambulance arrived, closely followed by a police car.

The paramedics peppered Griff with questions, which he was largely unable to answer. He just kept repeating he'd seen a man stagger to the door and run off, and that Tess looked like she'd been trying to get away from him.

The paramedics loaded Tess into the ambulance. They were concerned about the head injury. At the last second, Griff managed to stop Frank from getting into the ambulance by ushering him into the restaurant. Frank then stood on two legs, staring out of the window, his front paws against the glass, whining.

Griff watched them go, realising she was still wearing his coat and his wages from Maggie were in the pocket. He hoped the coat wouldn't be chucked away and the money lost.

A police officer approached, wanting to ask Griff more questions.

'I'm happy to answer questions, but we need to lock the place up and turn everything off, as she's running it on her own at the moment,' Griff said.

'So, you know the victim?'

'I do. I was here yesterday with Rob Fox putting a breakfast bar in.'

The PC gestured towards the restaurant, and they stepped inside. Griff closed the door and petted Frank, who was sat on his cushion, staring out of the window, whining softly.

'It's OK, Frank, you can come home with me,' Griff said.

The PC glanced around. 'There are signs of a struggle here,' he observed, taking in a chair on its side and the haphazard nature of some of the tables and other chairs.

'She looked upset, like she wanted to get away.' Griff recounted Tess running out into the road with blood on her face and a ripped shirt, and then the man in the doorway who ran off. He relayed the few words Tess had said before she passed out.

'Can you tell me your movements tonight, please?' the PC asked.

Griff outlined what he had been doing, and confirmed he had neither been drinking, nor taking drugs

The PC looked around the restaurant and noticed the CCTV in the corner.

'Hopefully that's working,' he said, nodding towards it. 'Any ideas where the recording might be?'

'No, but I'm sure she won't mind you looking,' Griff said.

The PC walked off towards the back of the restaurant and out into the storeroom. Griff heard his radio burbling quietly.

Frank left his cushion. He trotted over to Griff and jumped up onto his lap.

'Alright, mate,' he said absently, scratching him behind the ears. 'Did you have a fright tonight?'

The PC stuck his head around the corner. 'If you want to see what happened, I'm rewinding it.'

Griff put Frank down and went to the back of the restaurant where the PC was on his haunches in front of a small screen.

'So, one of this large party stayed in the loo after they left and waited until she was there alone,' the PC said grimly.

Griff watched with mounting anger as Tess tried to get away from the man. He saw him force her against the wall and then come after her. He saw it play out minute by minute as she became more desperate to get away. He clenched his fists when he saw him hit her, and then saw her scrabble for the door and run out straight in front of his car. He watched the man get unsteadily to his feet and then stagger to the door where he ran off.

'Wow,' the PC said. 'She had a lucky escape.'

'Until she ran into my car.'

'In some ways you did her a favour. If he'd caught her, the likelihood would be he'd have dragged her back in to finish what he'd started.'

'You taking the recording?' Griff asked.

'I am. When she's compos mentis I'll see if we can get a name. Maybe they paid with a card or something.'

Griff held up a hand. 'Right, there were nine of them. Look at all those empties; their bill would have been a lot.' He pressed the enter key on the till and picked up the last credit card receipt, which was for nearly £900.

'This looks about right,' Griff said. 'Look at the time. 9.55 p.m.'

The PC snapped a picture of the receipt, which Griff put back in the till.

The PC sat back down at one of the tables. 'Control tell me you're out on licence.'

Griff sighed. Here it came.

'I am. Few more months. Saw my offender manager yesterday.'

'You living around here now?'

'I am.' Griff reeled off his address. 'I've been working for Maggie at the Beach Cafe.'

'What were you in for?'

Griff eyed him. 'Control not tell you that?'

'You tell me.'

Griff told him.

'OK,' the PC said, standing up and shutting his notebook. 'You need to tell your offender manager about tonight. Only because your name will be on the system. I suggest you head it off with a well-scripted email tonight.'

'Will do.'

'You OK to lock up?'

'I am. Keys are in the till, I think.' Griff recalled Tess putting them in there when she'd unlocked the door for him and Foxy.

'OK.'

'I'll tidy up here for her and then move the car, OK? By the way, what was your name?'

'Ben Baker. I'll let myself out.'

Ben left and Griff surveyed the damage. He went into the kitchen, found a large deep tray and set about clearing away the empties. He tidied up the restaurant, put the chairs back and straightened tables.

Griff stood in the kitchen and assessed what Tess had been doing. He looked in the fridge and cold store, saw the meat for the next day, then noticed copies of the Sunday menu. He looked around. He could come and help tomorrow so at least she wouldn't lose a day's takings. He rang the hospital, saying he was her brother and wanted an update. They told him she'd been admitted because of concerns regarding her head injury, and she was sleeping.

He cleared up, grabbed Frank's lead and locked up.

Griff was almost asleep at the wheel when he got home. Frank snuffled about in the garden for a while, and then trotted in and sat next to Griff in the kitchen while he tapped out an email to his offender manager. He hoped to God he wouldn't say he had breached any rules, but he couldn't see how he had.

Griff got himself ready for bed. He was amused when Frank appeared on the bed next to him and settled down with a contented sigh.

CHAPTER 7

Griff woke early. There was a lot to do. He sprung out of bed and used the shower, all the time eyeing the large spider who was stalking him around the bathroom.

He let Frank out, wondering what to feed him. He made them both some scrambled eggs and then walked briskly along the beach to Tess's restaurant.

Griff got lost in preparation for Sunday lunches. He'd made desserts, sorted out the veg, done battle with the oven, and everything was on track. He was enjoying a coffee and a quick break, when a pretty teenager, with a boy of similar age, knocked on the door.

Griff let them in.

'Hi, guys,' he said. 'I'm guessing you both work here?'

They nodded. The boy stuck out his hand politely.

'I'm Linden. I work in the kitchen. This is Beth; she's the waitress. Where's Tess?'

'Tess was attacked last night; she's in hospital. I'm helping out today.'

'Who attacked Tess?' Beth asked. 'Was it the creep who felt her up?'

'Someone was inappropriate earlier on?'

Beth looked angry. 'Yeah, dirty pervert. Groping her at the table when she had her hands full.'

Griff recounted what had happened and how Tess had run out in front of his car.

'God. Is she OK?' Beth asked.

'I rang last night, but I was going to call again in a minute.'

'I'll do it; my mum's a Sister there. She'll get the deets,' Beth said.

'Are you another agency chef?' Linden asked.

'No. Is there supposed to be someone in to cook today?'

'Yeah, the bloke from yesterday.'

'He's agency?'

'Yeah. The old chef left and then Lorraine had the accident, so Tess has been lumbered. She got an agency chef to cover, but the first one didn't come back after a shift. Yesterday's bloke took the piss too.' He blushed. 'Sorry. He was useless, so I don't know if he's coming back today. Oh also, there's supposed to be a bloke coming in at five thirty to cook; he's applied for the job.'

'Right, OK. What time was the agency bloke due in?'

Linden blinked. 'Nine thirty, I think, but he was late yesterday too.'

'OK,' Griff said. 'No worries. I'll help out today. Don't worry, I'm a chef.'

Griff turned to Beth. 'Beth, are you OK to lay the tables and make them presentable?'

'Sure.'

'Thanks, Beth. So, we can open for coffee and cake at eleven, then our first lunch booking is at 12.15. Right?'

'Yeah.'

'Right, Linden. Let's get on. So, Beth, it says we are fully booked if I'm reading the system right, but we've got the chef's table now, so that's an extra two covers today if anyone comes in and they aren't booked.'

'OK. What's your name? I mean, what do we call you?'

'Griff is fine.'

'Griff?'

'Short for Griffin.'

'OK.'

Griff got Linden busy, while Beth laid up the tables for the lunch rush. A few people trickled in for coffee and cake, and Griff put some chilled music on low. He looked into the restaurant; it had a nice feel to it. A nice vibe.

'First booking here,' Beth announced.

'Showtime!' Griff called.

Lunch went without a hitch, and they managed to do extra covers, as well as some takeaway roast dinners. One woman was so enthralled with Griff's winter pudding she insisted on buying another four portions to take home.

Griff was in the kitchen using some of the leftover vegetables as a basis for a soup he was making for a special in the week when Beth came into the kitchen.

'Griff. That bloke's here.'

'What bloke?'

'The one to cook.'

'Coming.'

Griff left the kitchen and faced the small mouse-like man who was clutching a carrier bag and a roll of knives.

'Hi there,' he said, shaking his hand. 'I'm Griffin Jones.'

'I was looking for Tess,' he said stiffly. 'I am here to make her a meal.'

'Tess has had an accident. She's in hospital, but you're more than welcome to cook for us, though.'

'Who are you?' he asked haughtily.

'I'm a friend. This is Linden; he works in the kitchen, and this is Beth, our waitress.'

'I'd rather cook for the organ grinder, not the monkey,' the small man muttered.

'Sorry?' Griff swore he had misheard the man.

'I'll cook for her when she's back.'

'Erm, I'm not sure when it'll be. I'm sure she's got your number?'

'She has. I don't know why she didn't have the common courtesy to call me herself and postpone.'

Griff found the man irritating. He reckoned he'd give Tess a run for her money on the snippy front.

'She was knocked down by a car last night after being attacked by a customer and she left her phone here. I don't know her passcode otherwise I would have called you.'

'Hmm.' He looked around. 'Well, that will have to go,' he said, pointing to the chef's table. 'I won't have people watch me work.'

Griff raised an eyebrow. 'We had a great time with the couple who were sat there earlier at lunchtime. They said how nice it was to be able to watch.'

'Can't stand it. The menu needs an overhaul too; too much fresh stuff on there. That means too much prep time. We need more frozen stuff we can just defrost as it's ordered.'

'We don't work like that,' Linden said. 'We always have fresh, local produce.'

'I don't work that way,' he said.

'Tess and Lorraine won't like that approach,' Linden said, confident in talking about what he was passionate about. 'We strive to source and cook fresh, local and seasonal. No point having stuff on the menu that's totally out of season. People will know it's not fresh.'

Griff stayed quiet.

'What were you going to cook?' Linden asked. 'What's in the bag?'

'I was going to cook a spaghetti carbonara. It's everyone's favourite.'

Linden snorted. 'My cat could cook one of those with his eyes shut. That wouldn't have got you the job with Tess.'

The man's eyes narrowed. 'I am clearly dealing with a bunch of clueless amateurs who know nothing about running a restaurant. You'll be shut within the month with that attitude.'

'Time for you to leave, I think,' Griff said.

'I mean,' he said, walking around the restaurant. 'It's Sunday, so how many lunches have you sold? How many covers have you done? Twenty? Twenty-five?'

Griff's lips twitched. 'By my count, we've done around fifty roast meals today, plus another fourteen takeaways on Deliveroo. We've done another twelve, no, fourteen, pasta dishes. So, not a bad lunchtime by all accounts, and not a frozen meal in sight.'

'Hmm. I'm sure that's not true. This place isn't for me. I can tell. Too earthy for me.'

'OK. Sorry to hear that. Thanks for coming by though,' Griff said pleasantly.

The small man turned, viewing the place with distaste.

'Let me see you out,' Beth said, holding the door open.

The man marched out. The three of them looked at each other and laughed.

'Right,' Griff said. 'Let's get cleared up and we can head home.'

'Griff, what's this foil-covered dish in the oven?' Linden called.

'It's a roast dinner I'm taking in for Tess,' Griff replied. He turned to Beth. 'What's booked for tomorrow?'

Beth looked at the computer. 'Right, we have the Christmas menu starting tomorrow. We've got an office lunch booking. They've booked out the place for the afternoon. We have thirty for lunch tomorrow. Set menu. Nothing in the evening. She planned to close after the lunch.'

'Most of the stuff is here,' Linden said. 'I prepared the turkeys earlier. We've got locally made Christmas puddings. All we need to do is veg, make mince pies and a few bulk starters, which we can do tomorrow.'

'Sounds like a plan. Beth, are you working tomorrow?'

'Yes, but I can ask my sister to help if Tess is still out of action.'

'Great. Give me your number and I'll text you when I've seen Tess.'

The three worked to clear the restaurant and get it ready for the next day. Satisfied they had done as much as they could, Griff grabbed Tess's roast dinner. He set off for the hospital, with Frank sitting in the passenger seat.

Griff parked up and turned to Frank.

'You're going to have to wait here. You're not allowed in.'

Frank eyed him and lay down on the seat with a sigh.

Griff grabbed the cool bag carefully and stepped out into the frigid air, shivering because he didn't have a coat. He jogged over to the hospital entrance and looked for the ward Tess was in. Beth's mum had been helpful, providing an update and the name of the ward.

Griff located the ward and buzzed to be let in. Approaching the nurses' station he looked on the whiteboard for her name and which room she was in. He quietly approached the door, knocked lightly and stepped in.

Griff's first thought was how small she looked in the large hospital bed. She had a dressing over her head and a steri strip over a cut on her lip. There was a large bruise on the lower part of her jaw and Griff saw a large red graze up one arm. He felt a rush of anger at the man who had attacked her.

'Tess?' he whispered.

She opened an eye and looked surprised to see him.

'What are you doing here?' she asked, clearly embarrassed, hoisting the covers up to her chin.

'I've come to finish the job for good; to put you out of your misery,' he said lightly. 'If I can get you out into the car park, I'll reverse over you this time.'

She gave a half-laugh, then frowned as her lip cracked again. She touched it lightly and her finger came away with blood on it.

'Sorry,' he said ruefully. 'Also, sorry for almost running you over.'

She gave a wan smile. 'From what the policeman said, you did me a favour. He reckons if the guy had caught me, he would have dragged me back inside.' She paused. 'The policeman said he left you to lock up. Thanks for doing that.'

Griff gave a mock bow. 'No problem. Least I could do.' He smiled widely. 'Plus, you said I had a nice face and lovely eyes.'

'I did *not*!'

'Did.'

'When?'

'On the pavement.'

'When I was *clearly* out of my mind,' she said defensively.

'It's out there. You think I'm cute,' he said, amused.

'I do not!' She flushed and yanked the covers up further. 'What's in the bag?'

'Roast beef, Yorkshire pudding, all the trimmings.'

'You're kidding? My God, I'm starving.'

'Really.' He set about unpacking it and placed it in front of her. He produced a wooden knife and fork, and unscrewed a small Tupperware pot and poured over gravy.

'Oh, this looks divine. Thank you,' she said, pushing herself more upright in bed. She tucked in immediately, making appreciative noises.

'Don't suppose you still have my coat, do you?' he ventured.

She pointed to a tall cupboard with her knife. 'In there. Although that wodge of cash is in the drawer here.'

Griff retrieved his jacket, while she fished about in the drawer and passed the envelope to him.

'You always carry this much cash?'

'Wages from Mags.'

'Ahhh.' She pointed to the food with her knife. 'This is good. So, the agency chef turned up today then?'

'Not exactly.'

'This is nice. What is this?' she asked, holding up a forkful of veg.

'Parsnip, carrot and turnip puree, with black pepper.'

'Delicious!' Her cutlery stopped in mid-air, as she processed what he had said.

'What's not exactly?'

'Err, no one turned up. Except Linden and Beth and err… well. Me. I did today.'

She swallowed. 'What?'

'We had a good day. I think we did fifty roasts, another fourteen on takeaway and fourteen pasta dishes. Oh, and some woman bought a whole dessert to take away.'

Tess was wide-eyed. 'You did that many covers?'

'Uh-huh. Went really well. We had a couple at the chef's table too and they loved it. We had a great time with them. So much so, they've booked the same seats for Friday night.'

'I don't know what to say,' she stammered. 'I assumed the agency chef would have done the shift.'

'No idea what happened to him,' Griff said. 'Oh, I also brought your phone in.'

She took it from him. 'Thanks. Weren't you supposed to be working for Maggie, Sunday?'

'No, I finished, Saturday. So, I'm happy to help out.'

'I'm grateful.'

'There's something else,' he said, watching as she carried on eating.

'Which is?'

'That chef came in to cook for you.'

'How was he?'

'He said he wanted to speak to the organ grinder and not the monkey.'

'Did he now? Linden and Beth were there though?'

'They were.'

'And he didn't want to cook for them?'

'Apparently not.'

'What was he like?'

'My opinion? Bloody awful. He said there was too much fresh produce on the menu. It needed to be replaced with more food that could be easily frozen then defrosted when people ordered it. Less prep time for him. He wasn't interested in using seasonal or local fresh produce. Ask Linden, he was doing most of the talking.'

'Hmm. You aren't just saying that in the hope you might get the job?'

'Didn't even occur to me, to be honest. He was no competition though,' Griff said confidently. 'Any chef turning up to impress a potential boss with plans to cook spaghetti carbonara using dry pasta needs taking outside and shooting. But that's just my opinion.'

She looked surprised. 'That's what he was going to cook for me?'

'Linden was quite disparaging.'

'I'll bet!'

'He also said the chef's table would have to go; he refused to cook with anyone watching him.'

'He did, did he?'

'Uh-huh.'

'So, what did you cook today then?' she asked, finishing the last few things on her plate.

'The three roasts we had planned. All the veg, including a cauliflower and leek cheese. I made a few extra desserts with what we had lying about.'

'Such as?'

'A tarte Tatin. A winter pudding, using up those berries that were looking a bit manky, and a treacle tart with a stale loaf I found.'

'Wow.'

'Oh, and I started the makings of a soup to have as a lunchtime special this week. There was quite a bit of lamb left, so I was going to do a scotch broth. I just need to grab some pearl barley. We could do that as a special with a cheese toastie maybe. Or, I was thinking I could knock up some soda bread. Good return on very little.'

'Sounds brilliant,' she said, putting her knife and fork together. 'That was absolutely delicious.'

Griff pursed his lips. 'Bit dry; it's been in the bottom of the oven for a bit.'

'It was bloody heaven. Thank you.'

'You're welcome.'

'So, what are your plans now you've finished working for Maggie?'

'Tomorrow, I've got Christmas lunch for thirty people, and after that, it's anybody's guess.'

She yawned and lay back against the pillows, suddenly looking exhausted.

'Would you mind stepping in, just until I'm back and can sort stuff out?'

'Of course. No problem. Beth has said her sister can step in and help out waitressing tomorrow. Shall I see if she's free Tuesday too?'

'Maybe a good idea. I keep keeling over every time I stand up.'

'Don't worry, we've got it covered.'

'I can't believe you did so well yesterday lunchtime.'

'It was good. I loved it. Look, there's something I need to talk to you—'

The door opened and a tall man walked in followed by a nurse.

'Ah, Miss Dutton. I'm Dr Lynn. We are looking at a nasty old concussion—' He stopped when he saw Griff. 'Oh, I do apologise. Would you mind excusing us?'

'Sure.' Griff stood up and gathered his coat and the empty cool bag. He turned to Tess. 'I'll text you later.'

'OK, thanks,' she said, suddenly looking worried. 'Frank… what about…'

'He's with me. In the car. He's fine.'

She looked relieved.

Dr Lynn held the door open for Griff and gestured him through.

'Thanks,' he said, happy he had a few days more work in front of him. 'Don't worry about a thing. It's all covered.'

CHAPTER 8

Tess lay in her hospital bed in the semi-gloom and fretted about things. The doctor had been insistent she stay in hospital for at least another day. He was unhappy with her scan and wanted to wait a day to repeat it. Apparently, when the car had caught her, she had fallen and hit a vulnerable part of her head on the hard kerb stone.

In some small way she was relieved; every time she stood up, she wanted to either throw up or pass out. Being realistic, she knew there was no way she could run the restaurant.

She thought about Griffin and how he had stepped in quietly without fuss. She was thrilled with how busy they had been on Sunday. If her roast dinner had told her anything, it was that he was a great cook. She liked his approach to cooking; the fact he'd thought about using food sustainably, not just throwing it away. It was a sign of a good chef.

She had sent an apologetic email to the other chef, saying she was sorry to have missed him. She had received a curt response, saying now he'd seen the place and the 'set up' he was no longer interested unless she was going to completely overhaul the menu and get rid of the chef's table.

Annoyed at the cheek of the man, she responded, saying she was committed to fresh and local produce and she wouldn't be removing the chef's table. She wished him luck finding employment.

She decided not to tell her sister, who was safely ensconced at her friend's house, recovering slowly. Tess had managed to put her off chatting for a day or two, as she didn't want to worry her by telling her what had happened. She knew she would only fret. Tess was sure she'd be out soon enough, so she sent her an encouraging text about a good weekend's takings.

Lorraine replied with a thumbs up and they texted a few more times until Tess said she had to rush off. She promised to call her properly in a few days.

Beth and Linden had texted her separately; Linden saying what a superstar Griff was in the kitchen. He'd said Griff was really patient and happy to teach him whatever he was doing. Linden also mentioned what an idiot the chef who had turned up was. Beth had said similar; that Griff was chilled, but super efficient in the kitchen and lovely to be around. She also added he was totally 'buff'.

Tess laughed at the last bit. Griffin was attractive. He had a handsome face, which completely changed when he smiled, and it was one of those smiles that made *you* want to smile. Part of her was horrified she'd told him he had a lovely face and nice eyes. But in all honesty, he was exceptionally cute. She had always had a weakness for liquid brown eyes and a killer smile.

She wondered if he would want to work at the restaurant permanently. She realised she didn't really know anything about him.

§ § §

Griff arrived home exhausted. He made an omelette, which he

reluctantly shared with Frank, who had expressed more interest in it than the dog food Griff had purchased. They both stared at the TV for half an hour and then went to bed.

Griff was dreaming. He was standing on a motorway gantry, watching the cars whizz past below him. He was shouting a warning at something, shouting for all he was worth. Leaning far over the railing until his voice was hoarse and his throat hurt. He heard a phone ringing on the gantry and looked around, but he couldn't see one to answer. He was getting progressively more frantic looking for a phone when he felt a weight on his chest.

Struggling to the fringes of consciousness, he realised it was *his* phone ringing, and Frank was standing on his chest.

He pushed Frank off and scrabbled for his phone.

'Hello?' he said sleepily, looking at the digital alarm clock next to him: 2.43 a.m.

Silence.

'Hello?' Griff tried again.

'Your time is coming. You will die.' A disembodied voice echoed in the dark room.

Griff ended the call immediately. His heart thudded and he realised his hands were shaking. Who was ringing him? The number was unknown, so he quickly blocked it. He realised he should report this to the police in case it escalated.

He heard a smash of glass outside and hurried to the window to look out down the street. He saw two lads, one with a beer bottle, swaying about, and realised the breaking glass noise must have been them.

He sat back down on the bed and tried to think who it might be. Twice now someone had threatened that he was going to die. *What did that mean?* He lay back down and Frank, sensing unease, settled in the crook of his arm. Griff lay awake for hours wondering until he finally fell asleep.

Griff shifted from foot to foot outside the police station. He glanced at his watch and then took a breath and walked in. While he was waiting to be seen by the person manning reception, the PC who'd dealt with him the other night at Tess's restaurant, appeared behind the counter.

The officer frowned for a moment. 'Hello,' he called. 'Griffin, isn't it?'

Griffin gave him a quick smile. 'Don't suppose you have a quick sec, do you?'

'Course. Come through.'

Griff waited to be buzzed through and followed the PC down to an interview room. The PC gestured to a chair and grabbed his notebook from his pocket.

'What can I do for you?' he asked.

Griff took a breath. 'Sorry, I can't remember your name.'

'Ben Baker.'

'Sorry. So, you remember I'm on licence, right?'

'I remember. You told your offender manager about the other night?'

'I did.'

'Good.'

'But I've been getting these calls and I just think I ought to make you aware of them… just in case.'

'Just in case of?'

Griff looked uncomfortable. 'Twice I've had someone threatening to kill me.'

Ben's eyes widened. 'You've had a call with someone threatening your life?'

Griff nodded. 'And a text. The numbers are coming up as unknown.'

'What did they say, and when was it?'

Griff reeled off the details, finishing with the previous night's call.

Ben frowned. 'Any ideas who it might be?'

Griff shrugged. 'Not a clue.'

'Anyone connected to what you did time for?'

'I thought about that. There was a brother. He threatened to kill me plenty of times, but I think he ended up going abroad. I don't think he'd do anything like this.'

'I'll look into it. We have to take death threats seriously. Any unknown numbers come up and I want you to record the call, OK? There's loads of free apps that'll do it. But it's important.'

'Right. Thanks.'

'Anyone hanging about? Anything strange happening?'

'Nothing I can think of.'

Ben dug about in his pocket and produced a card. 'Take this. Call me if anything's off, yeah?'

'OK.'

'And just be careful. You still working at Maggie's?'

'No. I'm filling in at Tess's restaurant while she's still in hospital.'

'Keep in touch and be mindful.'

'Thanks, Ben.'

'No problem.' Ben opened the interview room door and then ushered Griff through to reception.

'Take care now,' Ben said.

Griff stepped out into weak sunshine. He checked his watch and picked up his pace. He needed to get on; he had lunch for thirty to cook for.

The day had gone well; the thirty had enjoyed their lunch and been good fun. Griff had been pleased to see them ordering lots of extras. All excellent for the bottom line. He made sure Linden, Beth, and her sister, all had a good meal each, and he did an extra one for Tess, thinking he'd deliver it later. He needed to ask her a few things that couldn't wait. They were running low on wine, and he had no funds to pay for some of the meat, fish and vegetables that he needed to order.

Once the office party left, Griff waved off Linden, Beth, and her sister and took a seat at the chef's table. He ate his dinner and made a list of what he needed to talk to Tess about. Then he set off to the hospital, with Frank hiding at the bottom of a large RNLI beach bag, next to the cool bag which held Tess's dinner. He figured it would do Frank good to see her; he wasn't sure if the feeling would be mutual.

§ § §

Tess received a follow-up call from a PC Ben Baker, who had visited her shortly after her attack. He called to tell her he'd managed to track down the name of the person who paid using the credit card and had spoken to him. He denied all knowledge of knowing Tess's assailant. However, when Ben mentioned he was in possession of video evidence of the attack and his colleagues in Cardiff would be visiting the man's chambers to locate the man in question, he'd immediately given up the name.

Ben told her that his colleagues in Cardiff were looking for the man in order to question him.

Exhausted by the conversation, Tess ended the call, and fell asleep almost instantly. Her attention span was incredibly low and the slightest thing exhausted her.

She was awoken by a nurse who was taking her for another scan. She endured it and then promptly fell asleep again.

Tess awoke to hear a light knocking at the door. She was surprised to see Griff push open the door quietly and step inside.

'They're only letting me in for a minute. I bribed them with mince pies,' he whispered conspiratorially. 'Visiting hours end at eight.'

'You didn't need to come in again.'

'I figured I'd bring you dinner.'

He dug about in the bag and produced a takeaway carton and another wooden knife and fork.

'Ooh, what's this?'

'Christmas dinner, and a special surprise.' He lifted Frank out of the bag and Tess squealed as Frank scuttled towards her on the bed, grunting and snaffling at her.

'Hey, Frank,' she said, stroking his face. 'I think you're growing on me. Are you OK?'

She set him next to her and started eating her food with enthusiasm.

'How you feeling?' Griff asked.

'Shattered. Keep falling asleep. Pretty embarrassing really.' She glanced up at him. 'Sorry if I drop off while you're here. Nothing personal.'

'I'm hoping my good looks and sparkling personality will be enough to keep you conscious,' he said mildly.

'This is delicious!' she said, ignoring the comment. 'What's this stuffing?'

'Chickpea, sage, onion and a few secret ingredients.'

'Is it gluten free?'

'It is. Saves a fortune fannying about for a gluten-free option.'

'Genius,' she said.

'Sorry, but I need to talk to you about the restaurant,' he started.

'It's OK,' she said, as she chewed. 'You need to be able to order food and you don't know what the arrangements are.'

'Yeah. We need some more wine. Today's crowd drank a lot!'

'That's great. Did it go well?'

'It did. They stayed for so long some of them ordered cheese and charcuterie platters too.'

Tess frowned. 'We're doing cheese and charcuterie platters?'

'We are. I struck a deal with the deli for a few days. They sell well. Quick turnaround and invariably people also have wine too.'

'Even better!' she agreed. 'Good idea.'

She carried on eating and motioned to his list. 'Go on. Fire away.'

Griff ran through the list, and she answered each query, telling him what to do or who to speak to. Suddenly, she lay back against the pillows, looking exhausted, and yawned.

'Thank you for… you know. Mucking in.'

'It's fine. No problem. Am thoroughly enjoying it.'

'You OK to stick around for a bit longer – maybe see us through Christmas?'

His eyes twinkled. 'Now, is it because you think I'm cute, or you think I'm not too shabby as a chef?'

Tess blushed. 'The second one obviously.'

'You did say I was cute though.'

'I had sustained a head injury, and I was in shock,' she insisted.

'If that's what you want to tell yourself,' he said lightly. He looked at his list. 'Last thing. Wine?'

'Order through James at the Harbour Vineyard. They supply all our wine. Run through what you've used and he'll drop it down the same day, I expect.'

'Great. I'll get onto him tomorrow.'

'Thank you. Look it's a long day for you doing all that and then coming in here. Hopefully, I'll be out tomorrow.'

'Let's wait and see. If you need a lift home, just holler. Look, there's something I need to tell you—'

'OK.'

The door opened and a nurse poked her head around the door and saw Frank. Her face changed immediately.

'God, sorry!' Griff said. 'My fault!' He scooped up a wriggling Frank and dropped him back in the bag.

'Oh, now he is adorable!' the nurse cooed, fussing Frank, who was busy snuffling from the bag.

'This is Frank,' Tess said. 'My sister's dog.'

'Hello, Frank,' she said, scratching him under the chin.

'I'm just going,' Griff said. He looked at Tess. 'Shout if you need picking up whenever.'

'She'll most probably go home tomorrow,' the nurse said. 'Plenty of bed rest though. No going back to work. Head injuries need lots of looking after. You'll have to keep her in bed for a while.'

'Quite the tempting proposition,' Griff said, raising an eyebrow. 'I'll bear that in mind, especially if it's doctor's orders.'

Tess looked at the nurse and then at Griff. 'Oh, he's not... We're not...' she stammered.

'See you tomorrow,' he said, winking at her. He left, with the nurse looking at him appreciatively and Tess flopping back against the pillows, bright red with embarrassment.

CHAPTER 9

Tess had seen the surgeon, who'd confirmed the nurse's words from the previous evening. She was allowed home as soon as her medication arrived, but bed rest was essential. Mindful of the three-hour wait for medication her sister had experienced, Tess decided she'd wait until it arrived, before calling a taxi.

The nurse appeared with the medication, which she proceeded to go through, and Tess wondered for a moment whether she'd remember it all. It was all she could do to keep her eyes open.

'OK. All done,' the nurse said, repacking everything into the bag.

'Thank you for everything. I just need to call a cab and then I'll be out of your hair,' she said.

'No need,' Griff said, walking in the door. He winked at the nurse and presented her with a large foil-wrapped package. 'Thank you for calling me.'

'My pleasure,' she beamed.

'Hope you enjoy,' he murmured.

'I can assure you, I will.'

'Are you bribing NHS staff now?' Tess demanded, vaguely amused. 'How come you're here?'

'He asked me to call him if you needed picking up. He didn't want you catching a cab.' The nurse turned to Griff. 'Can you grab that wheelchair out there? She can get to the front door in it.'

'I *do not* need a wheelchair!' Tess spluttered.

'You'll stay another night then,' the nurse said. 'I don't think you realise how much this will have taken it out of you. It's a good five-minute walk to the front entrance.'

'I'll get it,' Griff said.

The nurse sighed wistfully at his retreating back. 'I'd happily have someone like that pick me up and wheel me about. He's quite lovely.'

'Hmm.' Tess stood up and grabbed her bag, feeling momentarily dizzy.

'Take it easy,' admonished the nurse. 'Plenty of rest and relaxation.'

'You said she needed to be kept in bed for a while,' Griff said, pushing the wheelchair through the door. 'Does that mean I need to tie her to the bed?'

'Whatever floats your boat.' The nurse laughed and nudged Griff.

'Can we go?' Tess asked irritably. She plonked herself in the wheelchair.

'Your carriage awaits, m'lady,' Griff said.

Tess spoke to the nurse. 'Thanks for everything.'

'No problem, take care,' she said, holding open the door.

As Griff wheeled her down the corridor, Tess caught sight of herself in a window reflection and almost swore out loud. She looked like an absolute mess. Her hair was sticking up in all different directions, and she had her top on back to front with the label on full display. She realised she probably stank too; she hadn't had a proper shower since the accident.

'Sorry,' she said, over her shoulder.
'What for?'
'Being grumpy and looking a fright.'
'You're not either. It's fine.'
'Did you shut the restaurant?'
'Nope. Linden can cope for a couple of hours. It's the lull.'
'OK. Thanks for coming to get me.'
'No problem.'
'And thanks for keeping the nurses sweet.'
'Again. No problem.'
'Are you always so laid back?'
He was silent for a while.
'Well?' she demanded grumpily.
'I used to be much more stressed out,' he said quietly. 'Then I realised life was too short and you genuinely can't fret about the small stuff.'

Once Tess was safely in the car, Griff returned the wheelchair. He climbed into the driver's seat and snapped on his seat belt.

'OK?' He glanced at her as he started the car. 'What's up?' he asked, seeing her flushed face.

'Erm… I can't… reach across to get my seat belt on. It's too painful.'

He released his seatbelt and stretched across her to grab hers. As he leant across, she got a whiff of his aftershave, which smelt delicious. He glanced at her as he carefully drew the belt across her.

'That alright? Sorry if I'm invading your space.'

Their faces were inches apart, and for a second, she felt like a ridiculously nervous and inexperienced schoolgirl. She wondered why she was feeling this way. She scrutinised his face as he fiddled with the seatbelt, snapping it in over her coat, noticing his thick dark eyelashes and the blonde ends to his light brown hair.

'Feel OK?' he asked, looking at her quizzically.

She swallowed heavily. 'Yeah. Good. Sorry.'

'No probs.' He started the car.

'Thanks again for coming to get me,' she said, awkwardly trying to smooth out her crazy hair, wondering exactly how much she reeked in the small confines of his car.

'It's fine.'

As they drove, Tess stared out of the window and wondered when she would feel normal again.

'Do you live locally, Griff?' she asked.

'Uh-huh. My mum passed away a while back and left me the house. I opened it up again last week. Needs a helluva lot of work.'

'Where were you before?'

'I was in the navy for years.'

She raised an eyebrow. 'As a chef?'

'Yup.'

'Did you travel?'

'All over. Saw the world.'

'Wow. Best place you ever went?'

'Japan. The landscape and cherry blossoms are beautiful.'

'Miss it?' She yawned.

'Parts of it,' he said. 'Look. There's something I need to tell you.'

§ § §

Griff gripped the steering wheel tightly. He'd surprised himself with the thrill of attraction that had rushed through him as he'd buckled Tess in. He hadn't felt like that with anyone for a while. For so long he'd felt dead inside; like he was sleepwalking through life.

He needed to find the right moment to tell her. Maybe it would change everything. What if she wouldn't want him to work for her once she knew?

He swallowed nervously. 'OK. The thing is. I need to make you aware that… well, er, I went to prison and I'm on probation for another few months.' He inhaled as soon as he said it, holding his breath and waiting for her reaction. He felt pleased he'd done it. He'd plucked up the courage. At her silence, he glanced over, expecting a shocked expression. Instead, she was fast asleep.

'Shit,' he muttered. He'd have to pluck up the courage again to tell her another time.

§ § §

Tess had collapsed straight into bed and slept like the dead for at least four hours. When she awoke it was dark outside, so she staggered towards the bathroom and stood under the shower for as long as she dared. Drying herself off, she felt dizzy, so she lay back down. The next time she woke up it was 8 a.m. the following morning.

On her phone, there were a number of texts from Vincent – which she ignored – and a missed call from her sister. Texting her quickly, she said she was busy and would call later. Tess promptly dozed off again.

She was awoken by a gentle knocking at the flat door. Unsteadily, she got to her feet and carefully navigated the stairs, clutching the handrail like a wobbly pensioner.

Maggie was standing on the doorstep, holding a large takeaway drink and a paper bag displaying a few grease spots.

'Hey, Mags.' Tess held open the door and Maggie bustled past her and up the stairs.

'Come on,' she said. 'I've got breakfast and a special Christmas hot chocolate for you. Figured you'd be starving.'

Tess followed her up the stairs and sat at the small dining table obediently, while Maggie clucked around, unpacking the bag.

'One of my special rolls for you,' she said, sitting herself down. 'I know you like them.' She inclined her head towards the Christmas tree in the corner. 'See you got the tree up. Looks nice.'

'Thanks. God, I'm starving,' Tess said and took a huge bite of the roll. She sighed with pleasure. 'Oh, that's good.'

'So,' Maggie said. 'How's things?'

'OK.' Tess chewed. 'Griff's been a superstar stepping in to help out. He just did it, without me even asking.'

'He's a good boy. Great cook too.'

'Stroke of luck your guy coming back and him being able to step in.'

'Stroke of luck you running into his car, from what I hear.'

Tess shuddered at the memory. 'That awful man. Just thought he was… entitled…'

'Well, you gave him a good run for his money, didn't you? Kick in the balls and a bloody nose?'

'I don't really remember much. I just remember him all over me.' She shuddered again. 'Disgusting.'

She finished the roll and sat back in her chair. 'Mags. That was delicious. Thank you, you've all been so good to me.'

Her eyes filled with tears and she grabbed a tissue. 'Sorry.' She sniffed. 'This bang on the head has made me a bit of a wreck.'

'Don't you worry about it.' Maggie patted her arm. 'Come and have a little walk down to the beach. Get some fresh air. You look pale. Finish your drink and we'll go.'

Tess grasped her hand. 'Thanks for mothering me, Mags.'

'Any time, darling. Now drink up and we'll look for a coat and some shoes.'

Together, they walked down the high street and turned the corner to the slipway for Castle Beach, Maggie's cafe and the climbing centre. Maggie kept up a steady stream of chatter and town gossip and Tess breathed deeply, feeling much better.

It occurred to Tess she had no idea what was happening in the restaurant that day. She tried to remember; did they have bookings? What was on the menu? She frowned.

'What are you frowning about?' Maggie asked.

'Trying to remember what the bookings are for today,' she said. 'I've got no idea.'

'Good thing I'm all over it then, isn't it?' an amused voice said behind her.

Tess turned to see Griff, standing on the slipway, smiling at her. He had a rosy face from the cold wind, a red tip to his nose, and windblown hair. He wore a thick white cable-knit jumper with a dark blue pea coat and jeans. Frank was trotting happily alongside him, gazing up at him adoringly. On seeing Tess, Frank gave a small yip and strained to get to her.

Tess felt another pang of attraction towards Griff. She suddenly realised he was talking to her; his soft brown eyes were inspecting her face with concern.

'You OK? You're not going to fall asleep or keel over on me again, are you?'

'No,' she said defensively. 'Not intentionally anyway.'

'I mean, yesterday I'm chatting away to you and then realise you've fallen asleep. Not a great advert for my sparkling conversation, is it?'

She was mortified. 'Really? Sorry! I got home, fell asleep, then had a shower and promptly fell asleep again! It's ridiculous!'

Frank was bumping against her leg, desperate for attention, and she crouched down to pet him.

'Hello, you. Are you being good?'

Frank snuffled happily as she made a fuss of him.

'You certainly look better than you did yesterday,' Griff said.

Standing up, she said ruefully, 'I feel better. I terrified myself just looking in the mirror yesterday!'

He laughed. 'Everything's under control in the restaurant so nothing to worry about.'

'I'm so grateful you've stepped in,' she said, feeling suddenly nauseous and light-headed. 'I don't know—' She stretched an arm out to steady herself on one of the outside benches, only to find it wasn't as close as she thought.

'I'm sorry, I feel a bit…'

'Tess?'

Tess found herself looking into two deep brown eyes.

'Tess?' Griff repeated. 'Talk to me.'

Tess blinked and then realised with horror she was sprawled out on the road, surrounded by concerned faces.

'Oh God,' she said, trying to stand, but being overcome by a wave of nausea. She lay back down, breathing deeply.

'You look ever so pale, darling,' Maggie said anxiously. 'Shall we call an ambulance?'

'No. God no,' Tess said desperately. 'I just feel a little sick, that's all. I'll get up in a sec.'

She waited for the wave of sickness to pass, and once it lifted a little, she sat up slowly.

'Darling, do you want some water? A tea?' Maggie asked, as she held her arm.

Tess shook her head. 'I'm OK, thanks. Could you help me get up, please?'

Griff and Maggie helped her to her feet. She moved closer to one of the benches and sat down carefully, dropping her head low, breathing steadily.

'Did they say you'd feel like this?' Griff asked, looking concerned.

She nodded, eyes closed while she breathed.

'They gave me some anti-sickness pills.'

'They might help, dear,' Maggie said, sounding worried.

'Come on. I'll help you home,' Griff said. 'Do you feel up to walking?'

'In a sec,' she said.

Frank was butting her legs with his head and whining. She absently stroked his head and he nuzzled lovingly against her.

'I think he's missed you,' Griff observed.

Tess stood carefully and steadied herself on the bench.

'OK?' Maggie asked anxiously, gently brushing sand off Tess from where she had fallen.

'Yup,' she said. 'Thanks for earlier, Mags.'

'No problem, darling. I'll check on you later.'

Griff slid an arm around her waist. 'Come on,' he said. 'Lean on me.'

Together they set off, Tess leaning heavily against Griff as the road became steeper.

'You OK?' he asked. They made slow progress, Frank trotting along happily next to them.

'Why does this hill seem so much steeper than usual?' she grumbled. 'I'm sure it's not normally this bad. Could we just stop for a sec?'

'Is this a rouse to get me to carry you?' Griff asked, mischief in his eyes. 'Are you going to get all flaky again, so I absolutely *have* to carry you?'

She gave a small laugh. '*Flaky*? Oh, thanks for that.' She inhaled deeply again, trying to calm her roiling tummy. 'No disrespect and all that, but you don't seem the type to fling me over your shoulder and march up the hill with me.'

He raised an eyebrow, his lips twitching. 'I'm not sure whether to take offence or not. I would *obviously* be gentlemanly and ask whether you wanted a princess carry or a fireman's carry. I certainly wouldn't just assume you'd be happy being flung over someone's shoulder.'

'Oh? A choice? Well, that *is* very gentlemanly of you.'

'I thought so. So, which would it be? Just so I know for future reference. Fireman's carry or princess carry?'

'Princess carry, every time,' she said, deadpan.

'I'll bear it in mind,' he said mildly. 'Here we are. Where's your key?'

'I'm gonna come in and have a coffee for a bit. Then go back to the flat if that doesn't interfere with your plans? I feel like I need to be in the restaurant for a bit.'

'No probs. Your restaurant anyway!'

Tess spent an hour sat at the chef's table, chatting to Griff and drinking coffee. They agreed on some things going forwards, and rationalised the Christmas menu, making life easier for everyone. They settled on some different specials to rotate too. Linden arrived midway through the discussions and gave his opinion. He seemed to be learning a lot from Griff, and she could see his confidence growing.

Tess helped Beth prepare the restaurant for opening, until she was suddenly hit by a wave of dizziness. She grabbed the nearest table, realising she could barely keep her eyes open.

'Go and rest,' Griff said. 'You look exhausted.'

'I'll give you a hand, make sure you get up the stairs,' Beth said.

'Take this,' Griff said, handing over a Tupperware full of what looked like soup. 'Make sure you eat.'

'What is it?'

'Cauliflower cheese and bacon soup.'

'Sounds good.'

He dumped a hunk of bread wrapped in cling film on the lid. 'Go, sleep and recover.'

'I plan to sleep. Are you sure you're OK here?'

'We're all good.'

Beth helped Tess into her flat, up the steep stairs where she made sure she lay out on the sofa. She put her phone and a glass of water within easy reach. Tess was asleep before Beth had even left the room.

§ § §

The rest of the day flew by for Griff. The early lunch crowd had continued throughout the day and the restaurant had been booked out for a private party in the evening. Which, mercifully, started early and finished by nine. Beth's sister was helping out too.

As Griff and Linden were cleaning down surfaces, Beth stuck her head around the door and said in a low voice, 'Either of you guys meeting anyone after shift?'

'No, why?' Griff asked and Linden shook his head.

'Because there's a bloke in a dark coat with his hood up across the road in a doorway. Looks like he's waiting for something or someone. It's creeping me out a bit.'

'What does he look like?' Linden asked.

'Like a bloke in a dark coat, with the hood up,' Beth replied sarcastically. 'Creepy if you ask me.'

Griff peered through the opening by the chef's table and vaguely made out a dark figure in the doorway opposite.

'Is it raining?' he asked.

'Yup,' Beth said.

'Maybe he's sheltering, or waiting for a lift or something,' Griff mused, peering into the dark street.

'Maybe,' she agreed.

'Keep an eye,' he said. 'I'll walk you and your sister home if you're worried.'

'Thanks, Griff.'

Griff was tired. He was pleased with the feedback from the new lunchtime menu and the private evening party had loved the food and left an enormous tip too. Yawning, he turned the sign to 'Closed' after the girls and Linden left.

Locking the front door, he absently scanned the street and saw no sign of the person Beth had mentioned. He took a minute to look in the diary for what was happening the next day and then remembered the restaurant was closed on Wednesdays. He assessed what they'd need for the Thursday bookings and made the decision to get in early. He did some food ordering, cleared up, grabbed Frank and locked up.

As Griff left, he debated knocking on Tess's door, but then decided against it. It was late, and he was tired and just wanted to sleep.

CHAPTER 10

Frank's growling woke Griff. It was a sound he wasn't familiar with. He glanced at the clock; it was 1.30 a.m. He reached out a hand to stroke Frank and found nothing. He put on the light and saw him sitting by the bedroom door.

'What's up, buddy?' he asked sleepily.

Frank barked loudly and scratched at the door. Puzzled, Griff got out of bed and let him out. Frank hurtled down the stairs and launched himself at the back door. Griff opened it and Frank shot out. Concerned at the small dog's behaviour, Griff switched on the outside light and stared in disbelief at the kitchen window.

In huge red letters, the word KILLER had been scrawled across the window. The red paint gave the kitchen an obscene glow. With shaking hands, Griff grabbed a knife from the kitchen drawer and stepped outside. A foul smell assaulted his nostrils.

'I don't know who you are, but you can fuck right off,' he yelled in what he hoped sounded like a strong voice.

Silence.

Griff realised the stench was from dead animals that had been scattered around his back garden. Rotting badgers, dead foxes, a cat; they all looked like roadkill. The odour was awful. It filled his senses, the smell cloying in his nose and the back of his throat. It was like the smell of rank meat or poultry which nearly always made him retch. The animals were decomposing; infested with maggots and leaking fluids that pooled on the flagstones, leaving dark stains.

There was a bucket on its side, covered in something red. He wondered whether it was paint or blood.

Looking around in disbelief, his gut churned. His hands were shaking and the hand holding the knife looked like someone else's. White knuckled, gripping the handle tightly, shaking ridiculously. *Who the hell is doing this?*

A rustling sound in the nearby bush had him whirling around, brandishing the knife. When Frank appeared covered in the red matter, whining forlornly, Griff grabbed the small dog and rushed back inside, kicking the door shut behind him. Dumping the knife on the counter, he locked and bolted the door, then carried Frank up to the bathroom, where he gave him an impromptu bath.

As he washed Frank, Griff grew concerned it looked more like blood and less like paint. He wondered where anyone could get blood in such quantities.

After drying Frank off, Griff went back into the bedroom to call the police. When he picked up his phone, he saw a message from an unfamiliar number.

You will pay for what you did. Killer.

Griff stood at the kitchen doorway watching PC Ben Baker chat to the forensic officers moving about in his back garden. Ben was accompanied by a very tall, well-built police officer, PC Garland. Both officers headed towards Griff and he stood aside to let them in.

'Want a cuppa, fellas?' Griff asked.

'Why not?' Ben said good-naturedly, as he drew out his notebook.

Griff switched the kettle on and grabbed the milk. Frank was staring at the two PCs with an expectant expression.

'Is he alright?' Garland said, pointing to Frank. 'Why's he staring?'

'He does that,' Griff said. 'Milk?'

Both PCs nodded and Ben cleared his throat.

'So, you woke up to him growling last night about 1.30 a.m. and came downstairs and found this?'

'Correct,' Griff said, bringing over the teas. He placed a sugar bowl on the table.

'What had you been doing in the evening?' Ben asked.

'Working at The Fat Gannet,' Griff said. 'I've been there since Sunday.'

'Since you hit the owner with your car?' Ben asked.

'It wasn't an elaborate ruse to get a job, I can assure you.'

'What time did you get home?'

'About ten. I was knackered. Came home, went to bed.'

'And then the dog woke you?' Ben asked. 'No more calls or texts?'

Griff produced his phone. 'When I went to call you, this had come through.'

Ben inspected the text. 'Screenshot it and send it to me?'

Griff obliged.

'Anything else?' Ben asked. 'Weird or unusual?'

Griff started to shake his head and then stopped himself. 'Probably nothing,' he began.

'Might be relevant,' Ben prompted.

'There was a man standing opposite the cafe for ages yesterday. Creeped out one of the waitresses a bit.'

'What did he look like and are you sure it was a he?'

Griff thought for a minute. 'Now you ask, no, I'm not sure it was a man. I just assumed.' He looked rueful. 'The person had a dark jacket on, hood up. Couldn't make out a face.'

'How long were they there?'

'Not sure, maybe half an hour or so. Bit longer maybe. Just standing opposite.'

'And you've not had anything else?'

'Not that I haven't mentioned to you already. The calls and the text.'

'And now this, which is malicious and deliberate.'

One of the white-clad team knocked on the back door and pushed it open. 'We're done here. We'll remove the carcasses for you.'

'Thanks,' said Griff. 'Look, was that blood? Not paint? I mean, if it was blood, where do you even get that much of it?'

The forensic officer removed his mask to speak. 'I'm ninety-nine per cent sure it was theatrical blood. I've come across it before. I'd know the smell and consistency anywhere. You can buy it or make it yourself. Easy enough. Corn syrup, colouring, other bits and bobs.'

'*Fake* blood?' Griff echoed. 'Why?'

'Who knows?' Ben said. 'Easy to source, pretty untraceable I suspect.'

The forensic officer nodded. 'Absolutely. You could knock it up in here if you had the ingredients.'

'Jesus,' Griff said. 'So, I can clean it up now?'

'Yeah. Hot soapy water should do it, then a hose down. It'll be gone soon enough,' the forensic officer provided.

'Thanks.'

'I'll look into this number,' Ben said. 'I suspect it's a throwaway.' Ben and Garland stood. 'I'd think about getting some higher security for the back gate too, and perhaps cut down these weeds,' Ben suggested.

'That's today's job,' Griff said. 'This is my first day off since I got here, so the garden is being attacked.'

'Good luck,' Ben said. 'Anything else you're worried about, just call. You've got my number, but I'll leave both our cards here, so if you can't get hold of me, talk to Garland. I'll mention it to the detective in charge too, so he's aware.'

'Appreciate it.'

'You should email your offender manager too, so it's on record.'

'Will do. Have a good day fellas.'

'Thanks for the tea. Look after yourself.'

Griff watched as they all left via the side gate. He glanced down at Frank, who was looking pointedly at his bowl.

'Breakfast, then we get to work,' Griff said. 'A lot to do.'

§ § §

Tess had awoken feeling better. At some point in the night, she had left the sofa and crawled into bed. She estimated she'd slept for nearly eighteen hours. She felt wonderful. She was relieved the restaurant was shut which meant she could get on with some life admin and get back on her feet a bit more. While she felt strong, she called Lorraine, being careful to be vague about things, constantly turning the conversation back to what Lorraine was doing and how her leg was.

Vincent had sent more texts in the night telling her how much he missed her and asking her when she was coming back. She read the text and didn't reply. She didn't know what to say.

Tess had remembered when she woke, that the coming Saturday was a special day in the Christmas calendar for the town. It was Santa Saturday. The main high street was pedestrianised, and the road was filled with stalls carrying local homemade crafts and produce. There was street food and an opportunity for the kids to come and see Santa in his grotto. The town tradition was Santa was collected from a mystery location out at sea and brought into the harbour by the lifeboat. He was then driven up through the town on one of the RNLI buggies. He had a grotto by the church and sometimes he even brought with him a couple of his reindeers for the kids to see. There were Christmas carols from the choir and music from the local radio. When Santa arrived, there would be a countdown to him switching on the lights on the big Christmas tree.

Tess wanted to be well for Saturday; she saw it as a huge opportunity to sell street food that people could grab as they walked by. She wanted to talk to Griff about it; she knew he would come up with some good ideas.

She popped down to the restaurant and did a stocktake, ordering more drinks. She saw a long list of items to order in Griff's handwriting. She phoned the local suppliers to order the meat and cheese, and crossed them off his list.

On a whim, she texted him.

Hi, sorry to bother you on your day off, but I've ordered a few things off the list you made – hope that helps. Just thought I ought to let you know in case I'm out for the count again!'

She made herself a hot chocolate and was faffing with the fairy lights and other decorations, when there was a rap on the window. Maggie was outside, waving.

She opened the door. 'Hey, Mags! You coming in?'

'I won't thanks, my love. I was just passing and wanted to check how you were feeling today. You look better,' she observed. 'You're not opening on your own, are you?'

'Course not. Just getting sorted. I feel better,' she said. 'It's such a relief having someone as capable as Griff helping out.'

'The boy can cook,' Maggie said.

'He certainly can. Always surprising me with his ideas.'

'You heard from him today?'

Tess frowned. 'No, why?'

Maggie lowered her voice. 'Old bag Bennet, you won't know her, but she's a terrible gossip. Comes in every morning for a cup of tea and is always hopeful for a quick perve at Foxy. Mind you, love, we could all say that.' She tittered. 'Anyway, she lives a few doors along from Griff, and she said the police arrived at his place in the early hours of the morning.'

Tess's eyes widened. 'Really? Why?'

'I don't know, my love. That's why I'm asking.'

'Oh, I'm worried now,' Tess said.

'If you've a mind to go around, seen as you're off today, he lives in his mum's old place, number 60, Sutton Lane. You know, off the front.'

'I know it.'

'She died and left it to him. Needs love and affection, but then don't we all?' She tittered again. 'Gotta go. John will be livid otherwise.'

'OK. Why not come for some dinner with me tonight, just so I can say thanks for looking out for me.'

'Lovely. I'll be along just after we shut if that's OK? Early dinner for us both, eh?'

'Sounds good.'

'See you after six.'

'No probs!' Tess said, pondering on what Mags had said about Griff and the police last night. She locked the door, wondering whether it was appropriate if she popped in to see if he was alright. As she stood dithering, the postman rapped on the door and waited impatiently while she unlocked it.

'Here ya,' he said, handing her an A4 envelope and walking off.

'Thanks,' she replied. Turning the post over she saw it was addressed to Griff. That cemented it for her. It was an excuse to pop by and see him on the premise of not knowing if this letter was urgent or not.

§ § §

Griff had been busy. He had washed off the red letters from the large kitchen window and hosed down the back of the house. He'd found an old bottle of disinfectant and cleaned the back patio with it, scrubbing as much as he could. His next job was to clear the garden.

Rummaging about in the garage, he found some large garden waste bags, secateurs and a small saw. He also found gloves, which would be useful to save shredding his hands.

He'd found a small radio in the garage and was pleased to find it worked. He set about trying to clear the overgrown weeds, bushes and trees from the back garden. After an hour of heavy, back-breaking work, he stood back and admired his efforts. He remembered that under the overgrown brambles there was a decent lawn area.

He was hot despite the chilly air. Chugging back a large glass of water, he stripped off his jumper, and attacked the garden again. He'd had the good sense to dig out an ancient T-shirt and jeans, knowing clothes were likely to be ripped on the out-of-control brambles. The chef in him was a little sad at having to cut back the brambles; it looked like there had been a nice crop of blackberries, but he was a man on a mission.

It felt good to be doing something that required some brute strength and not much thought. He realised he was enjoying himself; he moved the radio nearer and sang along as he hacked, pruned and snipped.

§ § §

Tess knocked on the front door and waited. There was no sign of anyone coming to answer it. She could faintly hear a radio playing from somewhere, then she heard Frank barking. She rounded the corner of the house and tentatively pushed the back gate open, where the radio was much louder. Frank rushed over, yipping with glee, and rubbed himself against her legs.

Tess could see Griff's back. He was wearing an old pair of jeans with a tight-fitting dark blue T-shirt, which read, 'Once Navy, Always Navy' on the back. It clung to his well-toned torso. She admired his slim hips and wide shoulders. She watched him for a second, his methodical way of tackling the garden. It was the same methodical way he cooked. Frank barked again, breaking the spell, and she was embarrassed when Griff turned around and caught her gawping.

'Oh hi!' he said, stumbling as his foot got caught in a creeper.

'Oh! Are you OK?' she asked, trying not to laugh as he righted himself and extracted his foot.

He laughed. 'I'm fine. I'm being attacked from all angles! You alright?'

Tess felt stupid. 'Sorry to drop round, but this was delivered earlier when I was in the restaurant and I didn't know if it was urgent or anything, so I thought I'd bring it to you.'

He viewed her with a half-smile. 'Maggie tell you the police were here?'

Her eyes widened. 'Oh well, erm, she asked me if you were OK and I said I didn't know, so I kind of…, I thought I ought to… you know, um, check on you.' She finished, red-faced, and cursed herself for sounding like an idiot.

'I'm fine. Some vandals got in last night. Threw some paint around and stuff.'

'Why would anyone do that?' she asked.

He shrugged. 'It's been empty for years. Maybe they did it regularly and now can't, so they're pissed off.' As he talked, he was picking up armfuls of cut greenery and dumping them into large bags.

'Can I help with that?' Tess offered, holding the side of the bag wider to enable him to drop the stuff in.

'Ta. I was going to stop for a drink anyway. You want a cuppa?'

'Only if you've got time. Anyway, here you are,' she said, thrusting the rigid A4 envelope at him.

Yanking off his gloves, he took it, frowning. 'Don't know why anyone would send this to me at your place. Very few people know I'm there.'

'Perhaps it's a secret stalker,' Tess suggested lightly.

He pulled a face as he walked towards the back door. 'Tea coming up. Come on in.'

Striding across the kitchen, he switched the kettle on. He grabbed a couple of mugs off the draining board and threw a tea bag into each one.

'Don't you want to open it?' Tess asked, pointing to the envelope.

'Oh yeah.' He picked it up.

'Do you mind if I use your loo?' Tess asked.

'Course. It's a bit dated, so apologies up front. Just along the hall.'

'Thanks.'

§ § §

Griff stared at the envelope. *What the hell was this?* Feeling a sense of dread, he grabbed a knife and slit it open carefully. Peering in, he saw a single sheet of paper. He checked down the hall to make sure Tess wasn't returning and pulled out the paper. He gasped.

It was a photograph of Griff; black and white, like a photocopy. A crosshair target had been drawn on his face in thick red pen. The words, 'YOU WILL DIE' were scrawled across the bottom of the paper in red writing.

'Jesus,' Griff said, stuffing it back into the envelope as quickly as he could.

He heard the sound of flushing and busied himself making tea. Tess returned to the kitchen and pointed over her shoulder.

'You know people pay a bloody fortune for those types of decorative cisterns these days.'

He looked doubtful. 'Do they?'

'Uh huh. It's classed as an original feature. If I'm not mistaken, under the paint, it's an original Thomas Crapper.'

'Oh stop,' Griff said, passing over her tea. 'You're winding me up.'

She looked surprised. 'I promise you I'm not. It's the real thing. Google it.' Looking around she said, 'This house is what? Edwardian? Victorian? Probably full of original features that people love these days. I bought a Victorian flat once and uncovered all sorts of lovely features as I was doing it up.'

'I'll bear it in mind,' he said, sipping his tea. 'Perhaps you can be my original features consultant.'

'Perhaps I can,' she giggled.

'So, is this what you do then, when you're not running the restaurant? Something in property?' he asked.

'Not at all,' she said, drinking her tea. 'I was a nurse in Accident and Emergency for years, until recently.'

'Really?' Griff was surprised. 'What happened?'

'Covid happened,' she said, twirling her mug around on the table. 'It changed everything. I wasn't the same person afterwards. I'd lived on my nerves for nearly two years, under the worst pressure and stress that anyone can possibly imagine. I just couldn't cope with it any more. It's different now, the NHS. No one goes to bat for the nurses, it's shocking pay, and all the wrong people are making the decisions. I realised one day I spent more time covering my back and my team's decisions than I actually did making people better. To me, it was game over.'

'Sad. Do you miss it?'

'I miss some of the people. I liked the patients. In A&E though, you see people at their best and worst. Very little in between.

Sometimes it questions your faith in humanity; other days it reinforces it.'

'So, you've not worked at the restaurant for long then?'

'Off and on since Lorraine has had it. She got me drunk one night on Zoom and made me promise to come and help. She's tired and working far too much. When I arrived, I found her at the bottom of the stairs to the flat, with a broken leg, and here we are. She's living it up at her best mate's house and I'm running the restaurant.' She drained her tea and stood up. 'Look, I must go. I said I'd cook Maggie some dinner and I need to get started.'

'Tess, there's something I need to talk to you about—'

'Can we do it tomorrow? Maggie will be on her way.'

'Oh… OK. Tomorrow then,' he said, frustrated at yet another opportunity missed to tell her the truth.

'Thanks for the tea! See you tomorrow!' she said brightly.

'See you. Thanks for dropping that in.'

CHAPTER 11

Griff had awoken full of intentions to tell Tess exactly what had been happening. On his way in to work, he dropped the envelope into the police station and asked them to give it to PC Baker or Garland. He had also emailed his offender manager and updated him on recent events. He had received a curt email response saying they would discuss it at Maggie's on Monday.

Arriving at the restaurant, he left Frank to make himself comfortable in his usual spot by the window, put on his chef's jacket, washed his hands and rolled up his sleeves.

'Let the games begin,' he said, in a mock Sean Connery voice.

'Talking to yourself is the first sign of madness you know,' Tess quipped, walking into the kitchen.

She looked gorgeous that morning, in a blue shirt that enhanced the warm tones of her skin and complimented her colouring. Griff had found himself thinking about her more and more in recent days.

'It's the only way to get a sensible answer,' he retorted. 'You look like you slept well. How was Maggie?'

'She was good. Didn't complain about my cooking either. Right, now I need you to get your thinking cap on—'

'OK, look, before everyone gets in, can I talk to you about—'

'Morning, all,' Linden said happily, as he came into the kitchen peeling his coat off.

'Morning, Linden. Great, now who wants a coffee? We have some stuff to think about,' Tess said, rubbing her hands.

Griff gave her a thumbs up, frustrated once again he hadn't managed to have a conversation with her without anyone around. Accepting his coffee from Tess, he leant against the stainless-steel counter in the kitchen.

'So, what are we thinking about?' he asked.

§ § §

Tess knew Griff would suggest superb ideas for street food for Santa Saturday. He outlined a few; all utilising the current takeaway containers they used in the restaurant. He was careful to suggest they offer food that was different to their competitors in the town, to keep things friendly. He suggested a Christmas dinner, Yorkshire pudding wrap, a turkey and bacon bap and a halloumi, hummus and roast veggie wrap. He also suggested they do a few crumble and custard pots which were easy enough, and had good profit margins. He suggested three crumbles: apple and cinnamon, Christmas pudding and chocolate, vanilla and pear.

They also worked out they could slightly reconfigure the restaurant entrance to be able to take orders. They could borrow a bench from Endure and people could wait for orders on the street.

Heading into the storeroom to look for a couple of large blackboards she knew Lorraine had in there, Tess was overwhelmed with a wave of dizziness and clutched the wall for support. She grabbed a nearby stool and managed to sit down. She dropped her head and breathed deeply.

'I think you're overdoing it,' Griff said from behind her.

'I'm fine,' she said.

'Liar. It's OK to say you feel like shit. You're supposed to be in bed anyway.'

'I feel better. Apart from this stupid dizziness.'

'Come on. Come out and sit down properly. Have you eaten?' He held out a hand and pulled her up gently. She bumped against him. Her hands rested lightly on his chest, and their faces were almost level. Griff's eyes moved down to focus on her mouth; she felt a sudden thrill of anticipation and attraction.

'Are you OK?' he murmured softly, his eyes searching her face.

'Think so.' She allowed him to lead her into the restaurant to sit at one of the tables. 'I probably need to eat. Where's Linden?' she said, looking around.

'Popped out to get something,' Griff said. 'I'm going to make you breakfast. OK?'

'OK.'

'Omelette?'

'Fine. Let me make coffee.'

'I'll do it. Latte? Espresso?'

'Latte, please.'

Tess watched Griff use the coffee machine, admiring again, the methodical way he approached things. Preparation and then action. She found herself liking the colour of his skin tone against the white of his chef's jacket, and his strong lightly tanned forearms, against the rolled-up sleeves.

'There you go,' he said, putting the coffee down. 'Right, mushroom, cheese and ham in the omelette?'

'Just cheese and mushroom, please. Save the ham.'

'Very wise. I was about to make pea and ham soup. Just had a thought. We could offer it in the tall coffee cups with a buttered roll on Saturday. You up for that? What we don't sell, we can freeze for another day's soup special.'

'Brilliant plan,' she said. 'Do we need to order rolls?'

'Nope. We can make our own.' He smiled. 'Linden's gonna learn breadmaking.'

She sipped her coffee and then moved from her seat to go and sit at the chef's table, so she could watch him work.

'How do you feel now?' he asked.

'Better. Thank you. Sorry about all this… you know. It's a bit full on isn't it, considering you only stepped in to help.'

He glanced up as he grated some cheese. 'It's fine. It's how I like it. I like the vibe. Like the freedom of creation.' He dropped a knob of butter into a pan and expertly flicked it around, then threw in a handful of mushrooms.

'Did you always want to cook?' Tess asked, watching him.

'I always really enjoyed it. Even as a kid. I liked experimenting with food. But I always wanted to be in the navy too, so in the end, I decided to combine the two. I remember coming back from basic training one day; we'd been out for hours, and we were beyond starving. We dumped our stuff and sat down to this meal. I remember thinking the guys in the kitchen were pretty bloody amazing, because I think it was the best meal I ever tasted. The more I thought about it, the more I thought the kitchen of any ship is like another engine room really, because it *is* the engine room for the troops. You know? They can't operate properly without decent food. So that's how I ended up cooking. Loved every minute too. I was always really lucky with the folk I worked with.'

He added the eggs to the pan and sprinkled in cheese after a few moments. 'Did you always want to be a nurse?'

She nodded. 'I had an accident when I was a kid. I fell off my bike and went straight into a brick wall. Smashed up my face and hit my head badly. I was so frightened, and the nurses in the hospital were amazing. I decided then I wanted to be a nurse in emergency. To me, that's when people need the most help and comfort.'

Griff expertly flipped the omelette onto a plate and garnished it with a few pea shoots.

He placed it down in front of her. 'Get stuck in.'

Tess grabbed her cutlery and eyed the food appreciatively. 'Looks good.'

'Look, while it's just us, I need to talk to you ab—'

'Place up the road says they are doing street food on Saturday,' Linden announced breathlessly, as he walked back in to the restaurant. 'Although their menu is crap. Ours is much better.'

'What are they doing?' Tess asked, before she forked in another mouthful of food.

'Usual stuff. Small fish and chips, sausage and chips and some satay thing – all in a cone. Fairly uninspired.'

'They're welcome to do that,' Griff said, returning to a large pot on the stove. 'We're also doing a soup now, with a roll.'

'Are we breadmaking then?' Linden asked.

'You are. Let's get on.'

Tess finished her breakfast and was overcome with a wave of exhaustion, so she made her excuses and went back to the flat. She was just about to lie down when her phone rang.

'Hey, Lorraine. How are you?'

'I'm good. Look, just quickly. I forgot to tell you, it'll be Santa Saturday this weekend. I'm so sorry. You'll probably be busy for takeaway coffees and stuff. I probably should have given you a heads up.' She sounded apologetic.

'I know. I remembered. It's fine,' Tess assured her. 'All in hand. How are you feeling?'

'Better, apart from my bloody silly leg. I could get used to it here though. Honestly, it's so nice; the people are lovely and there's this incredibly hot baker. My God, I'm running out of excuses to go into the bakery, I can tell you. I'm sure I've put on a stone just buying excuse cakes.'

'Excuse cakes?'

'An excuse to go in and swoon over him.'

Tess laughed. 'That's good to hear. Look, I need to go. Can I ring you another time?'

'Absolutely. I just wanted to tell you about Santa Saturday.'

'OK. Take care, enjoy the baker!'

Tess chucked her phone onto the coffee table and sat back against the cushions. In a few moments, she was fast asleep.

§ § §

Griff was frustrated that, once again, he'd missed an opportunity to tell Tess what he'd been trying to tell her. He was, however, excited about the street food they were planning.

In the quiet moments between customers, Beth had been artistically painting the menu blackboards to advertise the street food. By the end of the day, Griff and Linden had got as much ready as they could for the following day.

That evening, they had a birthday party for thirty people who had booked out the whole restaurant and had offered to pay for the privilege. When Lorraine had taken the booking, the family had requested a set menu which had made life for Griff and Linden much easier. Griff also made them a birthday cake and was just icing it with a rich chocolate ganache when Beth appeared at the chef's table.

'Griff. Someone here to see you.'

Griff glanced up from pouring the icing and saw PC Ben Baker standing next to Beth.

'Hi,' he said. 'Sorry to disturb. That looks good.'

Griff was torn. He needed to finish icing the cake, but he didn't want Linden or Beth to know his business, or worse still, for Tess to appear and start asking questions before he'd had a chance to talk to her.

'Ben, can you give me a minute, mate? This is a little bit time-sensitive.'

'No probs. I've gotta pop over the road; I should be ten?'

'Perfect. I'll come and find you. OK?'

'OK.'

Griff carried on icing.

'What's that about?' Linden asked, chopping veg.

'Vandals got into my mum's place,' Griff said. 'I expect he's following up.'

Griff finished the ganache and cleared up, placing the cake carefully on a stand for final decorations. He washed his hands.

'I'll be back in a minute. You OK doing what you're doing?'

'Yes, Chef,' Linden said happily.

Griff left the restaurant and glanced up to Tess's flat, which was in darkness in the early evening light. He guessed she was still asleep after crashing out earlier. Seeing Ben ahead, stepping out of a shop, he called out, and jogged towards him.

'Hi. Sorry about a minute ago.'

'No problem. After I came in, I guessed I might have prompted some questions you maybe didn't want to answer,' Ben said.

Griff was surprised by his insight. 'Err... yeah. I'm still trying to tell Tess about my... past,' he finished. 'Every time I try, someone walks in, or we get interrupted. Anyway, what were you after?'

'My advice is you do it sooner rather than later. Anyway, I just wanted to check in to say there's no trace on the phone numbers sending you the messages. Whoever it is uses burner phones. But the lady who lives opposite you has Ring Doorbell footage of a figure in black, hauling a big old bag down the road and into yours. Can't make out gender or anything. Other Ring Doorbell footage further up the road has caught the figure getting out of a van and we're tracing it now. I just wanted to give you a heads-up really.'

Griff was surprised at what Ben had found. 'That's great. Thanks so much.'

'And you genuinely can't think of anyone who might hold a grudge?'

Griff was silent for a moment. 'Only her brother, maybe? Her parents?'

'I'm tracking down the brother. You were right, we think he went abroad. Parents are pretty infirm by all accounts.'

Griff pulled a worried face. 'I genuinely don't know who else would do this sort of thing.'

Ben clapped him on the shoulder. 'You're doing everything right. Tell us as soon as anything else happens, or if you're worried about something. Just call me. It's no problem.'

'OK. Thanks.'

'I'll let you get back.'

'Thanks, Ben.'

CHAPTER 12

The previous evening's birthday party had gone well. Tess was seeing profits increase with some of the new ideas with higher profit margins. She was under no illusions that the months of January and February were always deathly quiet.

She had awoken early, feeling much better, and had gone for a walk on the beach. She found herself missing Frank, which she couldn't quite understand since she had never been a pet person before. She supposed it was because she felt an obligation.

Maggie spied her coming off the beach and ushered her in for coffee and made her eat breakfast.

The previous evening, she had managed the entire evening shift without feeling wobbly. Later though, she sat down on her bed for a second and had woken up at 7 a.m. still fully dressed. She wasn't feeling as dizzy any more and felt much more like her old self.

She had been careful to stay in touch with Lorraine. Keeping her updated so she didn't discover Tess had been hurt and start panicking. Tess had firmly fudged over the news that Griff was the new chef by telling Lorraine he had been recommended by Mags. That alone had been enough for Lorraine.

Admiring the Christmas window displays, she walked back to the restaurant and realised she was following Griff and Frank up the hill. Griff was dressed in his navy-blue pea coat with jeans and brown boots. She admired his broad shoulders and tall build. She liked the way his hair tickled the collar of his coat. Her mind flitted back to when he pulled her against him the previous day.

'Hello!' he said, turning as Frank spotted her and strained on his lead, barking excitedly.

'Morning,' she smiled.

'Did you sleep well?'

'I fell asleep when I sat down on the bed for a moment. Woke up fully clothed eight hours later! So yes, you could say I slept well.'

Griff handed her Frank's lead. 'Hold him for a second.'

He dug about for keys and opened the restaurant door.

'Are you coming in?' he asked.

'Of course! I'm good to go. Lots to do today,' she said, watching as he walked through the restaurant, taking his coat off.

'I don't want you overdoing it. Tomorrow's going to be crazy,' he said over his shoulder as he stripped off his thick jumper.

'Nag, nag, nag!' she replied, covertly watching him. 'Honestly, I'm good.'

Frank jumped onto his bed in the window and promptly gave a series of excitable yips. Glancing up at the window, Tess was amused to see Frank nose to nose with Solo through the glass and Foxy looking on with a fond expression. She waved, beckoning them in.

'How are you?' she asked, opening the door, and using her foot to prevent Frank from flying out.

'Good,' Foxy said. 'More to the point, how are you?'

'I'm much better, thanks.'

'Not overdoing it?' Foxy asked.

'Err, exactly my point!' Griff called from the back. 'Got time for a coffee?'

Foxy rubbed his hands together. 'Always.' He closed the door behind him. 'How're you, Griff? Mags said there was some vandalism at your place the other night?'

Griff appeared, buttoning up his chef's jacket.

'Just some little twats arsing about, I expect,' he said, rolling up his sleeves. 'I called the police. They came and did their thing.'

'What did they say?'

'Still waiting to hear,' Griff said dismissively. 'Espresso?'

'Please.' Foxy gestured to the blackboards Beth had painted the day before, with the street food menu on, ready for the following day. 'That sounds amazing; a Christmas dinner, Yorkshire pudding wrap. Save me one. No, make it two.'

'Two?' Tess was incredulous.

He looked innocent. 'I'm a growing boy!'

'Here you go.' Griff handed Foxy a small cup and gave a coffee to Tess too.

'Thank you,' she said, touched he remembered how she liked her coffee in the morning.

Foxy drained his drink in a gulp and smacked his lips. 'Thanks for that.'

'Don't suppose you could give me a quick hand, could you, mate?' Griff asked. 'I don't want Tess to overdo it and she'll insist on helping.' He rolled his eyes, risking a glance at Tess.

'I am here, you know,' she said indignantly.

'What do you need?' Foxy asked, amused.

'I need to move a few of these around if you've got the time?'

'Cost you a wrap.' Foxy grinned.

'I'll be in the storeroom once you've finished bonding,' Tess said dryly, marching off with her coffee. She put the radio on as she passed the kitchen and hummed along while she looked for what she wanted in the storeroom. Vaguely, she heard the sound of furniture being moved and the scraping of chairs on the floor. She turned her attention to her mission.

She had gone through everything. She was sure last year Lorraine had ordered Christmas-print greaseproof paper liners for the takeaway boxes. She recalled Lorraine laughing about ordering too many and having no idea what to do with them. Tess remembered suggesting she made paper chains with them. If they were in the storeroom, then they would be perfect for the Santa Saturday street food. She was now on the last box on the shelf. It was old, battered cardboard, with holes in the corners, and shoved at the back on top of the shelving unit.

She stretched up and managed to touch it with her fingertips. Frustrated, she tried again and managed to catch the ripped corner of the box and pull it slightly towards her, before a bit of cardboard came off in her hand.

'Shit,' she said, her eyes scanning the room for something to stand on. She spied the catering-sized tins of tomatoes and plonked two of them on the floor, pushing them together.

'Perfect,' she said, and stood on them, stretching up. Realising the tins needed to be a little bit closer to the unit, she stepped off, pushed them forwards with her foot and then got back up again.

'Come… here… you… blood—' she muttered, trying to work the box towards her. She realised a corner had become caught and wouldn't budge. Tugging hard, the box shot towards her, and she teetered precariously on the tins.

'What the hell are you doing?' Griff's voice was incredulous. 'Christ alive. Do you even know what's in that? It could really hurt you if it falls on you and there's something heavy in there. Come here…'

'It's fine, it's almost there,' she said, struggling.

He stepped into the storeroom and stood close behind her, reaching up to try and take the weight of the box. Being taller than her, he reached easily.

'Christ, this looks like it's gonna fall apart,' he murmured close to her ear. 'Hang on, I've got this side. Hang onto your bit.'

Tess tried to regulate her breathing. She felt him pressed against the length of her and a thrill of attraction run through her. She closed her eyes for a second and breathed in his aftershave, feeling pure lust. She hadn't felt like this since Vincent.

'I've got it… hang on. Jesus… the corner is going to go,' Griff muttered. 'You hang onto that bit. Let's try and bring it around and down. I think the bottom is going to drop out of it.'

He manoeuvred it to the edge and together, holding onto respective sides, they lowered the box to the floor. They were so close; their faces were almost touching. Tess breathed in his aftershave again and noticed blond strands of hair threading through the brown. He flicked a glance over her.

'Are you OK? Not gonna pass out or anything?' he asked with concern, his eyes inspecting her face.

'I'm… I'm fine,' she stammered.

She stared at him, and it seemed like time stood still for a minute.

§ § §

Griff didn't know what to do with himself. It had been a long time since he had been up close with a woman, and he'd found the experience of pressing up against Tess more than arousing. He breathed in her heady perfume that was mixed with a faint scent of coconut.

They were so close he almost forgot himself and kissed her. In recent days he had realised he was incredibly attracted to her. What the hell was he doing just about to kiss her? He stared at her face for a moment. He was so close, he could just lean forwards and kiss her.

How would she react? Then he remembered what he needed to tell her.

'Tess,' he managed to croak out. 'Look… there's something I need to—'

'Morning, everyone!' Linden stood in the doorway. 'Ooh, what's in the box?'

'Not sure yet,' Tess grinned. 'We shall see. I think it's been here a while though.'

She opened the flaps of the box and pulled out a smaller cardboard box. She glanced up at Griff.

'What were you saying?'

Griff looked at Linden still in the doorway. 'It'll keep,' he said, sighing.

Tess opened the smaller box and squealed in delight.

'I *knew* she had some!' she said, pulling out a large packet of brightly covered greaseproof squares. 'These will be fantastic to use tomorrow.'

'That's what you were breaking your neck for?' Griff asked incredulously.

'It's Christmassy,' she said. 'Perfect for Santa Saturday.' She held them up closer to Griff. 'See how cute they are?'

Griff rolled his eyes and left the storeroom. He was irritated with himself. Both because he had almost kissed Tess, and because he still hadn't managed to tell her yet. It was getting ridiculous.

He heard Linden chatting to Tess as they emptied the box, and heard Frank barking as someone knocked on the door to the restaurant. Glancing at the clock, Griff saw it was still early. Clearly they weren't open yet. He dried his hands and opened the door. A delivery driver held a bunch of red roses and a bunch of large white trumpet lilies. The delivery man peered at his phone.

'Hiya. Got roses for a Tess Dutton and lilies for a Griffin Jones.'

'What? I'm not… I didn't order…'

'Take 'em, mate. I'm blocking the road. Have a good day!' He jogged back to his van and drove off.

Griff put the roses down on the table. There was a card nestled in amongst the blooms and he wondered for a moment who would be sending Tess flowers. He felt a spike of jealousy.

He looked at the lilies and also spotted a card. He opened it with a certain amount of trepidation.

Don't Rest In Peace. Burn in hell. You WILL die soon.

Griff dropped the card like it was on fire. He stepped back from the bouquet and stared at it, shaking his head. *Who the fuck?*

He breathed heavily for a second and then took out his phone and snapped a picture of the lilies and the card; front and back, so the name of the florist was clear.

He tapped out a text to PC Ben Baker and sent the pictures with it. Within a few minutes Ben had called him back.

'Griff, are you OK?'

'Yeah, I'm fine.'

'Are you in the restaurant? Do you wanna go somewhere so we can speak freely?'

'Uh huh.'

Griff stepped outside and walked across the road, leaning against the wall, watching the cafe as he spoke.

'I'm assuming you've seen the pictures. The flowers have literally just arrived.'

'I'll get onto the florist. I don't hold out much hope, but I'll try. I'm still trying to track down the brother. He goes off on these outward-bound type retreats in the Spanish mountains from what I understand. He won't be back for a week or so – but I am trying to verify it is actually him who's gone. Otherwise, it's all a bit of a convenient excuse.'

'I'm nervous about what's gonna happen next. I'm not gonna lie,' Griff said.

'Understandable. Leave it with me. I'll get on to the florist. Keep your wits about you.'

'Keep me posted, yeah?'

'Will do.'

Griff jogged back across the road and entered the restaurant, just as Tess was emerging from the storeroom.

'Who are these from?' she asked, her colour rising.

'The red ones are for you. I think there's a card.'

'Who are the lilies for?'

'Oh… erm… to put on Mum's grave. I haven't been yet. She always loved these, so I thought…'

'Oh, that's nice,' she said. 'Pop them in the back room. Cooler in there.' She dug about in the roses and produced the card. She flicked it open and read it with a frown.

'What the? It just says, "see you soon".' She showed him the card. 'There's no name here. Who would have sent me these?'

He shrugged. 'No idea. A secret admirer?'

She snorted. 'Hardly.' She inspected the flowers. 'They're beautiful, but anyone who knows me really well, will know I'm not a massive fan of red roses. I much prefer yellow ones.'

Griff raised an eyebrow. 'Noted.'

She guffawed. 'Oh stop.'

Beth arrived with a handful of holly covered in red berries.

'Morning,' she said. 'Mum said you're welcome to this. She went to the woods foraging at the weekend for her Christmas wreaths, and this was left over.' Beth pointed to the red roses. 'I could do something with all this.'

'Go for it,' Tess said. 'Might as well make them look their best.'

Griff put the lilies in the storeroom and decided he'd deal with them later. The next time he looked at the clock and registered what the time was, there was only a handful of customers left. One man had been sat at the chef's table for much of the evening, watching Griff closely and chatting to him.

As Tess went to get his coat, he waved a business card at Griff and left it on the counter.

'I'm David Watson. I'm opening a new business, and I need a good chef. I want you. Will you call me please?'

Griff didn't know what to say. 'I... er,' he started, just as Tess returned with the man's coat.

'Here you go,' she said, helping him into it. 'Thanks so much for coming.'

'Is this your place?' he asked, putting his coat on.

'It's my sister's. I'm just holding the fort since she was taken ill.'

'I was in here a few months back. It was different. Not as nice as now; there's a different vibe. How long have you been here?'

'Nearly three weeks.'

He looked as if he was thinking. 'I'm opening a new restaurant. All very hush-hush at the moment. But I am after a chef and a restaurant manager. I'd like you both to come and talk to me. You're a good team. You're a couple, yes?'

'What? Us? No... I mean... Griff is helping out... Oh, we're not...' She gestured vaguely, looking embarrassed.

The man raised an eyebrow. 'Oh, sorry, I just assumed.'

'We'll think about it and let you know,' Griff said, scooping up the man's card and waving it. 'We've got such a lot on in the next few weeks, it'll probably be January when we come up for air, won't it Tess?'

'Absolutely,' she said. 'Yes. January.'

'OK. Great. It was Tess and...?'

'Griffin Jones.'

Griff and Tess shook the man's hand in turn.

'Come and hear me out in January and see the space. Tell me your thoughts. OK?'

'Where is it?' Tess asked.

'It's fairly local. I can't say any more yet.'

'Very mysterious,' Tess said.

'So, I'll hear from you?'

'One way or the other,' Griff said, turning his attention to the stove. 'Have a good Christmas.'

'You too.'

'Bye now,' echoed Tess.

They both watched him go, before turning to each other and pulling surprised faces. Griff handed her David's business card. 'Put it somewhere safe and we'll think about it in the new year?'

§ § §

Tess put David's card safely in the till. It hadn't occurred to her things might come to an end. That other people would perhaps come and poach Griff. She found herself ridiculously upset at the prospect of it.

She glanced at Griff who was rubbing a hand over his face.

'Griff. Get off home. I'll lock up. You look done in.'

Griff looked around the kitchen and back at her. 'OK. How many are left out there?'

'Two couples. It's all good. Everyone's on coffee. I'm going to lock up when they go and get an early night.'

He pursed his lips.

'*Go*,' she said. 'It's going to be full on tomorrow.'

'OK. But text me when you've closed the door. I'll leave Frank.'

'OK. See you tomorrow.'

Tess busied herself doing bills and tried not to watch as Griff unbuttoned his chef's jacket. He was wearing a tight white T-shirt which clung to his torso, and she found herself wondering what he'd look like without it on.

'Excuse me?'

Tess jumped and faced the source of the voice. A woman at a nearby table was talking.

'Could we please get two more coffees and the bill?'

'Of course!' Tess said, momentarily flustered.

Tess quickly adjusted the bill, made the coffee and delivered both to the table.

'Just give me a shout if you need the card machine,' Tess said.

Tess cleared the remaining tables and walked back to the kitchen to find Griff doing up his coat. Linden and Beth had gone home earlier after the last main course had been served.

'Remember,' he said, 'text me when the last one's gone and you've locked the door.'

'Will do,' she saluted. 'See you tomorrow.'

'See you,' he said, easing past her. 'Oh, and don't even start getting boxes off high shelves or anything ridiculous like that.'

'Weren't you going?' Tess asked, amused.

'I'm going. Night.'

'Night.'

CHAPTER 13

Tess awoke on Santa Saturday feeling a frisson of excitement. She was keen to see how they did today; they'd not done anything like this before. She hoped the street food would do well, and she knew the configuration of the restaurant would certainly help to juggle customers wanting to eat in and have takeaways.

Frank, who had been asleep on the pillow next to her, noisily snoring, opened an eye and jumped off the bed. He sat at the top of the stairs, wearing a hopeful expression.

'OK,' she said, eyeing him. 'Quick walk on the beach, then it's all go.'

She was excited to watch Griff in action today. She enjoyed seeing him busy and seeing the contentment on his face when he was fully engrossed in something. So far, she had never seen him get flustered, even when they had been crazy busy. He just applied his methodical way of working to everything.

She dressed carefully. She wanted to make an effort with her appearance, so she took time over her hair and make-up, and chose a crisp white shirt and fitted black trousers. She added some subtle jewellery and felt good about herself. Unusually for her she was also having an excellent hair day. After a spray of perfume, she picked up Frank's lead and clipped him on.

'Off we go.'

She walked briskly down the hill towards the beach. Frank strained at the lead and yapped excitedly when he spotted Solo and Foxy coming down the outside stairs from the flat above the climbing centre.

'Morning,' Foxy said, doing a few leg stretches. 'You look nice.'

'Thank you,' she said, embarrassed. 'You off for a run?'

'I am.' He looked over at the two dogs who were nuzzling each other. 'Want me to take Frank? He can keep up. I've taken him before.'

'He'd love that! Thank you. Saved me a job today.'

'No problem.' He took Frank's lead, unclipped him and fastened the lead around his neck. 'Don't forget, two of those wraps have my name on them.'

'Text me when you want them, and I'll get them made up for you.'

'Look forward to it. See you later.'

Tess watched as Foxy winked and jogged off at a good pace, followed by Frank and Solo. Even as she rounded the corner, she could hear Frank's excitable barking, which she now realised he did when he was doing something he loved.

Glancing at her watch, she hurried up the road to the restaurant.

§ § §

Griff had slept well, apart from a mildly erotic dream he'd had about Tess, which he hadn't wanted to end. It had been so nice and full of promise. He'd tried to fall asleep again to see whether he could recapture it, but it proved elusive.

Slightly grumpy, he trudged off to the shower, undergoing his daily dance with the large spider. He thought about his dream with Tess. They had been in a big storeroom, looking for Yorkshire puddings which Griff knew he'd made, but couldn't work out where they'd been put. As they searched, he had gently backed her against the wall and kissed her. She had responded, wrapping her arms around him and pulling him close. At that point, much to his annoyance, he'd woken up.

He mused as he dried himself. He would like to kiss Tess but he didn't want to jeopardise a future job. He concluded he didn't really know what he was doing or what the job situation was either. With Lorraine being away, he assumed he would have to play it all by ear.

He planned to ask Tess if she wanted to come to lunch at a new restaurant that had opened in the next town. People were raving about it and he wanted to see what it was like. He could present it as checking out the competition, he concluded. Checking his watch, he dressed quickly, made sure the house was secure and headed off to work.

When Griff arrived, Tess was already in the restaurant, eating some toast, with a latte in front of her. She was making notes, oblivious to a small swipe of butter on her cheek.

'Morning,' he said, stripping off his coat. 'It smells of mulled wine in here. Are we selling it now?'

'Morning,' she said, smiling. 'No. It's a candle.'

'You look nice,' he said and leant over. 'You might want to lose this though.' He touched her cheek gently, swiping off the butter.

'What was…?'

'Butter,' he said, grinning. 'Much better.'

'Morning, Chef!' Linden called. 'First batch of yorkies is due out in five!'

'Perfect.'

'Coffee?' Tess asked, going to stand.

'I'll do it.'

While he made himself coffee, he decided to throw caution to the wind. 'You heard about that new bistro over in—'

'Yeah, a couple last night were raving about it.'

'Wondered if you fancied checking it out with me Wednesday? You know, see what the competition is doing. For lunch?'

She gave him a half-smile. 'I'd love to. It's important to check out the competition. Good idea. I'll book it.'

'I'm happy to.'

'It's fine,' she said, scribbling it on her list.

He glanced around while he sipped his coffee. 'Where's Frank?'

She gave a small laugh. 'He's gone off on a run with Foxy and Solo. Apparently, he can keep up.'

Griff laughed. 'He's going to be comatose by the time he gets back!'

'Exactly!' Tess said. 'All part of my cunning plan!'

'Chef! Can you come and have a look at this dough?'

'Coming.' Griff winked at her and went to help Linden.

§ § §

Tess opened the restaurant door and turned around the 'Open' sign. She hefted the blackboard out onto the pavement and noticed the town getting busier. She could hear Christmas music from further up the street and most of the stalls were all set out in the wider part of the high street, near the huge town Christmas tree by the church. The road leading up to it was strung with festive lights and the shop windows glowed warmly in the freezing air and dull sky. She knew the local radio station would start broadcasting around 1 p.m., and there were usually carol singers and other local bands playing until Santa turned up.

Humming along to a Christmas carol she could hear being played in a shop opposite, she finished setting up the outside menus and draped some extra twinkly lights around the blackboard. She also added some to the long bench they'd borrowed from Foxy for people to sit on to wait for food. A couple stopped and ordered coffees and cakes to go, so she hurried inside to make up their order.

'Showtime!' she called. 'Beth, two fudge cakes to go, please.' She made the drinks quickly, returning to where the couple were sat waiting. She handed everything over with napkins and forks and took another order, just as she finished with the first couple.

As she was scribbling down the final thing on her pad, she turned to go inside and almost bumped into a man standing near the doorway.

'Oh sorr—'

'Hello, Tess,' he said quietly. He inhaled deeply. 'God, I've missed you.'

She stopped dead in her tracks. 'Vincent?' She stared at him in disbelief. 'What the *hell* are you doing here?'

Tess couldn't believe what she was seeing. Vincent. Her ex. Gorgeous, handsome, rich Doctor Vincent. Cheating, deceitful, hurtful Vincent.

He gave a suave smile. 'Harder to ignore me in person.'

Flustered, she pointed vaguely. 'Hold on. I just need to…'

She walked inside, red-faced, her heart thumping, and asked Beth to make the drinks for a takeaway. She returned to the couple with the card machine and took payment. 'It won't be a sec,' she assured them. She moved to where Vincent stood, leaning casually against the wall, waiting. A thought of how incredibly handsome he looked skittered across her mind.

'What do you want, Vincent?' she asked. 'I'm super busy today.'

'To talk to you,' he said. 'Did you get my flowers?'

'Oh, were they from you?'

'Yes. Goodness, Tess, how many bunches of flowers do you receive?'

'Thank you.' She ignored his question. 'What are you doing here?'

'You aren't answering my texts,' he admonished lightly. 'I wanted to see you. Talk to you. Catch up.'

'You haven't come all this way to see me,' she said dismissively.

'I have.' His gaze travelled over her, and she felt her knees turn to jelly. He always had that effect on her. Forever handsome, lightly tanned, his dark hair peppered with grey, giving him a suave look. His eyes, bright blue against his tanned face. He was impeccable and expensively turned out, as he always used to be. Unwittingly, Tess found herself comparing him to Griff's jumpers, jeans and blue pea coat.

Beth appeared with the takeaway drinks and handed them over to the customers, eyeing Vincent as she returned inside.

Tess was on the verge of a flat spin. She didn't want Vincent there while Griff was inside.

'This is one of our busiest days, so I can't talk today,' Tess said desperately.

'What about later?' He trailed a finger across her hand. 'We could catch up then?'

She snatched her hand away even though she felt a thrill at his touch.

'I don't finish until about eleven.'

'Tomorrow then?' His glance flicked over to the restaurant's opening hours. 'Meet me for breakfast?'

'Why?'

'Because I want to talk to you.' He moved closer and she felt nostalgic and weak-kneed at the scent of his aftershave. 'I miss you, Tess,' he whispered in her ear. She felt her body betray her mind and start to respond.

'There's nothing to talk about, Vincent.' She tried to step away.

He took her hand. 'I think there is. I've waited long enough.'

'Waited for what?' She pulled her hand away.

'Waited for you. I can't live without you, Tess.'

She stared at him. 'Is this a joke?'

'Absolutely not. I want you, Tess.'

Her heart thumped wildly.

'Meet me for breakfast tomorrow. Least you can do as you don't seem to want to return my calls or texts.' He gave a charmingly rueful smile.

Tess saw Beth craning her neck to peer out of the window. Anything to get rid of him.

'Fine. Where?'

'What about the cafe at the top of the high street on the left?'

'The Kitchen Pantry?'

'Yes. Meet you there at eight thirty?'

'Fine.' She moved away as more people picked up a menu and decided what to order. 'What can I help you with, folks?' she asked pleasantly, hoping Vincent would get the hint.

He followed her, placed a warm hand possessively on her waist then leant over and whispered in her ear as he walked past. 'Can't wait until tomorrow.' He kissed her cheek briefly and she closed her eyes for a second, remembering the feel of him.

§ § §

Griff was in the restaurant near to the front window and glanced up to see a handsome man talking to Tess. He watched her step away and talk to some people reading menus. Who was he? Did she know him? He watched in surprise as he stepped towards Tess, touch her possessively and kiss her cheek. *Who the bloody hell is this guy?*

Realising he was staring, he turned away, wondering who the mystery man was. He found himself annoyed. Did she have a boyfriend? She hadn't mention it. Had *he* sent the flowers?

The local radio started broadcasting loudly and the restaurant got much busier. The orders were rolling in. People were getting their wraps and then coming back a little later for coffee and crumble, which were selling fast.

Foxy arrived, with an exhausted Frank, who jumped onto his cushion in the window and fell asleep instantly. Foxy took his two wraps with delight, sitting himself down at the chef's table to chomp on the first one. He announced it was even better than the breakfast burrito and insisted on having a third.

Loud Christmas music floated down the high street and as the afternoon skies grew dimmer, the place took on a slightly magical glow with all of the Christmas lights. The scent of hot chocolate and mulled wine filled the air. Tess glanced at her watch.

'Santa will be on his way!' she said and went to wait in the street to watch the procession up from the harbour.

'Griff! Come out and see!' Tess called.

The group from the restaurant stood outside the door as Santa rode on the back of the RNLI beach buggy, driven by a smiling Doug, the local lifeboat skipper. The buggy was flanked by other members of the crew, all wearing their yellow all-weather gear. The lights were flashing on the buggy and Santa was waving and 'ho ho ho-ing' all the way up the high street. Children were waving excitedly, desperate to see him.

Finally, Santa arrived at the enormous Christmas tree in the square. The radio DJ started a countdown and everyone joined in loudly. Finally, Santa switched on the tree lights and one of the nearby pubs made it snow from a machine on the roof. Children were gazing around in wonder, running about excitedly, trying to catch it.

'Only here would Santa arrive by lifeboat,' Griff said, smiling. He noticed some people looking at their menus and tapped Beth on the shoulder.

'More customers!' he said, heading back inside.

The celebrations went on for another few hours until the radio DJ said his goodbyes and the local choir sang their Christmas repertoire, as more snow fell from the pub. Parents with exhausted children started to head home, and the street vendors started packing up. The temperature had dropped, and many people were seeking out hot drinks, looking happy, with rosy faces, as the Christmas tunes blared out from a nearby pub. The team had another rush on hot drinks, soups and some crumbles.

'Wow,' Tess said, as she closed the door to the restaurant and turned over the 'Closed' sign. 'That was quite the day. Now who would like a drink and a sit down?'

'Thought you'd never ask,' said Griff. 'Come on Beth, Linden. Sit down and relax for a moment.'

They sat down, and Griff disappeared into the kitchen and came back with a hot dish. 'I know it's only simple, but I made macaroni cheese for everyone. I figured you'd all had enough of wraps and crumble for the day.'

'I think you should marry me,' murmured Tess, rubbing her aching feet. 'All this today and you thought about feeding us too. You are a superstar.'

'Goes to what I said about the engine room,' Griff said, collecting a stack of plates. 'Who wants some?'

Griff plonked the plates down and unbuttoned his chef's jacket, taking it off and throwing it on a nearby chair. He wore his usual tight white T-shirt underneath it. He dished up the pasta and Tess opened a bottle of wine. Linden and Beth had a beer each and there were a few moments of silence while everyone savoured the meal.

'We should have this on the menu, it's bloody lovely!' Beth exclaimed.

'Absolutely. It would do brilliantly as a lunch special,' Linden said.

'Agree,' said Tess, filling a glass each for herself and Griff. 'Right. Cheers to a fantastic day, team. I couldn't be prouder of you all. Griff, thank you so much for all your wonderful suggestions and you guys for making it all happen and working so hard. I appreciate it so much.'

'Our pleasure,' said Griff, taking a deep swig of wine. 'I can't believe how well we did. We sold out of practically everything. The soup, all the crumbles. We were down to the last Yorkshire pudding wrap too.'

The team spent the next hour chatting while they finished their meal, and Tess opened another bottle of wine. She was enjoying the downtime.

Griff was regaling them with stories of his time at sea, trying to cook while on the edges of a hurricane, and explaining how difficult it was to dish up food when everything was lurching about. Tess offered desserts and looked in horror at her watch when at 10 p.m., Beth's dad rapped on the door to take her home.

'Linden, Dad will give you a lift.' she said.

'Oh, I need to clear up,' he said.

'NO!' Tess said loudly, slightly tipsy. 'Off you go home! I'll clear up! I insist!'

'If you're sure?' Linden said.

'Definitely,' said Tess, waving her wineglass about.

'Go on, mate. I'll help clear up,' Griff said.

'You should go home too. You're probably knackered,' Tess said.

'It's fine.' He drained his glass. 'I'll help.'

He walked Linden and Beth to the door and locked it carefully. He switched off the main restaurant lights, leaving the glow of the Christmas tree and fairy lights.

Picking up an empty dish and a couple of plates, he took them into the kitchen and put them in a dishwasher crate. He returned to the restaurant just as Tess was stacking the plates and picking up some other glasses scattered about.

'Let me help,' he said, carrying some through.

'I want some music!' Tess said. 'Christmas music!'

She scrabbled about behind the counter and waved a CD triumphantly. 'This is it!' She inserted it and pressed play.

The sounds of Wham's, 'Last Christmas' blared out and she closed her eyes.

'God, I *love* this song!' she said, semi-dancing into the kitchen. 'It was so good! The perfect Christmas song!'

'You really do love this song, don't you?' Griff said, amused as he watched her dancing about.

'What's not to love?' she said, singing along while she loaded the dishwasher. The song ended and was replaced with 'Fairytale of New York' by The Pogues and Kirsty MacColl.

'I *love* this one too!' she said happily, singing along.

'You are really embracing the Christmas CD. Wait… exactly how *old* is this CD?' he teased, as he wiped down the surfaces.

'Oh stop.' She laughed. 'We've had this CD for years.'

'So that makes you old then?' he teased.

Laughing, she grabbed a tea towel and expertly wound it around, flicking him with the end.

'Ouch!' he said, laughing as it caught him on the leg.

'Payback for calling me old!' She giggled, flicking the tea towel again. He deftly caught the end of it and yanked it towards him, bringing her with it. Breathlessly, she bumped into him, her hands resting lightly on his chest as he pulled her towards him.

'Ha!' He wrestled the tea towel from her and chucked it over her head onto the counter. 'You are completely disarmed and at my mercy,' he said softly. 'What are you going to do about that?'

They were so close Tess could feel his heart thudding under her hands. Part of her wanted to reach up and run her fingers through his hair and pull him down to kiss her. She wanted to run her hands over the chest that she could see the outline of in his tight white T-shirt. She stared at him. His deep brown eyes met hers and then tentatively, he took her face in his hands and kissed her very gently.

She met his lips and kissed him back. With a groan, he wrapped his arms around her, pulling her close. She ran her hands through his thick hair and pressed herself closer. He backed her gently against the counter and pressed himself along the length of her.

'God, I've been wanting to do this all day,' Griff said, as he ran his hands over her back and through her hair.

'Me too,' she said breathlessly, shoving her hands up under his white T-shirt desperate to feel his skin against her hands.

He tugged her shirt out of her trousers and ran his hands over her back and cupped her breasts in his hands.

'You are so bloody sexy,' he murmured. 'And you smell absolutely amazing.'

'So do you,' she said, nuzzling his neck, feeling him hard against her.

§ § §

Griff's senses were in overdrive, and the Christmas music was blaring. He had his hands full of Tess's body and he was kissing her like his life depended on it. It had been so long since he'd felt this way. Wanting to kiss another woman, or better still, take her to bed. Not since before prison. He felt intoxicated by Tess, her response to him and her scent. His ears were ringing and he wondered if it was because it had been so long since he had his hands full of woman.

'Griff, your phone…' Tess gasped, pulling back slightly.

Then he realised the ringing was his phone in his pocket.

Dragging it out, he went to push the call to decline and saw it was PC Ben Baker.

Worried, he said, 'Hang on. God, I'm sorry. I probably should…'

'Hello?' he said. 'Everything OK, Ben?'

'Where are you, Griff?' Ben asked.

'I'm at the restaurant. Err, finishing up.' He raised an eyebrow at a giggling Tess. He ran a finger across her lips as he listened to Ben.

'Er, not *too* much to worry about, but I'm with the fire brigade at your house.'

CHAPTER 14

Griff inhaled sharply. 'Why's the fire brigade at my house, Ben?' he asked, with dread in his voice.

'Someone tried to pour petrol through the letter box and set fire to it. Mercifully, one of the neighbours saw them, so they could only manage to get it over the front door and porch before they ran off. The fire brigade caught it early, so the damage is minimal. But obviously, I'm worried this is escalating,' he finished.

'So am I,' Griff said.

'Can you come home?' Ben said.

'Yup. I'll come now.'

He ended the call and glanced at Tess, pulling a face. 'I need to go. I can categorically say I don't want to.' He leant forwards and kissed her gently.

'Is there a fire at your house?'

'Seems so. Police are there.'

'God. Are you OK?'

'Not really. Look I need to talk to you properly about this.' He gestured to them both. 'All this.'

'All what?'

'I'll tell you tomorrow. Do you want to meet for breakfast?'

She pulled a face. 'I can't tomorrow. I've got breakfast plans. After though? Before the others get in?'

'OK.'

'Go on. You need to go.'

He gently rubbed his thumb over her lips.

'I'll see you tomorrow,' he said, and kissed her gently.

'I'll see you then,' she said, blushing.

'Lock up after me.'

Griff arrived home, breathless from jogging most of the way. He looked with horror at the scene before him. The whole street was bathed in blue lights, and there were people standing watching the proceedings; a few were filming on their phones.

As Griff approached the scene, Ben spotted him and walked over.

'Sorry to be the bearer of bad news,' he said.

Griff pulled a face. 'How bad is it?'

'It's not as bad as it looks. Your neighbour opposite just happened to see it start, so called the fire brigade. Her husband went over with a fire extinguisher, which was enough to hold the fire at bay.'

'Nice of them. Where are they?'

'Over here.' Ben led Griff over to the pair and Griff thanked them profusely. Ben ushered them back inside and assured them he'd be over to collect the details from the Ring Doorbell.

The fire chief came over and spoke quietly to Griff. Together, they walked towards the front door and the fire chief switched on his torch.

'It's largely superficial. Wasn't going long enough to undermine the front door at all. In fact, most of the stuff fuelling the fire was the dry creepers on the porch, and the leaves. Your neighbour saved the day.'

'Thank God for nosy neighbours,' Griff murmured.

'If more people had the sense to have a fire extinguisher handy it would make our job easier sometimes,' the chief said mildly. 'Your neighbour had the foresight to direct the extinguisher through the letterbox too.'

'That it then?' Griff said.

'Boys will double-check the inside, now you're here, but it'll be fine. The door is still secure.'

'Thank you,' said Griff.

'No problem. You got lucky though.'

'I know.'

'I need to get on.'

'Thanks again.'

Ben appeared. 'Griff, I've just viewed the Ring Doorbell footage. Looks like it's the same person as the one who vandalised the back.'

'Christ, who the hell is it?' Griff asked, frustrated.

'We haven't got the manpower to keep someone here to wait for whenever they might strike next,' Ben said.

'What do you suggest I do?'

'You just need to be careful. Watch your back. Can you get any security here? Cameras and such?'

'With respect, how much use will it be if we've got them on camera twice and we're still none the wiser?'

'I see your point, but it may well act as a deterrent.'

'They seem fairly set on doing something to me.'

'Just need to watch your back. I'll make sure we do regular drive pasts when we're out on patrol.'

'Thanks, Ben. Appreciate it.'

'Try and rest up. You look knackered.'

Griff closed the door on Ben and locked up. Tired, he climbed the stairs to bed. His phone buzzed and he dragged it out. It was a message from Tess.

Is everything OK? How's the house?

He smiled, remembering their kiss and the feel of Tess beneath his hands.

It's fine. Not too much damage. Superficial. Helpful neighbour put it out. Then the fire brigade rocked up.

How did it start?

Don't know. Vandals, they think. Are you all locked up now?

Yup. Just going to hit the sack.

He texted. *I like that mental picture.*

She replied instantly. *Shame you had to go!*

I was thoroughly enjoying myself.

Me too. You know we quadrupled our takings today. Result!

Superb. So, I'll see you tomorrow.

Count on it. Night X

Night X

Griff quickly fell into a dreamless sleep. He didn't hear the three texts arriving in the middle of the night, or see the figure crouched outside his house in the early hours, who ran away when a squad car drove slowly by.

§ § §

Tess was nervous about meeting Vincent. She tried to unpick how she felt. Was it nerves? Anticipation? She remembered how he had looked, and the touch of his hand on her waist. But then she immediately felt guilty for kissing Griff and not wanting that to end.

Frustrated with herself, she walked into The Kitchen Pantry and viewed it with a critical eye. It was decorated with fairy lights and a large Christmas tree. Soft Christmas music played, and it had a nice feel to it. Cosy and Christmassy. She noted the Christmas special drinks – hot chocolate, mulled wine and cinnamon lattes – and made a note to copy them when she got back.

She spotted Vincent sitting at the rear of the cafe and fleetingly wondered why he hadn't chosen the best spot, by the window. She noticed he was in running gear but didn't look like he'd been running.

'Hello. Are you Lorraine's sister?' The woman behind the counter came out with a couple of menus and a black coffee which Tess instantly knew was for Vincent. 'You look so alike!'

'I am,' she said.

'You did well on food yesterday, didn't you?' she said. 'I saw your menu. Really good ideas there. I've been eyeing up your new chef, in more ways than one!'

'Yeah. Very busy day,' Tess agreed edgily, irritated at the woman for eyeing up Griff.

'Are you here to eat?' she asked.

'Meeting someone,' Tess said, pointing at Vincent.

'OK, I'll leave these for you both then,' she said, putting the menus and coffee down. 'Can I get you a drink?'

'Latte please?'

'Coming right up.'

Tess took a seat opposite Vincent. 'Morning,' she said.

'Morning to you,' he said warmly. 'How are you?'

'Good. You?'

'All the better for seeing you,' he said. 'Feels like forever since we've been together.'

'It's been months,' she said, picking up a menu and inspecting it. She looked at him over the menu. 'Vincent, why are you here?'

He took the menu from her hands. 'I came to see you.'

'I doubt that.' She plucked the menu back off him.

He looked hurt. 'I did. I miss you, Tess.' He reached out and touched her hair. 'More than you know. I like this longer on you now.'

She moved her head out of his reach.

'Latte?' the waitress said cheerfully, as she delivered Tess's coffee. 'Are you ready to order?'

Vincent beamed at the waitress. 'I'll have avocado on toast with the roasted tomatoes, please. Tess, you'll have it too, yes?'

Tess consulted the menu again, irritated that he felt he still knew her well enough to guess her breakfast.

'I'll have the toasted banana bread with seeds, please,' she said.

'But you don't like banana,' he said, frowning. 'Why would you have that?'

'I do like banana bread, not that you'd know,' she said sarcastically. 'Now, what are you doing here, Vincent?'

He sipped his coffee, looking relaxed.

'I want you, Tess. Simple as that. I want you to come back to me.'

'Oh please,' she snorted. 'Bit late now.'

'It isn't.' He leant forwards, grasping one of her hands. 'I miss you. Life is awful without you. I want you in my life. I want what we had before'

'You don't,' she said unforgivingly.

'I do. I miss you. I want you to come back to me.'

Tess was stumped. She wondered why he had suddenly turned up and seemed desperate to rekindle things.

'Why now?'

'I miss you, Tess. I realise it now.'

'You ended it. You were very clear about the reasons why, and that was months ago now.'

'I wasn't. I'm sure I didn't mean it,' he said defensively.

'Do I need to remind you?'

He shifted uncomfortably.

She took a sip of coffee – noting theirs at the restaurant was better – and sat back. She folded her arms and started speaking in a mock deep voice, imitating Vincent.

'Tess. We both want different things. We're just not on the same page any more. You're desperate for children, and I just don't want to accommodate them into my life. I want a life. I don't want to get married, and I feel this is something you want—'

'About the children thing—'

'I haven't finished,' she said, holding up her hand and continuing. 'Tess, I'm operating on a different level to you, and I just don't think you can keep up with me where I'm going. I'm mixing with different people, and quite frankly, they're just not your sort of people. I'm doing this for you, Tess. Not me.'

He sat back in his chair. 'I think differently now. I've changed.'

She choked back a laugh. 'Really?'

He adopted a hurt expression. 'Yes.'

Tess picked up her coffee. 'So why do you suddenly want me back? Not operating in the higher echelons any more? Can I now cope with who you mix with?' She adopted a high voice like a small child's. 'Will my wittle bwrain be able to cope with all the long words now?'

'Stop it.' He looked flushed and angry. 'I told you, I've changed.'

Their food arrived and Tess viewed hers critically. The banana bread looked good. Toasted, it was served with a vanilla ricotta, drizzled with honey, and sprinkled with seeds. Vincent was picking at his food, looking petulant. Tess remembered him always wearing the same expression when things weren't going his way.

'Why have you got your running gear on?' she asked.

'I was going for a run.'

'Was?'

'I came here. Didn't have time.'

'Are you on a schedule today?'

His eyes shifted to the large clock. 'No. Not at all.'

She chuckled. 'You were always a shit liar, Vincent.'

He winced. 'Still swearing, I see.'

'One of my many shortcomings, if I recall. It meant I wasn't suitable to mix with the toffs.'

'Tess, darling, when are you coming back to the hospital? No one seems to know,' he said, sounding desperate.

'I'm not.'

His knife and fork clattered on the plate. He stared at her. 'You're not?' He looked shocked. 'But you *must*.'

'Nope. Not going back.'

'That's ridiculous.' He wiped his mouth. 'But you're a nurse, Tess. A good one. Come back to the hospital. Come back to me.'

'I don't think so.'

He grasped her hand. 'Tess, I love you.'

Tess inhaled sharply. In all the time they had been together he had never said he loved her.

She eyed him. 'You've never said that before.'

'I mean it. I love you. I want you to come back. I miss the time we used to spend in your little cosy flat.'

'Only because you never wanted me to come to your flat.'

'You've still got your flat?' he asked.

'For now.'

'All the more reason to come back then. Come on, Tess. We can be together. Snuggled up there. I've missed you so much.'

She withdrew her hand. 'What exactly are you asking me, Vincent?'

'I'm asking you to come back to work, and to come back to me.'

'In what capacity?'

He blinked. 'What do you mean?'

'What I said.'

He looked nervous for a moment. 'Well... as it was before. I love you, Tess. I miss you. I want things to go back to how they were. You know I don't believe in marriage or anything like that.'

'I see. As I recall, I seemed to be very much your "bit on the side", along with a raft of other women. I'm certainly not returning to that.'

He put his napkin down. 'I'm not like that any more. I've changed. I've realised all I want is you. Missing you so much has taught me that. I don't want anyone else. I want you to be with me.'

He grasped her hand.

'This is a lot to take in. You just need to remember that I love you and I want to be with you. That's all that matters. We don't have to define it now or even put a label on it.'

Clicking his fingers at the woman behind the counter, he called out, 'Can I have the bill, please?' Turning his attention back to Tess he said, 'So, I'm asking you to think about. Yes? I love you and want you back. I miss you. Remember, we were good together.'

'I think there's a bit more to think about than that,' she said dryly. 'Like, how I might actually feel about it all.'

'Shush,' he said, placing a finger on her lips. She pulled away quickly. 'Just remember how we used to be. Let's talk later, or tomorrow. I'm going to give you some space to think.' Rising, he approached the counter and turned. 'I won't give up, Tess. I meant what I said.'

He touched his card to the machine and left the cafe without glancing back.

Tess sat there completely dumbstruck.

CHAPTER 15

Griff had awoken to the three texts. They were vicious, threatening, and all told him he was going to die horribly. He forwarded them to Ben and crafted another email to his offender manager with a view to discussing it on Monday. As an afterthought, he informed Ben of the meeting and told him when and where, just in case he felt it necessary to drop in.

Griff was slightly concerned the meeting was in Maggie's, which had a tendency to be a hotbed of gossip, but he figured people would find out sooner rather than later anyway.

Since he was awake early, he cleared the front door of debris and gave it a quick wash down. As he scrubbed, he concluded that he'd have to spend some serious time repainting it.

On his way to work, he popped over the road to thank his neighbours again. He explained someone was waging a hate campaign against him, but had no idea who they were, or why they were doing it. They promised to be super vigilant.

They also told him how much they missed his mother, and how she used to talk about him with regularity. He almost ended up sobbing over them both.

Arriving at work, he got started. Linden arrived and together they worked happily in companionable silence. Tess arrived later than usual, and Griff remembered she said she had plans for breakfast. He wondered for a split second who she had been with.

'Hey!' she said. 'Everything OK after last night?' She unclipped Frank's lead and he trotted off.

'Yeah, all sorted now. Gotta devote some time to sorting it out though.'

'Why would anyone do that?'

He pulled a face. 'I don't know. Are we shutting at five today, Tess?' he asked.

'Um, think so. Hang on.' She moved to the counter and glanced at the bookings on the screen in front of her.

'Yeah, Sunday lunch till 5 p.m.'

'OK.' He saw Linden had popped into the cold room for a second. 'Could we talk? Maybe go for a drink? I need to discuss some stuff.'

She looked concerned. 'Anything I need to worry about?'

He was about to speak when Linden returned. So instead, he winked and said, 'Hopefully not.'

'OK, after service then,' she replied.

'You're on.'

§ § §

The rest of the day passed by in a blur, with the restaurant having two sittings for lunch. People were still trying to get in when Tess had to turn the sign to 'Closed'.

'Don't know what's going on today with everyone!' she said to Beth.

'Word's got out about Griff's cooking. That's what a few people said to me anyway. People are keen to try it,' Beth said. 'Great for the restaurant. We've never been this busy. I think the changes to the menu help.'

Tess nodded. She had been looking at the books and they were doing better than they had done for years, even this early into December. Last time she'd spoken to Lorraine, she'd been thrilled at how busy they'd been. She wondered how her sister was because she hadn't answered her last two calls and had just sent texts saying she would ring her another time. She promised herself she'd call her later to put her mind at rest.

As Tess exchanged pleasantries with a couple of customers, she glanced out of the window and thought she saw Vincent disappearing hurriedly down the road. Before she could crane her neck to see if it was him, she was beckoned over by another customer.

Tess heard her phone ping in her pocket as she was taking payment from the last customer. She said goodbye and drew out her phone. It was a message from Vincent.

He had sent her a picture. It was taken a few years ago, in her flat, and it was one of the pair of them, snuggled up together on her sofa. He had accompanied it with the words:

Loved seeing you earlier. Think on what I said. Love you.

As Tess looked at the photograph, her mind wandered, and she thought back to breakfast. She was confused over Vincent showing up, telling her he loved her. She couldn't work out what his game was. He had never once told her he loved her. Not in their whole time together. He had ended the relationship, and it was only afterwards that Tess had heard the extent of his numerous infidelities. She had been shocked and genuinely heartbroken that all the time they had spent together was more than likely a lie. But now this?

She hated people who weren't honest and genuine, and she had vowed, after Vincent, she would never allow herself to be lied to again. She had felt like a gullible fool. Everyone had known, and no one had told her, or even suggested it.

She wondered why Vincent was here, saying all these things to her. She felt a pang of nostalgia. She had loved him. Deep down she wondered if she could ever trust him again. The part of her that loved him wondered whether he had changed. Had he *really*? Did he mean it when he said he loved her? She mentally shook herself. What was she thinking? Snogging Griff last night, then breakfast with Vincent. She *never* did things like that!

Her mind drifted to the kiss last night and she felt a tug of desire. Her gaze drifted to him in the kitchen and her stomach lurched when he looked up from what he was doing and gave her a huge smile. God, he was cute. She was finding him more and more attractive by the minute, and part of her was more than hopeful for another opportunity to be alone with him. She remembered his kiss, the feel of his hands on her body, the way his thumb had stroked—

'Tess?'

'Err, what?' she stammered, embarrassed about her train of thought.

'Griff says there's food for you if you want it. You OK? You look a bit hot and bothered.' Beth looked at her with concern.

'Oh, I'm fine. Thanks.'

'Food's up here,' Beth said, pointing to a steaming bowl on the chef's table.

'Oh, thanks. You eaten?'

'Yeah. Linden has too.'

Tess sat at the chef's table and accepted a basket of bread from Linden.

'Thanks,' she said, spooning in the soup. 'This is good.'

'I made it,' he said proudly.

Griff joined her with his own bowl of soup, his thigh brushing hers as he sat on the stool.

'Cosy up here, isn't it?' He grinned.

They ate in silence while they watched Linden and Beth clear up and chat.

'Good service today,' Griff said, as he dug out a notepad from his trouser pocket and a small pencil. 'The veg combo is really working.'

'Hardly any leftover veg now,' Linden agreed. 'I think people seem to like a more seasonal approach.'

'Good,' Griff said, scribbling on his pad.

'People said to me today the cauliflower cheese was amazing,' Beth said. 'We never used to do it, but it all gets eaten.'

'Can't have a roast without cauliflower cheese,' Griff said firmly.

Tess smiled. 'Well, long may it last.'

Griff glanced at her. 'OK, tomorrow. Normal lunchtime and then a private Christmas party for a local firm in the evening?'

'Yup,' she said. 'Let's push soup, the platters and a couple of specials at lunchtime.' She glanced at her phone. 'It's going to be wet and cold. So, maybe two soups, the platters and…'

'I think we should do a macaroni cheese special,' Linden said. 'Maybe with a side of garlic bread, or a green salad?'

'I like that idea,' Tess mused. 'Griff? What's your take?'

'I've got no issues with it. If we do it a certain way, what macaroni we don't use I can use in a soup the next day. Perhaps a take on winter minestrone.'

'Good thinking,' Tess said.

'So, how about a tomato and lentil soup and a chowder? I found some haddock in the freezer that needs using.'

'Perfect. People love chowder on a cold day.'

'We could do a cheese and leek soda bread?' Linden suggested.

'Good idea.'

Tess finished her soup, took her bowl through to the kitchen, and stacked it in the dishwasher.

Beth poked her head around the kitchen door.

'I'm off, Dad's outside. That person is over the road again. Like last time. Just staring. Hood up.'

'What person?' Tess said.

'There was someone acting a bit weird a few days back,' Griff said. 'I'll take a look.'

He slipped off the stool and walked towards the front of the restaurant. As he approached the window, the figure moved and walked off slowly.

'Not there now,' he said, as Tess headed towards him. 'Must have been a coincidence.'

Tess untied her apron. 'I need to give Frank a walk. Are you OK to lock up, Griff?'

'Sure. Err, what time shall we meet…?' He trailed off as Linden appeared.

'About half an hour?' Tess responded in a low voice.

'OK. Perfect.'

'See you in a bit.'

Tess grabbed Frank and slipped upstairs to change into some jeans and walking boots and threw a jumper over her white shirt.

She'd made the decision to hear Vincent out again and find out exactly what had prompted the change of heart and his declaration of love. She didn't really understand what he wanted from her. Part of her wondered if he wanted to move in together. Would he? She shook herself mentally. Ridiculous idea, surely? But then why was he here? Why was he suddenly telling her he loved her? Did she even want Vincent? Could she see herself living with him? But what did it mean that she had kissed Griff last night and couldn't stop thinking about it?

She grabbed a warm coat and marched down to the beach. Frank trotted about, disappearing into the darkness when she let him off the lead.

Her mind turned to Griff as she walked. She wondered what he needed to talk about. She had a sudden thought he might ask about Vincent. Had he seen them together? She wondered if he might say the kiss was a mistake, but then she remembered his cheeky wink. She concluded he wouldn't have done it if he was going to give her the brush off.

Then it occurred to her he might be after some more certainty with his role. Perhaps he wanted to know what would happen when Lorraine returned. Tess stopped walking for a minute. Wait. What *would* happen when Lorraine returned? She realised with a jolt she felt so at home in Castleby, she hadn't given her flat nor her other life a second thought. Did she actually *want* to go back?

Glancing at the time, she realised she was going to be late. She texted Griff.

Won't be long – just finding Frank in the dark!

Shivering, she called for Frank. She turned towards the slipway, where she saw Maggie wiping down tables in the window of the cafe. Frank appeared and they walked up the beach. Tess kicked the sand off her boots when she hit the tarmac. Clipping Frank on the lead, she walked briskly up the road and into the Hope and Anchor. The pub was warm, with a bright Christmassy theme to it. She spotted Griff waiting at the bar and joined him.

'Hey,' she said, nudging him.

'What are you drinking?'

'I'll have a glass of red, please. House is fine.'

Griff ordered and pointed to a corner. 'Why don't you grab that table?'

Tess took a seat. Griff followed a few moments later with the drinks, sitting opposite, with his back to the room.

'They're bringing a bowl of water for Frank,' he said, pushing her drink towards her.

'Thanks,' she said and took a sip.

He dug about in his pocket, producing a handful of dog biscuits.

'Free at the bar,' he said, handing one to Frank.

'Christ, he'll adore you for life,' she said, pointing to the look of adoration on Frank's face as he stared at Griff.

'Pure cupboard love,' said Griff.

'So,' Tess said. 'What do you want to talk to me about?'

'Few things,' Griff said, suddenly looking awkward, which surprised her, as she'd never seen him that way before. 'I wondered firstly, how you thought things were going, you know, with me being the chef.'

'Are you kidding?' Tess asked incredulously.

'No… I just wondered, you know… Checking in and all that.'

'You are single-handedly the best bloody thing that's happened to the restaurant for years,' Tess said. 'Can you not see that?'

'Er, I don't know. I didn't know the chef before, or what—'

'I think you're absolutely amazing,' Tess interrupted. 'Your ideas, the way you use food, reduce waste, think outside the box. I could gush on for hours but I'm sure you wouldn't want me to.'

Griff smiled. 'Fill your boots. Carry on gushing.'

She laughed. 'Seriously. Is that what you are worried about?'

'Well, no but…'

'Our takings mean people will get a Christmas bonus,' Tess said. 'Deservedly so. What you did for Santa Saturday was amazing! We've never taken money like it.'

'That's good to hear.'

'It's all down to you.'

'It's not. You had the idea. You just asked me to fill in the blanks,' he said.

Smiling, she took another sip of wine. 'OK. So, *I'm* the brilliant one then and you are my assistant.'

'Whatever works,' he said, laughing.

'Are you worried about when Lorraine gets back?' she asked, suddenly serious.

He pulled a face. 'I don't know. I'm just trying to get us through Christmas first and then have a think about it. There's the guy that offered us the gig together… I mean, that's gotta be worth a conversation at least.'

'True.'

'What about you? Thought any more about what you're going to do when your sister's better?'

Tess grimaced. 'It occurred to me earlier that I hadn't given back home a second thought. So, no plans. I'm just getting through Christmas really.' She gave a half-laugh. 'Looks like we're getting through it together by the sounds of it.'

'I'm game if you are,' Griff said, raising his glass. 'In it together!'

She raised her glass. 'In it together,' she echoed, clinking glasses.

§ § §

Griff was nervous, his stomach churned. *Tell her.* His inner voice screamed. *JUST TELL HER!*

What if she threw a fit? What if she sacked him on the spot?

'So, Tess. I need to talk to you about something else,' he muttered, unable to look her in the eye. He focused on his beer and started talking. 'So, I need to duck out after the lunch rush on Monday.'

'That's fine,' she said. 'It's good to have a few hours off before evening service.'

'OK. It's just, I have a meeting I've got to go to.'

'Griff, it's fine. Honestly.'

'Tess, I… look, the thing is. I've been trying to tell you for ages because you need to know. Not that it's a big thing. Erm, it *is* a big thing. But every time I go to tell you, someone appears, or I realise you're asleep, or a phone goes, or something, so I need to tell you this thing.' He paused. 'This big thing.'

He glanced up and found she was watching him closely.

'OK,' she said, drawing the word out slowly. 'This sounds ominous. You're scaring me now.'

§ § §

Tess stared at him. Shit. *Was he married?* What the bloody hell was it he needed to tell her? What was not a big thing, but actually was a big thing? Oh God, was he leaving?

'Are you leaving?' she asked.

'What? No, of course not,' he said, frowning.

She leant forwards. 'Don't tell me you're married?' she hissed.

He stared at her. 'Christ no. I would *never*—'

'Well, what then?' she said impatiently.

'It's just. God this is so hard to say out loud. I don't know how to say it.'

'Just say it.'

'OK. Just say it, Griff,' he half said to himself. He flicked a glance at her. 'Easier said than done, I can assure you.'

'You are totally freaking me out now,' she said. 'It genuinely can't be that bad.'

'Before I say,' he said, 'I just wanted to say, I really enjoyed last night. You know.' He met her eyes. 'With you in the kitchen. Once I'd disarmed you,' he said softly. He laid a hand over hers. 'I'd really like to take this… you know, explore… this with you.'

Tess's heart was thumping. The touch of his hand on hers had been electric and she stared into his liquid brown eyes as he talked quietly to her.

'Only if you want to,' he finished. 'You know, explore this thing with me.'

'I do,' she said, her breathing quick. 'Want to explore this with you. Now tell me this big thing.'

He dropped his head and stared into his beer for a second. 'Promise me you'll hear me out completely.'

'I promise. Christ, Griff, come on.'

'OK. So, I need to tell you that I—'

CHAPTER 16

Blood roared in Tess's ears. She saw Griff's lips moving but she couldn't hear the words. All she heard was the sound of the busy pub magnified. A loud, deafening, cacophony. She wanted it all to go quiet, so she could think. Her stomach churned. She suddenly felt faint. Was she going to be sick?

She stared in utter disbelief at the scene in front of her. She blinked again in case it was her mind playing cruel tricks on her. She was tired, maybe that was it. She had started to see things.

But she hadn't. It was real. Black and white real.

Vincent was in the pub, with a woman. Tess watched as he ushered the woman to the table and helped her take off her coat, revealing a pregnant tummy, made all the more obvious by the tight jersey dress.

Tess couldn't see the woman's face; her features were obscured by the thick curtain of glossy dark hair she wore loose. But there was an air of familiarity about her which Tess couldn't immediately place. The woman had her back to Tess, but as she ran her hands through her hair, Tess noted the set of rings on the woman's left hand. *What? No, it couldn't be!*

Her shock intensified as she watched Vincent approach the bar and pluck two menus from it before returning to the table. He rested his hand lightly on the woman's back as he bent and spoke to her. With mounting disbelief, Tess noted the thin gold band on his wedding finger. He certainly hadn't been wearing *that* when they'd met for breakfast.

Tess felt hot. She had to get out. She felt sick. She wondered fleetingly if she *was* going to be sick, right in the middle of the pub.

She felt bile rising.

'I've got to go,' she managed. 'I don't feel…'

Grabbing her coat, she yanked Frank's lead, and dashed out of the side door. Desperate to get away from Vincent's view. The door closed behind her and she steadied herself against the wall, drawing in deep breaths. Sweat broke out across her face and then she realised she was going to be sick.

Hurrying down the road, she stepped into a side alleyway and retched. She retched again, half sobbing, slumped weakly against the wall. Breathing deeply, she tried to calm down.

After a time, she realised she was freezing, so she shrugged into her coat and zipped it up. Her head was spinning and she still couldn't believe what she'd seen.

She felt the need to put distance between her and the pub. She walked quickly down the road, up onto Castle Mount. The wind was strong, buffeting her, drying the tears on her face.

Sitting on one of the benches, she fleetingly remembered seeing Griff in the same spot, crying. With horror, she realised she'd completely bailed on him, leaving him in the pub, with no explanation. She still had no idea what it was he wanted to tell her.

She hadn't heard a thing once she had seen lying, cheating, deceitful Vincent.

She couldn't believe she'd wasted time even thinking about him. That she'd actually thought about giving him a second chance! She realised that, deep down, she might have been open to it. But it had depended on what he would have said. She couldn't forget him saying he loved her and that he wanted her back. Now she realised she'd believed him. Was she really that dense? That fucking stupid? That *gullible?* She'd half believed him when he said they needed to be together. She'd thought about it. *Actually* thought about it.

Anger settled within her. She thought about the things he had said to her in the past. How he had been with her. Rage rushed in. What a *fucking* liar the man was.

She stood, not sure of what to do, but suddenly felt overwhelmed with exhaustion. Staggering slightly, she clutched the back of a bench to steady herself.

She felt weighed down with fatigue as she walked down the slope towards home. As she passed the pub, she couldn't help but glance in from the cover of darkness.

Through the large windows, she saw Vincent, chatting to a waitress, as he sat next to the dark-haired woman. He had a proprietary hand on the woman's belly. It was only when the dark-haired woman leant forwards slightly that Tess realised it was Karen; her old best friend and flatmate. The very same one who had disappeared and ghosted her with no explanation. Now Tess knew exactly why.

§ § §

Griff stopped talking and stared at Tess. She had gone deathly pale. Her eyes were huge and staring. He sat silently, waiting for her to respond to the epic news he'd taken ages to pluck up the courage to tell her. She made a strangled sound.

'I've got to go,' she said. 'I don't feel…'

Griff stared at her as she got up from the table, grabbed her coat and yanked Frank out of the door with her.

'What? Come on! You said you'd hear me out…' he called to her retreating back. Frustrated, he watched her leave.

'Fuck,' he said, dropping his head into his hands. 'Looks like you're out of a job, mate,' he muttered bitterly. He sat morosely for a while, replaying the conversation in his head.

'Promise me you'll hear me out completely,' he'd said.

'I promise. Christ, Griff, come on.'

He had taken a deep breath and told her.

So that was it. He'd finally said it, and she bailed. Hadn't heard him out. Just left. Looking like she was going to throw up. Christ, he'd actually made her sick. He pushed his half-empty glass away in disgust, grabbed his coat and left. It wasn't the first time this had happened to him since he'd left prison.

Griff walked home. He assumed Tess would sack him now. He wasn't quite sure how she would do it but he supposed it would be at some point the next day. He felt sad. He loved working in the restaurant. Working with Tess. It had begun to drizzle, so he tucked himself deeper into his coat and picked up his pace.

He was deep in thought about his exchange with Tess as he walked down the side of his house. He wished he had kept the card with the man's name on it who had offered him a job. He tried to rationalise the evening with Tess. Surely she wasn't so unreasonable that she wouldn't even hear him out. Wouldn't even talk to him about it? He opened the back gate, registering too late, the security light he had installed wasn't working. He heard a shout and then everything went black.

§ § §

Through the window, Tess stared at her old best friend and flatmate in total confusion, trying to work it out. Tears filled her eyes and she let out a sob, but quickly clapped a hand over her mouth.

How could she? With Vincent? She'd always known how Tess felt about Vincent. They dissected it for hours; she knew *everything*. Stifling further sobs, she ran up the road to the flat.

Safely inside, she unclipped Frank and trudged up the stairs. She grabbed a bottle of Lorraine's brandy from the kitchen and took a deep swig as she sat down on the sofa and tried to work it all out.

How did he know her? When had they met? Karen had moved out *months* ago. Tess had sensed there was an issue; Karen had been cold and distant for a while and was hardly ever home. Karen said repeatedly there was no issue; she just wanted to live alone.

As Tess took another swig of brandy, she wondered whether they'd been having an affair the whole time Karen had lived with her. The brash liquid burnt her throat as she took another gulp. She cast her mind back, desperate to remember any evidence.

She remembered coming home midway through a shift when she had felt unwell and finding a man's jacket on the sofa. Because she had felt so wretched, she went straight to bed. She heard low voices and the front door closing a few minutes after she had arrived. Now she wondered whether that had actually been Vincent. How had she not known her old best friend and her ex were *married?* When did that bloody happen?

Angry, she moved over to her laptop and opened the lid. She opened Facebook, then Instagram, and scrolled through them to find Karen's accounts, but couldn't see them. She found a mutual friend's Instagram; she sat back and stared at the screen. This would teach her not to keep in touch with her friends. It was all there. The wedding, three months ago. The scan picture – congratulations posted – four weeks before that. The past few months – all in glorious technicolour.

Tess slammed the laptop closed. What a *fucking* bastard. Here, with his pregnant wife all along! All that crap at breakfast about wanting to get together again. How much he missed them being together! Wanting to be a couple again, when all the time Tess would be his "bit on the side". Tess took another swig, swallowed hard and choked a little. Then the tears really came.

Tess awoke the next morning with a bad taste in her mouth, hugging an empty brandy bottle. She moved her head to peer at the clock and winced as she felt the loose-brain feeling of a bad hangover.

'Ouch,' she grumbled, as she swung her legs over the side of the bed and sat for a minute. Frank eyed her knowingly from his position by the door.

'You can stop with the judgey looks as well,' she mumbled, staggering to the bathroom.

Ten minutes later, she gulped down a couple of painkillers with some breakfast, and decided Frank needed a walk on the beach. She was concerned she had walked out on Griff last night with no explanation at all. He must genuinely think she was crazy. She decided to speak to Griff when he was in, to explain and try to finish their conversation.

She thought back to how worried he'd looked when he'd been talking. She genuinely hadn't heard a thing he'd said as soon as she spotted Vincent. Lying. Cheating. Bastard Vincent.

As she passed Maggie's she waved and Maggie bustled out.

'Glad I caught you. Little party, Christmas Day, for those of us on our lonesome,' she said. 'You up for it?'

'Yes. I'll be shutting the doors at six and that's it for me for a good few days!'

'You'll come then?'

'Of course. Tell me what to bring.'

She waved the comment away. 'I'll tell Griff. We'll work it out.'

'OK. See you later!'

'Have a good day!'

Back at the restaurant she found Linden waiting outside, stamping his feet in the cold.

'Hi,' she said in surprise. 'Griff not here?'

He shrugged. 'If he is, he can't hear me knocking.'

She frowned. It was unusual for Griff not to be in on time. She thought about what he'd been trying to tell her last night. She wondered whether anything she'd said or done would mean he wouldn't turn up. She opened the door to the restaurant; there was still no sign of Griff.

Frowning, Tess checked her phone. No messages from him. She texted him.

Everything OK with you today?

She waited a few seconds, staring at the screen, and then put her phone down. She would give it another few minutes.

After ten minutes with no response, she decided to give him a call. She waited as it rang and rang and then eventually clicked to voicemail.

'Griff, it's me. Erm… Just wondering if everything is OK with you? Umm, sorry about last night too. We er… do need to finish our chat. Call me when you can?'

Tess carried on in the hope that there would be a message from him, but her phone remained annoyingly silent.

§ § §

Griff awoke to sunlight streaming through his window at an angle, catching him directly in the face. He fleetingly wondered why he hadn't closed his curtains, then, when he moved, he remembered.

He gingerly rolled onto his side and pushed himself to a sitting position, gasping in pain as his ribs protested. He saw his pillow and saw it spotted with bloodstains. His face felt swollen and sore, and his lips were stuck together. When he tried to lick his lips, he felt a stab of pain and tasted blood.

He managed to stand and shuffled into the bathroom where he inspected his face in the mirror.

'Shit,' he muttered, turning his face to see the extent of the damage. Gingerly, he tried to strip off the T-shirt he was wearing, but it hurt to raise his arms. Eventually, he managed to get it off by bending slightly and dragging it off so he didn't have to raise his arms too high. His ribs were covered in black and blue bruising.

His hands shook from the pain as he steadied himself on the basin. He breathed deeply, trying to push down the nausea.

The front doorbell rang shrilly in the quiet house, making him jump and his heart thud.

Griff closed his eyes. Flashes of the previous evening came to him but he was unable to piece them together fully. He just remembered the pain. Lying on the ground, cold, gritty and wet against his cheek, while someone viciously kicked him.

He remembered hearing voices, shouts, and then strong arms under his to help him up. He remembered falling onto his bed desperate for sleep. Desperate to be left alone.

Shirtless, he made his way downstairs to answer the door. He opened it to find PC Ben Baker on the doorstep.

'Christ, they weren't exaggerating,' he exclaimed, wincing. 'Why aren't you in hospital?'

Griff slumped against the doorframe.

'Who wasn't exaggerating? Sorry, I've only just woken up.'

'Your neighbours opposite. They left a message for me. I've just come on shift and picked it up. They said they interrupted someone giving you a kicking last night and helped you inside. You refused police and an ambulance apparently.'

Ben turned, raised an arm and gave a thumbs up to a face at the window, in the house opposite. He turned back. 'I genuinely think one of them has been up all night watching your place for unwanted visitors.'

Griff peered around Ben and saw his neighbour at the window. He raised an arm and winced, then gave a small wave. He received one in return.

Ben studied him. 'You look terrible. Can I come in?'

Griff stood aside, and Ben walked through to the kitchen and unlocked the back door.

'Have you been to hospital?' he asked.

'No, it was just a beating; I've had enough in my life.'

Ben shook his head and tutted as he peered outside. 'So, whoever it was, smashed the bulb to your security light. That's why they jumped you back there.'

Griff gingerly sat down at the table. 'Ben, what time is it?'

Ben glanced at his watch. 'Ten forty-five.'

'Shit, I'm late.'

'Griff, you need to rest.'

'I'm fine. Been worse.'

'Come on. You need to rest up and recover.'

'Can't do that. Got a meeting later, too.'

'Oh. Your offender manager. I'll join you for a while to confirm our concerns.'

'Appreciate that.'

'I need my phone.' Griff felt the pockets of the jeans he was still wearing from the previous evening.

'Coat?' Ben pointed to Griff's coat, hung on one of the chairs.

Griff dug about in a pocket and found his phone; the screen was cracked, and it was dead. He plugged it into the wall but it remained lifeless.

'Look,' Ben said. 'Hop in the shower. No offence, but you stink and look terrible. I'll drop you into town. The time it would take you to walk is better spent in the shower.'

'Sure?'

'Go.'

Griff hustled upstairs as quickly as his ribs would allow and he painfully peeled off his jeans and underwear. He stepped into the shower. He was still waging the battle for control of the bathroom with the enormous spider he'd seen on his first day in the house. They had been chasing each other around the room and there now seemed to be an element of comedy about it. As the spider sat on the edge of the vent, Griff glanced at it.

'You win today,' he told it. 'I haven't got the energy.'

He felt better after letting the hot water assault his fragile face. He stepped out of the shower, wincing as he overstretched for his towel. He managed to get dressed and appeared downstairs to a grinning Ben.

'Wish my girlfriend would shower and get dressed that quickly. You ready?'

'Thanks, Ben.'

Ben locked the back door for Griff and helped him into his coat. He opened the squad car door for him, and Griff bent to get in and gasped at the pain that shot through him. He winced as he settled in the seat. He closed his eyes and leant his head against the headrest.

'See? You shouldn't be working. You're exhausted already.'

'God, you nag more than my mother did,' Griff said, eyes still closed. He was just drifting off to sleep when Ben pulled up outside the restaurant.

'Cab for Jones arriving at destination,' he quipped.

Griff unsnapped his seat belt. 'Thanks, mate. Appreciate it.'

Griff closed the car door and took a breath. He remembered telling Tess last night and watching her run out of the pub without looking back. He wondered if he still had a job.

He tried to push open the door to the restaurant. It was locked, so he tapped on the glass. Tess walked towards him with an expression he couldn't quite place.

'Oh my God! Are you OK? I've been so worried about you! I've been ringing and leaving messages. What the hell happened?'

He stepped in. 'Sorry I'm late…'

She tutted. 'Stop! What happened? Are you OK? You look terrible.'

'Someone jumped me, late last night,' he said. 'They were waiting for me at home. I was knocked out; I don't remember much.'

'Was it the vandals?'

'What?'

'The vandals? From the other day. Was it them?'

Griff had to think for a minute. 'Possibly, yes.'

'You've been to hospital?'

'No, but—'

'You must go!' Tess insisted.

'I'm fine. I just took a kicking, that's all. But my phone was a casualty.'

'Tess, any news on… *Jesus Christ,* what happened to you?' Linden said, coming out of the kitchen.

'He was set upon,' Tess said.

'You've been to hospital?'

'Don't you start,' grumbled Griff, starting to take off his coat.

'You're not working today,' Tess said.

'I'm fine,' he insisted. It occurred to him she hadn't mentioned the previous evening. 'I need to get a few things done, then I'll sit down for a bit.'

'Can you sit down in the kitchen and direct Linden?'

'It's fine. Stop fretting. I'm just a bit sore.'

'I'm not happy about you being here in this state. You need to be at home.'

'And I said I'm fine.'

The phone rang and Tess snatched it up.

'Oh hi,' she said, smiling, 'I've been trying to get hold of you.'

Griff went into the kitchen, ignoring Tess's gesticulating for him to sit down. He heard her laughing and saying, '*you did what?*' followed by more guffawing. He assumed it was maybe her new boyfriend ringing or the sender of the red roses. He shook his head, angry that she hadn't even mentioned what he'd told her last night. How could she not even discuss it with him?

He snatched up an apron and tied it around himself, unable to face wrestling himself into a chef's jacket. He got Linden to bring round one of the stools from the chef's table and sank onto it gratefully. He directed Linden on what was a priority and started peeling vegetables.

He heard Tess finish her call, promising someone they'd talk later. He heard her tell someone she loved them, and he banged down a pot on the side.

'You OK, Chef?' Linden said. 'You seem pretty pissed off about something.'

'I'm fine,' Griff mumbled.

'I read an article in one of my sister's magazines. It said ten things the phrase, "I'm fine" actually means. One is… I'm not fine and I need someone to ask me again, two is—'

'Why are you reading your sister's magazines?'

Linden shrugged. 'She leaves them in the loo. Nothing else to read in there.'

Griff rolled his eyes.

'Are you really fine? Or not fine?'

'Linden. Make the soup. I'm fine.'

'Yes, Chef.'

The lunchtime session was busy, but many customers wanted soup, cheese or meat platters. Linden was delighted the macaroni cheese special was sold out within the first two hours. As things calmed down, Griff made Linden start getting ready for the evening shift, knowing he had a meeting in the next hour or so.

'I'm not sure how much use I'll be later so let's get ahead on what we can do now,' Griff said.

'Good plan,' Linden said. 'I'm all for life being easier.'

As Griff watched the time tick round, he hoped his offender manager hadn't needed to get in touch with him today. At that moment, Tess arrived in the kitchen with a handful of black wire.

'Look,' she said. 'This is an old phone, so if your SIM fits it, you're welcome to use it until you get a replacement. I'll leave it here.'

Griff glanced up at her. 'Thanks,' he said.

'Come here,' Linden said, holding out his hand. 'I'll see if I can sort it.'

Griff pulled his broken phone out of his pocket and handed it over to Linden. Within a few minutes, the new phone had flickered into life, and a series of electronic beeps sounded.

'You've got some messages,' Linden said.

'Thanks,' Griff said, taking the phone. The messages were the same as last time. He was going to die. Next time they wouldn't get interrupted. Griff closed his eyes and tried to ignore them.

Tess breezed back into the kitchen.

'We're shutting for a few hours now. No one about. Can you be back here by 6 p.m? Party is booked for 8 p.m. We know what they're eating. Is that enough time for you guys?' She directed her comments at Griff and Linden.

Linden nodded. 'Yeah, we've done as much as we can.'

'Good. Right. See you all later then.' She left the room and Griff sighed heavily. Clearly, she was going to ignore everything and carry on as if he hadn't said a word.

He picked up his coat and walked out of the restaurant, tickling a forlorn-looking Frank under the chin as he went.

CHAPTER 17

Griff walked painfully down the hill towards Maggie's. He bundled himself up in his coat and sat on one of the benches outside the cafe, facing the beach. He breathed in the sea air as much as his ribs allowed and closed his eyes.

Maybe this wasn't the right place for a fresh start. Maybe he should find that guy's card, and just go and talk to him. He'd get builders in to fix his mum's house, get it shipshape and then sell it. Make a new start elsewhere. But he knew from bitter experience that changing his postcode wouldn't mean he'd forget all of his problems. They'd just go with him.

He felt a hand on his back. It was Maggie.

'What in the world has happened to you, my love?' she said, full of sympathy for him.

He struggled to form the words. 'Someone's out to get me.'

'Tell me,' she demanded, taking a seat next to him.

Griff outlined everything that had been happening. He showed her the texts and told her about the fire and the beating the night before.

'Police know?'

'Uh huh.'

'What does Tess say?'

Griff stared stonily ahead. 'She's not saying anything, Mags.'

'You told her?'

'I did. About prison. I didn't mention what's happening now.'

'What happened?'

'She left the pub. Didn't discuss it. Just ran out.'

Maggie frowned. 'Unlike her.'

'Is it? I have no idea.'

He glanced at his watch. 'Look, I'm meeting my offender manager here. Ben Baker said he was gonna swing by too. OK to have a quiet corner?'

'Of course.'

'He's mainly coming to see you though,' Griff said. 'I've told him I think you have a boyfriend as he seemed to have very fond memories of you.'

Maggie tittered. 'Stop. Now come and wait in the warm. There's tea and cake with your name on it.'

Griff dragged himself inside and made himself as comfortable as his ribs allowed. At exactly 4.45 p.m., Peter Denton walked in and scanned the room.

Griff wasn't sure who he was looking for – Maggie or him – but he raised a hand anyway.

Peter walked over, shook Griff's hand, and took a seat opposite him.

'What in the hell happened to you? You know there's no fighting allowed under your licence.'

'Good thing I was set upon and didn't know a thing about it then, due to being knocked unconscious,' Griff retorted.

Peter looked concerned. 'Is this the trouble you've been emailing me about?'

'Well, if it isn't one of my favourite men,' Maggie said, appearing at Peter's elbow and laying a hand on his shoulder. 'Aren't you going to say hello properly?'

Peter's face broke out into a huge smile, and he got up to kiss Maggie chastely on the cheek.

'Oh, come here,' she said, throwing her arms around him for a hug. 'So good to see you, Pete,' she said. She winked at Griff over Peter's shoulder. 'Now, what's it going to be? Welsh cake? Coffee? Sponge cake?'

Peter sat down, looking flushed, and Maggie nudged him with her hip. 'You used to love a Welsh cake, if I recall,' she said.

'That would be lovely, Maggie. You look quite wonderful,' Peter said, resembling a lovesick puppy.

'Griff darling. Same?'

'Go on then.'

Maggie squeezed Peter's shoulder. 'I can't tell you how worried I am about this one. Hate campaign it is. Poor boy is trying to get on with his life and this is what he gets. I hope you're being nice to him,' she said, giving Peter the benefit of one of her death stares.

'Absolutely. Yes,' stammered Peter.

'Tea and Welsh cakes coming right up,' she said, bustling off.

The door opened and Ben Baker stepped in. Griff saw Maggie point to him in the corner. The next hour passed in a blur. He was fighting fatigue and a banging headache. All he wanted to do was lay down in bed and sleep. Ben spoke about Griff being persecuted and also outlined what an upstanding citizen Griff had been, rescuing Tess from an attack and stepping in to help her out as she recovered. Ben was soon called away but gave Peter his details.

By the time the hour had gone, Peter gave a rueful smile and closed his notebook. 'I think we'll meet once a month now,' he said.

'You seem to be doing well. Settling in and building a community, which is important. Are you planning to stay where you are working?'

'I don't know yet,' Griff said. 'I was offered something else but it was only to have a conversation.'

'OK, well you have to do what you think's right and what suits you. Let me know of any changes. Shall we meet here again?' he said, wistfully eyeing up Maggie who was serving some customers with takeaway drinks.

'Sounds good.'

They settled on the next date after Christmas. While Peter said goodbye to Maggie, Griff waited by the door, and they walked out together.

'Good to see you doing well, considering,' Peter said gruffly. 'Good to have Maggie in your corner too.'

'She's a diamond all right.'

'Shame she has a boyfriend,' Peter said wistfully.

'Not sure if it's serious though, so there's always hope.'

Peter beamed. 'I like that idea. Take care of yourself.' He extended his hand and shook Griff's. 'See you soon and let me know of any changes or if you need to move the date to sooner. It's absolutely no problem.'

'Bye, Peter,' Griff said, watching him walk up the hill with a spring in his step.

Griff poked his head in the door and blew Maggie a kiss. 'I owe you.'

She waved the comment away. 'Hush now. Take care, sweetheart,' she said.

Griff closed the door and walked slowly back up the hill to the restaurant.

§ § §

Tess was on Castle Mount, coming down the hill after walking Frank. As she walked down the path opposite Maggie's cafe, she stopped in her tracks. She watched Griff leave the cafe with a man in a suit who shook Griff's hand enthusiastically.

She wondered who the man was. She caught the words, 'Let me know of any changes or if you need to move the date to sooner. It's absolutely no problem.'

Tess stared. *Was he getting another job?* Had he decided to bail just because she left last night?

He'd been grumpy all day, so she wondered if he had arranged it as a last-minute thing. Last night he'd been talking about getting through Christmas. She huffed as she marched down the path. Just getting through Christmas, eh? Was it such an ordeal working for her? Clearly, he'd arranged a job for himself to start after Christmas. The cheek of it! She dropped down off the steps onto the beach and passed the cafe, just as Maggie was collecting in her specials blackboards.

'Alright, Tess?'

'Fine thanks, Mags,' Tess said.

'You taking good care of Griff?' Maggie asked.

Tess stomped off up the road. 'Seems like he's taking care of himself pretty well without me!' she threw over her shoulder.

She fumed as she marched up the road. After the kiss the other night, she had expected a little more loyalty from him.

§ § §

Griff bought himself a packet of heavy-duty painkillers and a bottle of water and walked back to the restaurant. His phone pinged again and he almost didn't want to look at it, but did so in case it was Ben with some news. It was another vile text.

I'm coming for you. You will die.

He forwarded it to Ben and put the phone away. He took two painkillers, chugging them down with some water. As he approached the restaurant, Linden was coming in the opposite direction with Tess. Griff gave a wan smile and waited for Tess to unlock the door, before slowly making his way through to the kitchen.

Linden followed. 'Did I just see you taking painkillers?' he asked.

'What of it?' Griff said, an edge to his voice.

'You need something to eat if you're taking them. My mum says it's no good for your stomach lining if you don't. I'll make you some food.'

'It's fine. Stop mothering me.'

'I'm making it anyway, so eat it, don't eat it. Your choice.'

Griff's stomach rumbled and Linden heard it.

'Guess you are eating it,' he said, turning away with a half-smile.

Griff felt marginally better after eating. Linden had insisted the three of them sat at a table and ate together, but Griff, not wanting to talk, ate his food quickly, returning to the kitchen as soon as he could.

'What's up with Griff?' Linden said quietly to Tess as they watched him slowly move around back to the kitchen.

'Not a hundred per cent sure,' Tess said.

'Have you asked him?' Linden said. 'He won't talk to me.'

'I will.'

'Well, can you do it soon, as I'd like the old Griff back, please?'

Tess watched Linden go back into the kitchen. She sat for a while wondering how to approach Griff, particularly in light of how she left the pub last night, plus what she'd overheard him say to the other man earlier. She tried to remember exactly what was said. It sounded just like he had lined himself up to go and work somewhere else, but surely he'd tell her and not just bail?

Beth arrived. 'I think tonight's party is just behind me. They're coming out of the cocktail bar,' she said, stripping off her coat.

'Better they drink here rather than there!' Tess said, opening the door as she saw people approaching.

'Let's get cracking then,' Griff muttered. 'Come on, Linden.'

Griff glanced at Tess from the kitchen. He saw her chatting to the customers as she filled wine glasses. He tutted. Clearly, she didn't care about what he'd told her last night. He frowned; perhaps she wasn't the person he thought she was.

'What are you frowning about?' Beth said, picking up a tray of appetisers from the side.

'Nothing much,' Griff said. 'Come back for the hot ones next? I'm getting them out in a couple of minutes.'

'Yes, Chef!' She winked, whirled around and returned to the restaurant.

Griff worked methodically. If he could just get through the next couple of hours, he could sleep. His ribs were hurting, his face was sore, and his lip kept splitting. He had a banging headache and a huge lump on the back of his head where he had been clouted. He just wanted to sleep with no interruptions and not worry about someone setting fire to his house with him in it.

He'd thought about checking into the local hotel but he couldn't afford what they were asking for a room. He resigned himself to having to chance it and hope that there'd be regular patrol cars past his house.

Mercifully, the private party was well behaved. They sat for food on schedule and once desserts were out of the way, a few of them asked if they could move some of the tables to create a small dance floor. While Linden helped some of the men do this, Griff took the opportunity to slip by Tess and head home.

As he walked, he waited for a car to pass so he could cross the road, but the car slowed. Griff braced himself instantly, drawing on what few reserves he had left. The window buzzed down.

'Let me give you a lift home. Man in your state shouldn't be walking.'

'You're a sight for sore eyes, Mags.'

'Hop in, gorgeous.'

Griff climbed in, inhaling sharply as the pain hit. Maggie viewed him critically.

'You look shattered, Griff.'

'I am. I just want to sleep without—' He stopped himself, the trauma of the last few days catching him unaware and closing his throat. He knew he was tired and emotional.

'Without worrying if someone's coming for you?'

'Pretty much,' he croaked.

Maggie glanced at him. 'You are coming home with me. Rest, be safe and not worry.'

Griff closed his eyes in relief.

'Thanks, Mags,' he managed, as silent tears poured down his face.

Maggie continued driving but reached across and took one of his hands.

'It'll be OK,' she said softly.

CHAPTER 18

Maggie woke Griff as she was leaving. She put a cup of tea down next to him and said she would be back in two hours with breakfast. Griff drank down the tea and promptly fell asleep again, waking an hour later and feeling much better. He had slept so deeply, he had missed the series of texts that had arrived in the night. More of the same, telling him he was going to die.

He sat up in bed and looked around the room. He had barely taken it in when he'd arrived with Maggie last night. There was a pile of his clothes on the chair; he had fallen into bed and gone straight to sleep. He looked at the bedcovers. He was sure he hadn't moved at all in the night.

There was a large, folded towel and a note from Mags telling him the bathroom was across the hall.

Griff ventured out, admiring Maggie's house, peering through windows to get his bearings. It was a beautiful old cottage nestled on a hill overlooking the town. He found it strangely comforting to be in Maggie's house.

He spent far longer in the shower than he should have, enjoying the hot water; it was a respite from his usual practice of playing hide and seek with a large beady-eyed spider.

He dressed carefully, trying to avoid causing himself too much pain. He made the bed and arrived in the kitchen just as Maggie let herself in the front door.

'Morning, my love,' she said. 'You look so much better than last night.'

'I feel much better. Thanks, Mags. You don't know what you did for me last night.'

She tittered loudly. 'Say that again and I'll open the door so the neighbours can hear! They'll be scandalised!' She placed a hand on his arm. 'No arguments. You're staying here until this business is over.'

'I won't put you at risk, Mags.'

'Nonsense,' she said. 'Much as I like Ben Baker, although his girlfriend could do with less make-up and more brain cells if you ask me, I'm going to take matters into my own hands.'

Griff looked at her suspiciously. 'In what way?'

She tapped the side of her nose. 'Trust me. Now, get this down your neck and I'll drop you into work.' She held out her hand. 'House keys, please.'

'Why do you want my house keys?'

She grinned. 'Never tell anyone anything they don't need to know.'

'But it's my house. I kind of need to know.'

She clicked her fingers. Griff rummaged in his coat pocket and produced the keys.

'You'll get them back later,' she said. 'Don't worry.'

'But I need to get some stuff.'

'I'll sort that. You're not going back there for a bit.'

He frowned.

'Do you trust me?' Maggie demanded.
'Of course I do.'
'Well shut up and eat then.'
Griff knew better than to argue, so he tucked into his breakfast roll.

Waving goodbye to Maggie, he realised he didn't have the keys to the restaurant, so he stood awkwardly outside until he realised Linden had made an early start. He tapped on the door and was surprised to see Tess walking through the restaurant to let him in. Frank gave an excitable yip, launched himself off his cushion and nuzzled Griff's legs as he stepped inside.
'Thanks. I left my keys…'
'You look better,' she said.
'Sorry for bailing early last night. Dead on my feet.'
'No problem. Appreciated you staying to help. The party last night was really happy. I mean *really* happy. Pretty much drank us out of wine, so I need to restock before lunchtime. You OK to be here?'
'Fine.'
'If you're sure,' she said. 'I need to get on.'
She walked back through to the storeroom and Griff heard the clinking of bottles.
'Morning, Chef!' Linden called.
'Morning, Linden,' Griff said. 'You want coffee?'
'Go on then!'
Griff made the coffees quickly, debating whether to make one for Tess or not. He gave up wondering and stuck his head in the storeroom.
'You want coffee?'
She was engrossed in her phone. 'What? Oh. No… Thanks though.'

Griff and Linden were discussing bookings for the next few days and planning specials when Tess appeared in the kitchen.

'I'm going to the Harbour Vineyard to order more wine,' she said. 'I won't be long. Do we need anything?'

Both shook their head, so Tess left.

'How long did you stay for last night?' Griff asked, remembering people had been dancing and becoming rowdy when he left.

'They insisted on buying me, Tess and Beth a drink, so I stayed for a bit then their taxis started arriving for them. Thank God! Some of them were in a right state! I stuck around to help move the tables back and then we locked up and left together. I think Tess was in early to finish the clearing up.' Linden tilted his head. 'Are you OK? You don't seem your usual self?'

Griff carried on slicing onions. 'I'm not sure what my usual self is, to be honest,' he said. 'I'm beginning to wonder if it wasn't a mistake coming back.'

'I think you've turned this place around,' Linden said.

Griff inclined his head. 'Nice of you to say. Now, how about we do a veg curry as a special today, with rice and maybe a naan bread?'

Linden grinned. 'Guess I'm making naan bread then.'

§ § §

Tess walked briskly down the hill, her head full of thoughts of ordering wine and some of the local gin. She had received a few late-night texts from Vincent asking if she was free for a nightcap and a chat. She had read them, fumed, and then ignored them. She supposed his pregnant wife was fast asleep and he fancied some late-night activity. She remembered back to how it used to be a habit. Suddenly turn up late at night often citing he'd been in surgery. Now she didn't believe a single word he had ever said to her. Even this morning she was still fuming about it all. She felt like she was a stupid, gullible idiot for even believing he might have ever felt something for her.

Part of her wanted to confront his wife and tell her what Vincent had been doing, but she had been so hurt by her so-called best friend ghosting her and the betrayal, she figured she'd find out soon enough all by herself.

Tutting, she rounded the corner and stepped into the Harbour Vineyard, which housed a bar, tables and racks of wine which customers could sample before they purchased. She jogged lightly up the stairs towards James's office. The office door was open and his chair empty. She strode over to the window to see if he was out the front.

Her eyes scanned the street below. She jumped as her phone rang. It was Vincent. She debated answering it. In the end, she thought it might be quite illuminating. She answered just as she saw him through the window in the street below.

'Hello?'

'Darling, it's me.' His voice was soft.

'Who's this?' she demanded, from her position above the street. She watched as he rolled his eyes and glanced at his watch.

'That's not funny.' He sounded irritated.

She was silent for a moment. 'What do you want, Vincent?'

She watched as he leant casually against the wall and watched the passers-by.

'I meant what I said over breakfast. Every word. Have you been thinking about it?' he probed.

'Thinking about what?' Tess asked innocently.

'Tess,' he chided.

'I'm still not quite clear about exactly what you're asking me,' Tess said. 'By the sounds of it, you just want me back in my flat, or should I say, flat on my back?'

'Nothing wrong with that,' he said. 'We had a lot of fun as I recall.'

She peered down at him. He idly picked a piece of fluff off himself and smoothed down his coat.

'That was then,' she said briskly.

'What does that mean? It wasn't that long ago.'

'Feels like a lifetime ago. I mean, anything could have happened in that time,' Tess said, fully aware this would irritate him.

'Like what?' He frowned.

'I don't know. I mean, I could have got married for all you know. You could have got married.'

He laughed incredulously. 'Don't be ridiculous.'

This irked her. 'Why's it ridiculous?'

'It just is. Come on, darling.'

She tutted. 'I'm busy, Vincent, what do you want?'

'I've told you. I want you to come back to the hospital. Come back to your flat and then back to me.'

'I'm hearing a lot about what you want, Vincent. Nothing about what I want.'

She watched his face change as he spotted someone down the street. He waved and Tess saw his wife walking towards him.

'I think my phone's going to die,' he said quickly. 'I'll call you later.'

Tess was left listening to silence, as she watched him smile and kiss his wife.

'Lying snake,' she murmured.

'Tess!' A voice behind her made her jump.

'James. Hi.' She abandoned Vincent-watching. 'I am in need of a load of wine. Last night's party almost emptied stocks!'

'OK. Let's get an order together. I have a couple coming in for a tasting session in a mo, so I need to be quick. Plus, if we do it now, we can put it on the delivery van for later.'

'Perfect.'

Together, they disappeared into the office, where Tess settled the last bill, and they arranged for extra stock to cover the rest of Christmas. As they were finishing up, James glanced at his watch.

'Christ, I need to go.'

'Go on. I'll finish the order here and leave it on the desk. I only need a few more.'

'Thanks, Tess.' He rose from the desk and hurried down the stairs. Tess heard the murmur of voices from below. She finished the order and left it on his desk with a Post-it note of a smiley face. She was about to go down the stairs when she heard Vincent's voice.

'This is delicious. We're also looking for some palatable alcohol-free wines for my wife here.'

Tess froze. *Shit*! She had no desire to see either of them. Wildly, she looked around and saw the spiral staircase the staff used which led to the back of the shop and through a small courtyard to the street. Quietly, she made her way down the stairs, avoiding them.

§ § §

Griff was exhausted. Everything hurt. To add insult to injury, he'd picked up a large pan of soup and almost dropped it when his ribs had protested, screaming in pain. He had slopped carrot and coriander soup all down the side of his chef's jacket, which had soaked through to his T-shirt. Linden had rescued the rest of the pot and hefted it into the large cold room, and Griff had gone to the storeroom to change his jacket. He usually kept spare T-shirts and jackets wherever he worked; a lesson learnt on day two of working in a navy kitchen.

He unbuttoned the jacket, painfully shrugging it off, and put it aside to take home and wash. He braced himself. He was dreading having to take off his T-shirt. It had been a marathon just to get it on that morning. Any activity which involved twisting, or raising his arms, was agony. He debated cutting it off for a second but then decided against it when he realised he still had to get another one on.

Readying himself for the pain, he breathed out and managed to lift the bottom of it, his ribs screaming in agony as he raised his arms. Feeling slightly sick, he leant against the shelving unit and tried to work the T-shirt upwards without raising his arms too much, half bending over.

The door opened and Tess walked in, reading something on her notepad. As she looked up, her eyes settled on his torso, which resembled a blue and purple abstract art painting.

'*Jeeeesus*,' she said, frowning. 'That looks like bloody agony.'

'Yup.' Griff turned away from her slightly, suddenly embarrassed. Unsure of how to be with her after the other night.

'Are you trying to take it off?'

'Yup.'

'Do you want help?' she asked, stepping forwards. 'Come on.'

Gently, she took the bottom of his T-shirt and hitched it up slowly, carefully trying not to touch his sides. As she moved it upwards, she stepped forwards and slipped her hand inside the T-shirt to help work it over his shoulders and arms.

'OK?' she said, concentrating on her task. 'Bend forwards a little more.'

'Yup,' he said through gritted teeth.

'What's this anyway?' she asked. 'Soup? That's never gonna come out.'

'Carrot.'

'Ahh.'

'OK. Last bit.' She stepped closer, working the T-shirt up over his head. He winced as his arms were raised higher than he wanted them to be.

'Sorry... sorry,' she said softly. 'There. All done.'

'Just the clean one to go on now,' he said, taking a breath and reaching for it.

'Why don't you just wear the jacket?'

He shook his head. 'I need another layer. Trust me.'

'OK. Here goes then.'

Together, they managed to get the T-shirt and jacket on without it causing Griff too much agony.

'Jesus, Griff, you're clammy and you look like you're in so much pain. I think you should go home.'

'I will, in a couple of hours. We're too busy to leave Linden.'

She glanced at him. 'Are you even safe to go home? What if the people who mugged you come back? Surely you shouldn't go home for a bit?'

He shot her a sideways look. 'I stayed at Maggie's last night.' He gave a half-smile. 'To be fair, I think she did it to get the neighbours talking.'

Tess burst out laughing. 'I expect that's happening anyway!'

He chuckled.

Tess looked sympathetic. 'Stay here. Upstairs. In Lorraine's room. It's all yours. Please. I insist. Do the last few covers and then head straight up and go to bed. I feel terrible that you're working to help me out and you shouldn't be.'

It was a sorely tempting offer. He was almost asleep standing up; his pain levels had worn him down so much. He nodded.

'OK. I just need to sleep. That's all. Without…'

'I know. Without worrying.'

'I don't know if Mags is expecting me…'

'I'll call her. Go finish up.'

'OK.'

§ § §

Tess tapped out a quick text to Maggie to let her know Griff was staying upstairs. Maggie replied with a thumbs up.

Tess watched Griff covertly. He was clearly in a lot of pain. His typically efficient movements were even more efficient as he worked with Linden. When she saw the last main course go out, she walked into the kitchen.

'Griff. Come on. That's it.'

'But I need to —'

'You don't need to do anything. Come on.'

She gestured to the door and followed him through, telling Beth she'd be back in five minutes. She opened the door to the flat and gestured for him to go up, following his slow progress up the steep stairs.

'OK,' she said briskly. 'This is you.' She opened the door to Lorraine's room which was already made up and ready for when her sister got home.

'Bathroom is through there.' She opened a cupboard and drew out a large towel. 'Help yourself to a shower or bath, or whatever.'

'Thanks.' He took the towel.

'Do you need help with the jacket and T-shirt?'

He looked embarrassed. 'Please. Sorry.'

'It's fine.' Wordlessly, she unbuttoned his jacket and slid it off his shoulders. She repeated the earlier process with his T-shirt and folded it, leaving it on the chair. She turned and lifted an eyebrow.

'I'm assuming you're OK getting your trousers off?'

He gave a wan smile. 'If I was in a better state, I'd take that as a challenge.'

She gave a half-laugh. 'Gotta go. I can't leave Beth.'

'Thanks,' he said awkwardly.

Tess flicked a glance over his firm chest and torso, mottled with bruises, and flushed when she caught him looking at her. Flustered, she turned and clattered down the stairs, slightly faster than she'd intended, ending up clumsily falling against the door.

'You OK?' she heard him call.

'Fine! See you later.'

§ § §

Griff heard the door slam. He unbuckled his trousers and slid them off. He padded towards the bathroom in his underwear, with the towel slung over his shoulder, and stood under the hot shower for as long as he could stand it without falling asleep. Stepping out, he dried off, slung the towel around his waist, and cleaned his teeth with a spare toothbrush he found in a packet in the bathroom cabinet.

Padding back towards Lorraine's bedroom he closed the shutters and sat down gingerly on the bed. He lay back, trying to pluck up the energy to put his underwear back on, and didn't know another thing.

CHAPTER 19

Tess peered out of the restaurant window. Beth had mentioned a dark-clad figure over the road, waiting, who had been there before. Every time Tess checked, they were still standing there. As she said goodbye to the last few customers she noted the figure again. Frustrated, she decided to confront them as pleasantly as she could. Just in case it was someone homeless, or hungry, who needed food. She opened the restaurant door and marched purposefully towards the figure. As she approached, the figure turned and jogged down the road. She couldn't catch a glimpse of the face.

She watched them go, making sure they were out of sight, and returned inside. She tidied up a little but was so tired she decided she would finish up the next day since they were closed. Locking up, she set off with Frank for a quick walk before bed.

As she reached home, she glanced up at the flat's top windows, noting that Lorraine's bedroom light was still on. She half hoped that

Griff would still be awake, as she felt she really ought to talk to him about the other night when she had run off, and try to explain.

When she reached the top of the stairs, Lorraine's bedroom door was ajar, and the light was still on. She hesitated, wondering whether to knock or not. She pushed the door open slightly, and saw Griff on his side, fast asleep on top of the duvet, wearing the towel, obviously from the shower. Stepping in, she pulled the duvet over him, turned off the light and closed the door.

§ § §

PC Ben Baker knocked again on Griffin Jones's front door and stood back to peer up at the first-floor windows. He had been trying his phone repeatedly, with no luck, so now he had come round in person.

'He's not been home,' Griff's elderly neighbour called from his open front door.

'Since?'

'Couple of nights now.'

'Thanks, I'll try him at work. Appreciate you looking out for him.'

'We look out for each other around here,' he replied shortly and closed the door.

Ben climbed back into the police car and went in search of Griff. He would try the restaurant first and if all else failed, he'd ask the oracle that was Maggie.

Ben pulled over in the high street, seeing a rare space. He knew it was early, but hoped Griff might be at work. Locking the car, he strode off down the street and stopped in front of the restaurant.

He knocked on the huge plate glass window and peered in. There were no signs of life inside so he moved to the next door knowing it led to the flat above. He rang the doorbell and heard feet thumping down the stairs. Tess opened the door, holding a struggling Frank on the lead, as she tried to put a coat on.

'Hi,' she said brightly, then her face fell. 'Oh God. What's happened?'

'Looking for Griff. Thought he might be in early next door.'

'Is his house OK?'

'It's fine, I've just come from there.'

'He slept here last night. Maggie's the night before. I think he just wants to sleep, without being half-awake all night worrying.'

'Is it OK to go up?'

'Feel free. I'm on my way out. He's in my sister's room. First door on the right. Don't think he's up yet.'

'Thanks.' He waited to the side for her to pass and then climbed the steep stairs.

Knocking gently on the door, he called out, 'Griff? It's Ben. Tess said it was OK to come up.'

He knocked gently again and pushed the door open. He saw a mound of covers and spoke again.

'Griff. It's Ben. I need a word.'

The covers shifted and Griff's head poked out from beneath.

Ben felt awkward. 'Tess let me in.'

'Oh. Sorry.' Griff rubbed his face. 'Give me a sec and I'll be out in a minute.'

Ben backed out of the door and walked into the lounge area. He admired the Christmas tree twinkling warmly in the corner. He stood at the large window, looking up the high street, his attention piqued by a figure in black jeans and a black hoody who was standing in the doorway of the shop opposite. Ben drew out his phone and went to take a picture just as a builder's van stopped and hooted the horn. The figure moved towards it, climbing into the passenger seat. It was only when the man turned that Ben saw the logo of the roofing company on his back.

'Sorry. I was out for the count,' Griff said, his hair crazy, barefoot, and dressed only in a pair of jeans. 'Sorry.' He gestured to himself. 'Getting a T-shirt on is a bit of a marathon.'

'Did you get checked out?' Ben asked, pointing to Griff's bruised and angry-looking torso.

'Nope. What's up?' He looked worried. 'Everything alright at the house?'

'Yup. What's with the sofa surfing? Don't wanna go home?'

'Not really. Not until I feel like I can fight someone off, to be honest.'

'I get that.' Ben drew out his notebook. 'Do you wanna sit down?'

Griff sat down gingerly at the small dining table. 'Why do I feel like this is bad news?'

Ben sighed. 'Look, I'm sorry to bring it up. I know it'll be painful. But did Gabriella ever talk to you about work?'

§ § §

Griff stared at Ben in disbelief. He hadn't been expecting questions about Gabby, his fiancée. He wasn't ready. His heart started thudding and his throat closed. Grief bubbled up, threatening to release.

'*What?*' he whispered.

'Did Gabriella ever talk to you about stuff at work?'

Griff leant forwards and put his head in his hands. Part of him didn't want to think about it. Think about her. Think about what he'd done. He'd learnt to live with the ache of missing her. And the weight of the guilt. The crushing shame he felt.

Griff tried to compose himself.

'Sorry to ask,' Ben supplied awkwardly.

'Erm. No, she didn't. Not really. She always said if she'd had a shit day, but she didn't talk about it much.'

'She didn't mention anyone specific?'

Griff narrowed his eyes. 'Why all the questions?'

'Did you know she had reported an individual for harassment and stalking?'

Griff stared at him. 'What? Who?'

Ben referred to his notebook. 'Yeah. About three years ago she made a complaint about an ex-client of hers who had started to behave inappropriately. He was turning up at the office, sending flowers, waiting by her car.'

'She never said.'

'Were you around then?'

Griff shook his head. 'Back then? Er, I think I was somewhere in the Pacific then.'

'Maybe she didn't want to worry you?'

'What happened, who was it?' Griff asked.

'I don't know really. I'm still digging. At first glance, I don't think it was dealt with very well.'

'How so?'

'It was bad enough that she felt she had to report it, but nothing seemed to happen as a result. It looks like maybe the police up there tried to talk to him about it but couldn't find him.'

'So, nothing happened?'

'As I said, I'm still digging.'

'But you have a name?'

'I do.'

'Who was it? What was she seeing him for?'

'I can't say much. But I think it was a child custody issue.'

'Where is he now?'

'No idea,' Ben said, closing his notebook. 'I'm trying to find him. I'm onto my colleagues in that area so we'll see what they dig up. I am just grasping at straws here. It's pretty unlikely he'd be doing this to you, particularly if there's a risk of him losing custody if he gets caught.'

'But you're taking it seriously enough to tell me and to look into it further?'

'I want to cover all bases. I wondered if she'd mentioned it back then.'

Griff shook his head. 'Nope. Any news on her brother?'

'Hmm, he's disappeared it seems. Parents are too old to do anything really. Both of them are in sheltered housing. I don't think two pensioners would have the savvy to send the text messages, daub your back wall with mock blood, pick up roadkill, and give you a kicking.'

'Probably right,' Griff admitted glumly. 'Doesn't help me though.'

'I just wanted to make sure your fiancée hadn't mentioned anything else to you along these lines.'

Griff shook his head. 'Nope. She came across all sorts in her job, but most people were OK, I think. I can't believe she never mentioned this guy.'

'Maybe she didn't want to worry you.'

'It was bad enough to report it.'

'Maybe she had to report it. I expect her work made her. There has to be a trail of evidence for stalking to be prosecuted. Maybe reporting it officially was enough to stop it.'

Griff looked out of the window, remembering her. He felt his throat close, his eyes fill.

'I'm sorry to bring it up,' Ben said quietly. 'I'll let myself out. I'll keep on it.'

'Thanks, Ben.'

Griff barely heard Ben move down the stairs. The grief had overtaken him, and he laid his head in his hands and let the tears come. He sobbed for his lost fiancée and lost child. Sobbed for what he had done, and for what he'd lost.

§ § §

Tess arrived back and opened the door to the flat. As she stepped in, she heard a noise. She stood poised, her head on one side, listening. What was that? Then she realised; it was the sound of sobbing. Proper, heart-wrenching sobs. Griff. Her mind flew back to seeing him on the bench on Castle Mount where she had seen him crying.

Quietly, she reversed out of the front door and closed it gently, wondering what Ben had said to him. She decided to start clearing the restaurant, ready for reopening on Thursday, to give Griff some time. As Tess tidied up, she thought about Griff, wondering what he was so upset about. She wondered about his past and whether that was the cause of his tears.

Mechanically, she got the place tidy. She noticed Griff's phone on the side, showing he had numerous text messages. Idly, she wondered who they were from.

A tapping on the window made her look up and she saw Vincent cupping his eyes against the glass, peering in. She dived behind the counter and stayed there until she peeked out and saw he had gone. She just didn't have the energy to face him today and hear his lies; not knowing what she knew. She finished up her admin in the kitchen, out of sight.

She heard more tapping on the window and peeked around the corner. Griff was standing there fully dressed. He looked like he'd just stepped out of the shower. He gave a small wave when he saw her.

She moved over to the door and let him in.

'You OK?' she asked, noting his red-rimmed eyes.

'Uh huh.' He shivered. 'God, it's cold today. We're off to check out the competition, aren't we?'

'Oh, I assumed…'

'You booked a table, didn't you?'

'Yeah, but if you're not up for—'

'Are you OK to drive?'

'Oh OK. Fine, yeah. I'll drive.'

Half an hour later, Tess and Griff walked into the newly opened The Larder and were shown to their table. Conversation had been light on the journey and Tess had mainly talked about specials and what she had ordered. She hadn't been sure how to bring up the other night.

The place was decorated in a plain Christmas theme, with a vaguely Scandinavian vibe. There was a simple Christmas tree, with a few sparse wooden decorations, strung artistically with white lights. Holly seemed to be the other primary festive decor, fixed attractively around walls and in small vases on tables.

The waitress seated them in a small booth that was relatively private. The place wasn't busy and the diners were evenly spread out.

'Decent menu,' Griff observed. 'Not sure how much of it is fresh though?'

'Hmm,' Tess said. 'Especially some of the fish. Red Snapper certainly isn't local or seasonal. I like the idea of the stew bowls though – brilliant for really cold days.'

The waitress breezed up and rattled off the specials, took drink orders and informed them she would return in a moment to get their food order.

'Why does it seem that absolutely everything comes in a bowl?' Tess muttered. 'What are you having?'

'I think I'll try one of these chicken shawarma bowls.'

Tess laughed. 'I was going to have that! I like the idea of these one-bowl salads.'

'My thoughts exactly.'

'I'll have the Bombay poke bowl then.'

'Good choice. These aren't a bad price either. You know we could do them, or a better version of them,' Griff suggested.

'They'd go down well, I think. We'd need to make them slightly simpler; fresh ingredients and such. Maybe with a side of something to add texture.'

'Exactly.'

'Right then. What are we having?' the waitress asked.

'Everything OK with Ben this morning?' Tess asked, once they were alone again. 'Sorry I just let him in.'

'It's OK. It's your flat.'

'Everything alright with your house though?'

'Yeah. He just had some follow-up stuff.'

'Oh, that's good.'

Griff focused on the water glass in front of him and looked awkward.

Tess said quietly, 'I think I need to apologise for the other night.'

Griff raised his eyes to meet hers. 'I wondered if we'd talk about it.'

'I'm sorry for bailing. I saw...' She fumbled for the words for a moment, finding herself slightly tearful. 'I saw something upsetting... it really affected me. Sorry.'

He looked concerned. 'What was it?'

'I feel sure you don't want to be bored senseless by the saga of it all.'

'Try me. I'm a captive audience.'

'Here we go.' The waitress put down their drinks. 'Food won't be a tick.'

'Go on.' Griff gestured.

'Let's just say, I saw someone, with someone I wasn't expecting to see them with.'

'Ahh. Is this red roses man?'

'Apparently so.'

'So, who was red roses man with?'

Tess gave a twisted smile. 'Ahh well, red roses man was with his *new* wife. His new *pregnant* wife.'

Griff pulled a face. 'Ouch. And he's sending you red roses?'

'He is.'

Their food arrived and they started eating.

Griff chewed, thoughtful. 'Sounds a bit snakish,' he said, finally. 'I'm assuming you didn't know about the new wife?'

Tess waved her fork. 'Let's be clear. The new *pregnant* wife.'

'Yeah.'

Tess tilted her head. 'You really don't want the whole sordid detail?'

'I genuinely do.' He pointed his fork at her bowl. 'How is it?'

'Good. I'd do less of this,' she pointed, 'and maybe more of that. There's far too much dressing too.'

Griff pointed to his. 'And I'd do more of this and a lot less of this. Either way, I like the idea. If we do these for lunch we could use the bowls we use for mussels or chowder.'

Tess pulled an impressed face. 'Now you're talking.'

Griff carried on eating. 'Come on then. Out with all the sordid details.'

Tess chewed while she thought.

'OK, potted version. Then I get to ask you a question.'

'Deal. Go on.'

'Ex-boyfriend. Together a number of years.'

'Red roses man?'

'Yeah. Doctor. Dumped me because apparently, in his opinion, I couldn't operate in his circles, and I *apparently* – which was news to me – wanted to get married and have children. So, I was dumped. Because, and I quote, "he didn't want to be tied down" with things like that.'

'Nice.'

'Oh yeah. And—'

'There's more?'

'There is. Pregnant wife was actually my flatmate bestie for years. We were really close until suddenly one day she upped and left, saying she didn't want to share any more, then *completely* ghosted me.'

'You had no idea they were seeing each other?'

'None at all. What a mug, eh? No idea until they walked into the pub the other night.'

'Ah.'

'Interestingly though, he'd asked me to meet for breakfast earlier that same morning to ask me to go back to him. Apparently, he loved me and wanted us to be together. But he wanted to keep the arrangement "loose", you know, "no ties".'

'However did you resist?'

Tess chuckled. 'Exactly.'

'How've you left it?'

'He's still waiting for an answer.'

'What are you going to do?'

She met his eyes. 'Absolutely nothing. He's a lying, cheating snake. Mind you, so's she. They're welcome to each other.'

Griff nodded. 'Seems sensible.'

Tess focused on her food. 'I get to ask you a question now.'

'How is everything?' the waitress interrupted. 'Any more drinks?'

'I think we're fine, thanks,' Griff said, and she repeated her mantra to the next table.

'So, my question?' Tess asked.

'Go for it.'

'Have you got another job lined up?' she blurted out suddenly, remembering him and the man in the suit outside Maggie's.

Griff sighed heavily and met her eyes. 'No. Do I need to have another job lined up?'

She stared at him. 'Of course not.'

'What about when Lorraine gets back?'

'She won't be back until January and she'll still need someone.'

Griff was quiet for a moment.

'And what will you do?' Griff asked softly. 'I don't know if I'd want to work there without you around.'

Tess stared at him.

Awkwardly he said, 'You know, we work well together, you're flexible, happy to make changes and stuff.'

'Lorraine might be too.'

He shrugged. 'How is she anyway?'

'OK, I think. I haven't had a proper chat with her for a little while. She's always doing something.'

'Do you miss her?'

'Yeah. I miss nattering to her. We used to do that a lot. It's tailed off a bit in the last couple of weeks. But thinking about the restaurant, in some ways it's nice that she isn't around. She's not very amenable to change.' She paused. 'I know you lost your mum. Do you have any other family?'

He shook his head. 'Nope. All on my lonesome.'

They ate in silence for a while, making the odd comment about ingredients or what they would change. The waitress appeared to clear their plates and asked if they'd like desserts. Both declined and they asked for the bill.

'Is it OK if we call into one of the new farm shops on the way back? I want to see if we can get some of our produce from there and save ordering in,' Tess said.

'No problem.'

CHAPTER 20

Griff sat in the car, watching the countryside whizz past. He concluded from lunch that Tess didn't want to discuss his prison sentence. Perhaps she just wanted to pretend it didn't happen. Surely if she wanted to know more then she would have said something? Asked something? He decided he wouldn't bring it up again unless she did. He closed his eyes, suddenly exhausted, immediately drifting off to sleep.

Griff insisted on going home when they returned. He knew he had to sometime. Although he didn't feel that strong, he felt like he needed to check on the house and be there. In his mind, he refused to be chased out of his own house by whoever this was. Ben had assured him his neighbours were keeping a fairly close eye, so he felt reassured to a certain extent. He'd grabbed his keys off Maggie, who had winked but was too busy with customers to chat.

Inside, he checked around, going in and out of each room and greeting the large spider he shared the bathroom with. Then he got on with the kind of mundane chores people did on a day off.

He put the spider on notice to hide and ran himself a bath. He climbed in, grateful as he felt his aching muscles relax in the heat.

He checked his new phone. (A new one had arrived and was surprisingly easy to set up.) He ignored all the unknown number messages and tapped on a message from the solicitor confirming various details. He figured when he felt stronger, he would look at the rest of the messages, knowing they would all contain death threats of some description.

He climbed out of the bath and dressed warmly. Starving and feeling a wave of nostalgia, he decided to cook one of his mother's favourites. He missed her.

Coming downstairs, he jumped when he saw the outline of a large figure on the other side of the front door. Expecting the worst, Griff grabbed a cricket bat he'd found and left by the door and yanked it open.

'Who the bloody hell…' he began and then realised the huge figure was Foxy.

'I think your doorbell's knackered,' Foxy said mildly. 'I've been ringing a while.' He pointed to the cricket bat. 'I don't really play, but if you insist…'

'Sorry,' Griff said with relief, lowering the bat. 'Come on in.'

He replaced the bat near the door.

'Maggie told me what's been going on and about you taking a beating. Mate, this is not good.'

'Tell me about it.'

'So don't freak, but me and my mate, Rudi, have got to work.'

'Got to work, how?' Griff was suspicious.

'Stick the kettle on and give me your phone,' Foxy ordered.

Griff hesitated and then realised the futility.

'Don't look at the messages. They'll be all about someone wanting to kill me.'

'Police involved?'

'Yeah. They've been great. Do you know Ben?'

'Only to nod to. He's quite new, isn't he?'

'So I hear. Drink?'

'Go on then.'

'Beer OK?'

Foxy nodded and accepted a bottle from Griff, as he finished fiddling with his phone.

'Done.'

'If you've set me up on Tinder, I swear I'll kill you with my bare hands.'

Foxy barked with laughter. 'Right. Paying attention?'

'Yes.'

'Me and Rudi have set up CCTV all around the place. Mainly outside. Vulnerable points. You can access it all here.' He fiddled with Griff's phone and opened an app. 'See? We've done motion sensors too, so you get a notification if there's something a bit off.'

Griff stared at him. 'Christ, how much did that cost?'

Foxy waved his hand. 'Rudi's trialling the gear. He's ex-forces too. Now he's a tree surgeon but he does security consulting on the side. We've got this on loan to see if it's any good.'

'Thank you,' was all Griff could manage. He was deeply touched.

'Now, I've been keeping an eye. But nothing has shown up so far, which is good. We're covered for the side alley, back door, front porch, garage, etc. There's even a few up the street each way too. It won't go off constantly. Like if a cat or something goes past. This is state of the art; it looks for people-shaped things and determines whether a notification is needed. All very clever.'

'That's great. I don't know what to say. I can't thank you guys enough.'

Foxy sipped his beer. 'We have to stick together, don't we? You can buy me and Rudi a pint once we've caught this prick. Are you OK if I keep an eye on my phone in case you need help? You couldn't fight off much in your state.'

Griff waved a hand. 'Knock yourself out. I could do with all the help I can get.'

Foxy regarded him quietly. 'Do you know who it might be?'

Griff closed his eyes. 'Been wracking my brains.' He exhaled forcefully and sipped his beer. 'How much has Maggie told you?'

'She says it's your tale to tell. She just told me you were in trouble and needed help. That's good enough for me.'

Griff tried to push down the wave of emotion that had closed his throat. He felt his eyes prickle with tears and sniffed.

'I'm always happy to listen, mate,' Foxy said quietly. 'I've had plenty of issues of my own.'

Griff suddenly felt like he wanted to talk. He had spent so long keeping it inside, keeping it locked away. The enormity of it had been like a huge weight that he dragged around with him day after day.

He met Foxy's gaze. 'Sure you wanna listen?'

Foxy nodded. 'I am.'

Griff took a deep breath. 'It's about as bad as it gets.' He paused and swallowed hard. 'I fell asleep at the wheel and killed someone,' he said softly.

Foxy remained quiet, but took a deep breath, then laid a hand on Griff's shoulder. The weight of it alone was welcome. He realised how much he missed having friends close by.

'The person I killed. She was my fiancée. She was pregnant.' Griff stared blindly through the sheen of tears at his beer bottle. 'I will never ever forgive myself,' he whispered.

'Tell me how it happened,' Foxy prompted gently.

Griff's hands shook as he held his beer. He tried to clear the lump of grief that had settled in his throat.

'I'd come home for a rare leave weekend. She'd been waiting to surprise me; tell me face-to-face about the baby. She always said she wanted to see my face when she told me.' He sniffed. 'I think it had been about four months since I was home last, so it had happened then. Anyway, her car wouldn't start, so her brother lent her one of his old bangers. Apparently he was going to do it up. He'd bought it at some auction. I think it was a write-off.

'She hated it because it was a manual and she liked automatics, so she asked me to drive.' He grimaced. 'She'd booked a cottage for the weekend in Cornwall, so she picked me up from Portsmouth. She couldn't wait to tell me she was expecting. Told me as soon as she saw me. Just blurted it out right then and there on the dockside. Couldn't wait.' Griff smiled, remembering.

'Go on.'

'I was beyond knackered; just come off a long shift. It's chaos when you're coming back to shore. We set off in the bloody rust bucket. I was tired, but it turned out there was a leak in the exhaust that was quietly filling the car with fumes. So slight that we didn't really notice or smell it until it was too late. Both of us were sleepy because of it. The car was too old for airbags too, so she died of a head injury.' Griff tried to stop his voice from cracking as he said it, as he blinked back the tears. 'The baby... it was too small to survive...'

'Mate,' Foxy said sadly. 'I am so sorry. Were you hurt?'

'Both of us had head injuries. I was out for a few days, apparently. Broken collar bone and a cracked rib from the wheel. I didn't know anything about it. The police said the vehicle wasn't even roadworthy. They wanted to prosecute for that, as well as for death by dangerous driving.'

Foxy looked annoyed. 'But you said it was her brother's car?'

'It was. He denied all knowledge of it. Said I'd helped myself to it.' He laughed bitterly. 'Not quite sure how I could have done that when I was still on duty on the way into port, but no one listened. I pled guilty anyway. Maybe if I hadn't been so tired I would have been OK.'

Foxy sighed. 'How long were you sent to prison for?'

'Two years, but I was out after sixteen months on licence. Dishonourable discharge from the navy too. It's the gift that keeps on giving.'

'That sucks,' Foxy said. 'What news of the brother?'

'He wrote to me every month in prison telling me he was going to kill me when I was released.'

'Nice fellow.'

'Thankfully, I got released early; good behaviour. I managed to get a chef's job in Newcastle and I tried to get my life back on track. Pretty hard when you've got a record. Even harder when the hotel folded.'

'I'll bet.'

Griff cleared his throat. 'So, I'm back now. Trying to pick up the pieces and start again. Bless Mum for leaving me some cash to do the house up.'

'Maybe you should think about staying. See how the place fits. Might be the best thing. Settle down and stop going all over.'

Griff gazed around the kitchen of the house he had always loved as a child. Before this persecution had started he had always felt safe and settled here.

'Maybe you're right.'

Foxy squeezed his arm. 'Anything I can do to help, Griff,' he said. 'I mean it.'

'You've done a lot more than you know,' Griff said gratefully. 'Considering you don't really know me.'

'Anyone who can cook like you is a top man in my book,' Foxy said, standing up. 'Slightest thing – holler. Me and Solo will be round.'

'Copy that.' Griff followed Foxy down the corridor. 'Appreciate it,' Griff said awkwardly.

'No problem. Anything I can do. I mean it. See you later.'

Feeling better and slightly more protected, Griff spent some time familiarising himself with the app and the cameras around the house. His stomach rumbled in earnest so he knocked himself up a pasta dish and then fell into bed, reassured he'd be woken by the movement alarm if anything happened overnight.

§ § §

Tess treated herself to a takeaway and a bottle of wine. She had arranged to Facetime Lorraine, so she set herself up at the dining table so they could eat together while they chatted. It was something they used to do regularly when Tess was back at her own flat.

She dished herself up some food, poured a large glass of wine and dialled her sister.

It rang for ages until a slightly dishevelled Lorraine answered the phone breathlessly.

'Did you forget?' Tess asked.

'Er. No. Erm… yes. Sorry.'

Tess narrowed her eyes. 'What you been up to?' she asked suspiciously.

'Hang on a mo,' Lorraine said, disappearing off-screen.

Tess carried on with her dinner, peering at the screen. She heard the deep timbre of a male voice. Lorraine reappeared a few minutes later, looking slightly neater and holding a glass of wine.

'Did you have company?' Tess asked.

'What makes you say that?' Lorraine asked, glancing behind her.

Tess knew the look. 'Oh my God, you're shagging the hot baker,' she said triumphantly.

Lorraine almost spat her wine out. 'What? I'm—' She blushed.

'Don't lie. I *know* this look.'

Lorraine laughed. She glanced behind her before leaning in close to the screen. 'I just can't help myself,' she whispered. 'The man's a genuine God.' And promptly collapsed into giggles, taking Tess with her.

Lorraine told Tess everything; she tended to overshare. But by the end of it, Tess knew her sister had completely fallen for the baker, and it appeared as though the feeling was mutual.

'So let me get this straight,' Tess said. 'I'm working my arse off here, while you're basically shagging your way through the week without a care in the world. Is that correct?'

'Bang on, I'd say,' Lorraine said, collapsing into giggles again.

'Sorry,' she said, after she'd stopped laughing. 'How are things going?'

Tess gave her an update on the last week or so and proposed some new ideas. By the end of it, Lorraine was looking impressed.

'You're doing amazingly. The takings are off the charts.'

'Griff is pretty fantastic,' Tess admitted. 'We work well together.'

Lorraine was quiet for a moment. 'Buy me out,' she said quietly.

'WHAT?'

'I'm serious. I've been thinking about it for a while. You could run it. Sell your flat, buy me out. Run it how *you* would run it. You're clearly really cut out for it. I'm jaded. Can't be bothered to try anything new. I'm tired of it. I would never have thought to do what you did for Santa Saturday.'

'Are you not coming back?' Tess asked.

Lorraine smiled. 'He's asked me to think about staying,' she said. 'The place next door to his bakery is up for sale. We think we might buy it and make it a cafe, just for the daytime, so I'd finally get evenings back.'

'Wow.'

'Don't give me an answer now,' Lorraine said. 'Think on it.'

'I don't even know if I can afford it,' Tess said.

'If you sell your flat you could.'

Tess was stunned. It hadn't occurred to her that this would ever be an option. 'Can you give me some time to think about it?'

'Course.'

'I need to go. Think about this.'

'OK.'

'When do I get to meet the hot baker?'

'Soon. Promise.'

'OK. I'll think about it and speak to you in a few days. Let me know what you might want for it.'

'OK. Don't forget you've got those investments from Mum and Dad – they're probably worth a bit.'

'I'd forgotten all about those,' Tess mused.

'It doesn't have to be difficult. We could do this really easily.'

'You've been thinking about this for a while, haven't you?'

'I have. Maybe it's time for you to think about a change. Anyway, speak soon. Love you.'

'Love you too,' Tess said and ended the call. This was something she needed to think about properly.

Her phone buzzed and she looked down hoping it was from Griff, but it was another text from Vincent.

I'm leaving tomorrow, I hoped I might see more of you while I was here, but clearly you don't feel for me what I feel for you.

Tess felt a flash of anger. She responded irritably. *I don't know what you want from me, Vincent.*

He replied. *I've told you; I love you. I want you to come back to the hospital and your flat. We can be together. We are so good together. I can't wait to be tucked up in your flat with you.*

Tess tapped out a response, calling Vincent various names under her breath. 'This will be interesting,' she murmured, pressing send.

But what if I want more? What if I want commitment?

Vincent replied. *Babe, you know I'm not into that. I just want us to be together and not put a label on it.*

But when would we see each other? Tess chuckled as she typed.

We'd see each other at work and after work.

Tess didn't reply for a while.

Tess, darling. Come on, give me an answer.

I'm selling my flat, but I could come and live with you. She giggled as she typed.

Babe, you know I like my space. Don't sell your flat. I love it. It's the perfect place for us. So cosy! Darling Tess, come back to me. I miss you so much.

I'm not sure.

What aren't you sure about? Tell me. I'll try and change it.

Well, I'm not sure your pregnant wife will like any of this – but do tell me how you think you can change this.

Tess, come on. I don't know where you think you got that information from.

Tess scrolled through her friend's Instagram page and took a screenshot of his wedding day. She sent it to him.

Don't take me for a fucking idiot, Vincent. You are a despicable snake. Contact me again and I'll tell her everything and make sure everyone we know, knows too. You're a couple of liars and cheats and you're welcome to each other.

§ § §

Griff awoke feeling much better. He'd slept deeply with no alerts or texts coming during the night. He'd been hoping the persecution would just stop one day and never start again.

His body felt a little more flexible, so he managed to get dressed without too much pain and set off for a walk along the beach, promising himself breakfast at Maggie's. He shivered in the cold, biting wind and burrowed deeper into his coat. He thought about his chat with Foxy the day before and concluded he was a top bloke for helping out someone who was, essentially, a stranger.

Pushing open the door to Maggie's, he was enveloped in the warm air and bustle of the cafe. Festive music played softly, and the Christmas tree sparkled in the warm lights. He spotted Foxy chatting to Mags, with Solo by his side.

'Hey, buddy. You had breakfast yet?' Griff asked. 'Wanna join me, my treat?'

Foxy beamed. 'My favourite set of words. Love to. Maggie, heart attack in a roll, please.'

'Make that two and I'll have an americano, please,' Griff said, grinning.

'Go sit,' Maggie said. 'I'll bring it over.'

'You look better this morning,' Foxy remarked, sitting opposite Griff.

'I feel better. What you've done has given me real peace of mind.'

'Perhaps this might be the end of it. I was keeping an eye last night and there was nothing going on.'

'Let's hope it stays that way.'

'You feeling OK today?' Foxy asked. 'Don't feel bad for sharing.'

'Just don't really like talking about it.'

'Better out than in.' He rested his elbows on the table. 'When I first came here, I'd left the forces and was spiralling because my daughter had died. I blamed myself. Completely.'

'Jesus. I'm so sorry,' Griff said.

Foxy gave a quick smile. 'What I learnt was to let people in who I trusted. Talk to them about it. Let it out and allow the mind to make room for better things. Nicer memories. Slowly that happened.'

'Why did you blame yourself?'

'Because I was late. If I had been there, it wouldn't have happened.'

'Outside of your control, mate.'

Foxy sighed. 'I know that now. Bit like the leak in the exhaust was completely out of your control.'

Griff gave a wan smile. 'I see where you're going with this.'

'Someone very wise said to me once that every time you share the worst thing in your world, it makes room for something better to replace it. Think on that.'

Griff stared at him. 'I like that.' He had a sudden flashback to kissing Tess. Perhaps it was a good memory, he wondered fleetingly.

Maggie bustled over with their order. 'Seeing you two in here this morning has brightened up my day no end,' she said. 'The image of you both sat here will live rent free in my head today.'

'I don't even know what that means,' muttered Griff, sinking his teeth into the roll.

'Just nod and go with it,' Foxy replied, doing exactly the same.

CHAPTER 21

Griff's friendship with Foxy strengthened over the week following Foxy turning up at Griff's house to tell him about the security system he and Rudi had installed. Since then, the texts had ceased, but Griff was still alert to the fact that they could start again at any minute. Foxy had given him a few free climbs which had rekindled his love for climbing and helped him gently regain his strength.

Things had been extremely busy in the restaurant. The past week had whizzed by in a flurry of Christmas parties, private bookings and it was now only two days until Christmas. He'd been busy and occupied but in a positive way. His grief felt like it had shifted slightly.

Tess hadn't mentioned him being in prison since the night he told her, so he assumed she didn't want to discuss it.

It was nine in the morning and Griff was dangling from a rope at the top of the large wall at the rear of the climbing centre.

His friendship with Foxy had extended to Rudi, and they had spent a very pleasant few hours in the pub. They reminisced about life in the forces and tried to work out whether their paths might ever have crossed. Griff was beginning to feel part of something again, and the crushing grief was lessening. He felt more like himself again.

He was confused about the situation with Tess. Since their lunch checking out the competition, they hadn't spent any time together alone, as the restaurant was always so busy. The days were long and, invariably, Griff left to go home slightly before Tess. He started earlier and she finished later, and that seemed to be the rhythm they worked to. Griff was looking forward to some time off after Christmas. The restaurant was closed from 6.00 p.m. on Christmas Day until they reopened on the day before New Year's Eve.

Griff realised he was happy. Happier than he had expected to be and he concluded that it was enough for now. He had contacted a friend who was a semi-retired painter and decorator, and, after Christmas, he would repaint the house inside and out. The roof quotes were much more reasonable than Griff had been expecting, so he had more money to spend on the house than he thought he had. He figured he'd update it as much as he could. His painter friend would also stay in the house, so they struck a deal that worked for both of them. All that was required was for Griff to have a clear idea of colour schemes before he started. As usual, Griff had forgotten all about it until his friend texted that morning to remind him. He had toyed with the idea of asking Tess to help, but he decided he'd play it by ear.

As he slid down the wall deftly, using the rope, he saw Tess chatting to Foxy inside, so he tapped on the window and waved. She waved back, smiling. Griff stepped out of his safety harness, slipped off his climbing shoes and headed inside.

Frank was straining at the lead, nuzzling Solo, and seeing Griff put him into a flat spin about who to be affectionate to next. He nuzzled Griff, allowed himself to be patted, and then turned back adoringly to Solo.

'Morning,' Griff said to Tess, nudging her gently. 'Checking up on me?'

'Hardly. I didn't even know you climbed.'

'Got back into it. Totally strong-armed by this one.' He gestured to Foxy.

'Guilty,' Foxy said deadpan, holding up his hands in surrender. 'I'm shameless. I'll drum up business anywhere.'

'I'm grabbing coffee from Mags's and ten minutes' fresh air before I start. You want to join me?' Tess asked Griff.

'Sure, just let me grab my stuff.'

'Foxy? You got time?'

'Alas no. Need to get on.'

'OK. Usual coffee, Griff?'

'Please.'

'See you over there.'

Griff grabbed his stuff and threw a thick jumper over his T-shirt. His movements were easier, and the climbing was helping him stretch out the stiffness a little more.

Zipping up his jacket, he walked towards the outside table and sat down opposite Tess, who had her face turned towards the weak December sun.

'Nice to take a few minutes out to stop, isn't it?' he said. 'Thanks for this.' He picked up the coffee.

'It is. It's been crazy!' she said. 'Maggie wants to know what we're bringing to the party after we shut, Christmas Day.'

'Oh OK, I'll talk to her.'

'Lorraine's asked me to buy her out,' Tess blurted out suddenly. 'She's banging a baker where she's staying and she's totally fallen for him.'

'There's a gag there about a cream horn,' Griff said dryly, smiling.

'Or nice buns,' she quipped, laughing.

Griff studied her for a minute. 'Will you? Buy her out?' he asked.

'I'm still thinking about it. I guess it depends on a few things,' she ventured.

'Like?'

'Future plans and all that,' she said vaguely.

'What happened to red roses man?'

'Oh, he was persistent, I'll give him that. I told him to leave me alone or I'd tell his wife.'

'And has he?'

'He has. Can you believe he tried to deny he had a pregnant wife?'

Griff raised an eyebrow. 'From what you said about him. Absolutely. Best rid of him.'

'Absolutely.'

'You OK about it though?' Griff probed.

'Yup. Been there and done that with him once. Not going back.' She glanced away and sipped her coffee.

'OK. So, I've got a bit of a weird ask,' Griff said, suddenly deciding to seize the moment.

'Oh?'

Griff explained about the decorating and how he needed help with colour schemes. 'I remembered what you said about doing up your place and I wondered whether maybe you'd come and help me with some colours so I can at least tell him colours for a few rooms?'

'Have you got colour charts?'

'Christ, I think I've got every single colour chart on the planet.'

'I'd love to,' she said. 'I adore doing things like that.'

'Thing is, he's starting a few days after Christmas, so I need to let him know sooner rather than later, in case he has to order anything.'

Tess thought for a moment. 'OK. The only real time we have is later after we close, but we'll probably be done by seven-ish as it's a late lunch office party. I know they have a table booked at the cocktail bar for seven thirty anyway.'

'OK. How about I do us some dinner to take back to my place and we can make a start if that's OK?'

'Yup. Can I bring Frank? He chews the Christmas tree if I leave him alone.'

'Course.'

'Done then!' She drained her drink. 'Right, let's get on.'

§ § §

Tess turned the restaurant sign to 'Closed'.

'Griff! I'm just whipping upstairs to change and then I'll be back. OK? Five minutes?'

He gave her a thumbs up from the kitchen as he packed their dinner into a bag.

She jogged up the stairs and threw on a pair of jeans and a thick jumper, fluffed her hair and gave herself a quick spray of perfume. She grabbed her laptop and a big notebook, chucked it into a tote bag and scuttled back downstairs. Griff was leaving and he passed her Frank's lead as he locked the door.

'Good to go?' he asked.

'Yup. I've got my laptop, because of Pinterest, and a notebook.'

'What the hell is Pinterest?' he asked, as they walked through town.

She stared at him. 'Clearly, you've been living under a stone for the last *however* long.'

Griff gave an awkward laugh and slid her a look as they walked. But she knew where he'd been; not much social media or whatever it was, in prison these days. They carried on, dodging the few roads where most of the bars spilt out onto the streets with raucous music blaring and drunk people in Christmas jumpers and hats staggering about.

'What's for dinner?' Tess asked, nudging him. 'I'm starving.'

'Now that would ruin the surprise!' Griff said, grinning.

'Not even a clue?'

'Nope.'

They arrived at Griff's place, and he raised an arm to wave at his neighbour who was standing at the window as soon as Griff's security light came on over the front door.

'Curtain twitcher?' Tess asked, eyeing him.

'Bloody life saver more like.'

Inside, they shrugged off their coats. Griff turned on a few lights and led the way towards the kitchen.

Frank trotted to the back door and scratched to go out.

'He seems at home,' Tess said.

'He quite likes it here, I think,' Griff said, switching on the outside light and checking everything was OK. He let Frank back in and put a bowl of water down for him. He set the oven to warm and unpacked the bag.

'Wine?'

'Please.'

Griff poured them both a glass. He handed Tess hers and opened a small tub, offering it to her.

'What are these?'

'Cheese straws. I thought they are quite good nibbles for New Year's Eve. Small quiches as well. Or some sort of twist on sausage rolls. Soak up the alcohol and all that?'

She sampled one. 'These are delicious. Good idea. They're eating early, so they'll definitely snack once they've been out in the town square for a while.'

'Exactly what I thought!' He busied himself removing the foil covering from a dish and slid it into the oven. He opened another Tupperware and shook a salad out into a serving bowl.

'Dinner's half an hour or so.'

'OK,' she said, sounding businesslike. She drank a glug of wine. 'Which room's first?'

'Er, they all pretty much need doing…'

'Better give me a tour then?'

He picked up his wine and gestured towards the doorway. 'Madam, if you will, your tour will begin in just a moment.'

Tess laughed, grabbed her wine and stepped into the hallway.

Griff adopted an upper-class accent. 'And we see here on my right we have an excellent example of an original water closet, manufactured by the renowned company known as Thomas Crapper, and moving into the lounge area, we have original features—'

'Oh, this is lovely,' Tess said, as she looked around the room. 'Look at this cornicing!' She pointed to the fireplace. 'That's beautiful. Does it work?'

'Yeah. Want a fire?'

'I'd love one,' she said. 'I miss a real fire. It makes it so Christmassy too! Oh, look at your tree. I love it.'

Griff had found the old Christmas tree his mum had always used and had spent a happy hour one evening putting it up. He switched the lights on, and it glowed and sparkled from the bay window.

'Mum had this tree for as long as I can remember. She was allergic to real trees. I think the lights are actually older than me. Come on, we'll whizz round, then I'll start a fire.'

He showed her the rest of the house, chuckling as she spotted the enormous spider in the bathroom and shuddered.

'So, what are you thinking? Modern, but with a nod to traditional?' Tess asked, as she followed him down the stairs into the lounge.

'Pretty much. Not too modern. But nothing dark. I can't stand dark colours. Depressing.' He had a sudden flash to the colour palette of the prison and gave an involuntary shudder.

'OK. Keeping it light.' She grabbed her tote bag from the hall and plonked herself down on the sofa, drawing out her laptop as Griff bent to light the fire. She switched it on and settled back down, opening Pinterest. She typed in a few key words and was rewarded with a series of pictures to scroll through.

§ § §

Griff busied himself with the fire until he was happy it would look after itself. He checked on dinner, then grabbed the wine bottle and cheese straws, and returned to the lounge. He switched on a couple of table lamps which gave the room a much warmer glow with the tree and light from the fire.

Topping off Tess's glass, he sat next to her on the sofa and passed her the cheese straws.

'What you thinking?' he asked, amused as she munched on the cheese straws.

Tess talked him through some of her ideas and they scrolled through pictures, with Griff picking the themes he liked.

'I like this look,' she said, showing him a colour palette in a similar room. 'It's nice and light.'

'Yeah. I like it.'

'How about this for the kitchen? You know, if you change the cabinet doors to something like this and drop in new worktops the whole look changes and it's so cheap to do.'

'I like that idea. I've got a butcher's block too. My mate, Tina, in Pembroke – her partner's dad is closing his butcher's shop. He's got a beautiful block that's really old, and he said I could have it.'

'That will break up the space really nicely in there,' she agreed. 'I don't think there's much you can do with the bathrooms but paint them and maybe update the floors and blinds.'

'Umm.'

'Are you selling it or staying?'

He sipped his wine and met her eyes. His thigh was sat comfortably alongside hers and he felt a sudden intense pull of desire for her.

'I'm not sure yet, to be honest.' His phone buzzed. 'Dinner's ready,' he murmured.

'Oh good.'

'Do you want to eat here or in the kitchen?'

'Let's eat in here. The fire's so lovely.'

Griff dished up dinner. He rough chopped the salad, dished up, and carried the food back through to the lounge.

'Here you go,' he said, handing her a plate.

'Smells to die for,' she said. 'What is it?'

'Salmon gratin.'

She forked in a mouthful and closed her eyes. 'Oh my God. You really are a bloody magician in the kitchen.'

Griff watched her as she ate. She had a rosy glow from the wine or the fire and he found himself incredibly attracted to her. He was even happier that red roses man had buggered off. For a while, they sat eating in a comfortable silence.

'What sort of food did you cook in the navy?' she asked, taking a mouthful.

'Depended on who we were cooking it for. Sometimes it was bog basic, hearty grub, but sometimes the captain and senior staff entertained local dignitaries, so it was banquet standards. They expected top restaurant type quality and that's what it had to be.'

'Which did you prefer? Cooking for the crew or the brass?'

'I didn't mind either.'

She smiled at him. 'You have to be the most easy-going person I know. How come you're so laid back?'

'I don't think I'm laid back.'

'I do.'

She finished her plate and drained her glass of wine. 'Do you want some more wine?' she said, offering the bottle.

'Yup.'

She filled both glasses.

'Thanks.'

He finished eating and put his plate on the coffee table.

'Not bad.'

'It was bloody delicious and you know it,' she chided.

'I am afraid I don't have any dessert,' he said.

'It's fine,' she said. 'That was enough. Shit, I forgot to bring some food for Frank.'

'I've got food for him. Come on, buddy,' he said to Frank, who had been dozing by the fire.

He went to pick up her plate. 'I'll wash,' she said, waving him away and following him to the kitchen. 'You feed Frank. Least I can do.'

Griff fed Frank and tidied away leftovers, while Tess washed the dishes.

'Right. Now we need to think about what we're going to do upstairs,' she said, following Griff back into the lounge.

Griff raised an eyebrow.

'Decor wise,' she stammered.

Suddenly the house went dark.

'What the…' Tess exclaimed, almost bumping into the back of Griff who had stopped dead in the hall.

'Sh,' he whispered, holding her back with his arm. 'Quiet for a minute. Don't move.'

'What?' she whispered. 'Why?'

He grabbed his phone from his pocket and activated the CCTV app, scrolling through the images. There were no warnings; there was nothing obvious to worry about. He heard his heart thumping in the quiet and realised he was breathing heavily. Tess was standing next to him in the gloom.

'It's OK,' he said. He jumped at the sound of a large bang outside and grabbed the cricket bat.

'Jesus!' whispered Tess. 'Is it the vandals? Should we call the police?'

'Hang on.'

He consulted the app again. A car drove down the street and then the loud bang sounded again.

'What are you looking at?'

'Foxy put in some cameras for me.'

'Why? After the fire?'

'Yeah.' He tried to sound dismissive. 'They needed somewhere to trial a new system, so they're using this place.' He exhaled heavily. 'I think it's a car backfiring,' he said, replacing the bat. He slowly opened the door and looked out into the street. It was in darkness. No lights were on; not even street lights. His neighbour opposite opened his front door.

'This whole part of town is out,' he called.

'Oh great!' called Griff. 'Thanks for letting me know.'

He closed the door and turned around, bumping into Tess who was close behind him in the gloom, wide-eyed.

'What did he say?' she whispered.

'Power cut,' he whispered back.

'Why are we whispering?' she said, giggling.

They were face-to-face and Griff couldn't help himself any longer. He bent his head and kissed her.

She responded, winding her arms around his neck and made a small noise. He deepened the kiss and pulled her closer.

Griff pushed her gently backwards, so she was against the wall, and ran his hands over her, enjoying the feeling as she responded to him. His senses were in overdrive. He hadn't been with anyone since his fiancée and this was the first time he had really wanted to be. He yanked her jumper over her head and kissed her again.

She had burrowed her hands up his jumper and she pulled it off, his T-shirt coming with it. She ran her hands over his chest and torso, making an appreciative noise.

He wasted no time in pulling her top off so she was in her jeans and a bra.

'I think we should go and review the decor upstairs,' he murmured.

'Good idea,' she said breathlessly.

He grabbed her hand and pulled her up the stairs and into his bedroom. Grabbing her again, he kissed her and together they fell onto the bed.

'Sure you're OK with this?' he asked, stroking her face gently.

'Shut up and kiss me again,' she said, grabbing him and undoing his jeans.

CHAPTER 22

Tess awoke to a delicious smell of bacon wafting through the house. She lay for a moment, cosy and comfortable in the soft bed, comforted by the weight of the warm, heavy duvet. Her mind floated back to the previous evening. She smiled as she thought about Griff. She had been deeply touched by his concern that she was happy for them to be together. She snuggled deeper, smiling to herself as she remembered their lovemaking.

Eventually, the pressure on her bladder forced her from the bed. She grabbed one of Griff's T-shirts and padded along to the bathroom, checking for the large spider. Contented that it must be hiding, she quickly used the loo, sluiced her mouth out with mouthwash and followed the smell of food to the kitchen.

She stood quietly in the kitchen doorway, watching him as he methodically stirred, buttered and arranged. Each movement was fluid and intentional. She had never seen him flustered and she loved his methodical approach to pretty much everything. The radio was on, and she watched as he leant over, turned up a song and started singing along to it, tapping the spoon he was using, on the side of the pan.

'I didn't know you could sing,' she said dryly, from the doorway.

He jumped, looked embarrassed and then walked over to her. Sliding an arm around her waist, he kissed her gently on the lips.

'I can't. Good morning.'

'Good morning,' she said. 'Something smells gorgeous.'

He hugged her and stepped away slightly. 'Thought you might like breakfast,' he said, passing her a coffee.

'You know how to spoil a girl, don't you?' she said, amused, and accepted the coffee. 'Thank you. Much more treatment like this and I'll move in.'

He winked. 'This is nothing. I have planned a full kitchen repertoire to get through.'

She arched a brow. 'Intriguing. What does it consist of?'

He leant in and kissed her again. 'Well, phase one of my kitchen repertoire consists of you having breakfast and then you wearing a lot less than you are now.'

She burst out laughing. 'And what will you be wearing?'

He gave her a disarming look. 'Nothing but a smile. You in?' He grabbed the pan off the stove.

She gave a casual shrug. 'Umm, depends how good breakfast is.'

Chuckling, he pointed to the table. 'Oh, it'll be good. Sit… round one incoming.'

§ § §

Griff finished buttoning his shirt and enjoyed the feel of Tess sliding her hands around his waist from behind. She rested her head on his back and sighed heavily.

'Seems a shame to have to go to work and spend the day feeding people,' she said. 'I'd like to stay here.'

'It's a crying shame,' he agreed. 'I had phase two of my kitchen repertoire to put into action.'

'There's a phase two?' she said, surprised. 'I thought phase one was pretty thorough.'

He leant his head back to kiss her.

'Wouldn't you like to know what it is?'

'I think I would, yes.'

He smiled. 'All good things come to those who wait.' He glanced at his watch. 'We need to get moving. I've got birds to stuff.'

She laughed. 'There's a joke about you doing that already this morning. Perhaps you'll tire of it.'

He turned and grabbed her waist. 'Never,' he said, burying his face in her neck and nipping it lightly. 'Come on, we can get in a walk on the beach.'

The morning was freezing, with a brisk wind. Frost had settled on the pavements and roofs overnight and they sparkled in the weak winter sunlight. House windows glowed with Christmas lights and decorations. On the beach, they walked at pace, with Frank happily scampering about.

'This is a nice walk to work,' Tess said, as Griff captured her hand and tucked it into his pocket. She felt ridiculously happy that Griff was so affectionate; from his casual tactile touches, to him happily holding her hand as they walked to work.

'I usually plan my day as I walk but you are completely distracting me,' he said, pulling her closer to him, draping an arm across her shoulders. He dropped a kiss on the top of her head. 'Bloody hope my cooking doesn't go to pot because of it.'

'Breakfast was more than acceptable,' she said, chuckling. 'I think you'll be fine.'

Together, they left the beach, walking past Maggie's and up the high street. Griff dug about in his pocket for the keys and opened the door.

Tess moved around the restaurant switching on lights. It was looking so Christmassy she had a sudden rush of festive excitement and decided to put on an upbeat playlist of Christmas songs. She chuckled to herself, remembering the last time she'd played the CD; it was the night they had first kissed.

She heard Griff whistling in the kitchen and leant over the chef's table.

'Envelope for you,' she said, handing it over.

He took it, looking puzzled. 'Where was that?'

'On the mat when we came in.'

'Cheers.' He glanced at the clock and swore under his breath. He put the envelope aside and busied himself putting the turkeys in the oven. They had a number of bookings at lunchtime, with many people ordering the Christmas menu in advance.

'Once I've done this, I'm gonna go and get the other turkeys so we have them early. If we leave it, we'll be late on the delivery round. OK? I'll only be half an hour.'

'No probs, it's only coffee and cake time anyway. Do you want to take my car?'

'Brilliant. Saves me getting mine.'

Linden arrived and got busy in the kitchen, while Tess bustled about laying tables and adding crackers and holly to each.

Griff appeared, wiping his hands and unbuttoning his chef's jacket.

'Can I grab your keys?'

'Sure. Below the till,' she called,

'Back in half an hour,' he said, winking at her.

A few couples came in for takeaway coffees, and another couple with a baby, popped in for cake and coffee. As Tess was putting one of the specials blackboards advertising Christmas hot drinks outside, a man in black joggers and a black North Face puffa jacket stopped next to her. He was dark-haired and unshaven, and Tess estimated him to be in his early forties. He had, what she could only describe as, a 'hard face'.

'Excuse me, love,' he said, in a pronounced Liverpudlian accent. 'Does Griffin Jones work here?'

'Yes!' Tess said, smiling warmly. 'He's just popped out for a bit. Should be back in half an hour or so. Can I help with anything?'

The man dug his hands in his pockets a little more and hunched his shoulders.

'No, it's fine. It's him I need.'

'OK. I'm not gonna lie, we are going to be hellishly busy when he gets back. We're fully booked for the rest of the day really. Does he have a number for you? Can I get him to call you later or—?'

'How long's he been working here?' he interrupted.

'Oh... er, about a month, I think.'

'This your place?'

'Kinda. My sister's.'

He considered her response. 'Nice of you... considering.' He looked at her expectantly.

'Considering what?' she said, confused.

'Considering he did time in prison for murder.'

The blood in Tess's ears roared. She felt momentarily dizzy and grabbed the blackboard for support.

'What?' she managed, struggling to maintain focus. *How could this be true? Was this a sick joke? How could this man even say this?*

The man leant forwards, and Tess caught a whiff of strong unpleasant body odour. She recoiled slightly, stumbling against the blackboard, moving it so it was a barrier between them.

He tilted his head. 'He murdered a woman. Went down for it.'

Tess was stunned. She didn't know what to say.

'Guess he didn't share that little morsel, did he now?' he said. 'No worries, love, I'll call back another time. I'm around for a bit now.'

Tess tried to gather herself. 'Who… who shall I say was asking?' she managed, her voice shaky.

'Let's keep it a surprise, eh, love?'

He winked and sauntered off down the street, whistling loudly.

Tess leant against the wall, breathing deeply. This couldn't be true, could it? Griff wouldn't have lied to her, would he? Not after everything? She heard a noise behind her and turned. Frank was scrabbling at the window, up on two legs, as he did when he was anxious.

She made her way back into the restaurant and stroked Frank.

'Boss!' Linden called.

'What's up?' she managed, pasting on a smile, her mind still whirling.

'Can you take this and put it by the till? I think Griff forgot to put it in his bag. It got wet.'

Tess leant through the chef's table and plucked the sopping envelope she had given Griff earlier from Linden's hand.

'Oh God,' she said. 'It's falling apart.'

'Sorry,' Linden called.

The moisture on the paper had freed the lip of the envelope so it was no longer stuck down. Tess decided she would try and save whatever was inside from ruin, so she pulled it out and laid it flat. She stared in disbelief.

It was an order of service, for a funeral.

The funeral was for Griffin Jones.

She suddenly remembered the envelope. Grabbing it, she realised it had been hand-delivered. There was no postmark, no stamp, just a hand-printed name.

She opened one of the drawers in the unit below the till and laid the paper and envelope inside gently, hoping it would dry. She'd have to give this to Griff later. What did it mean though? She wondered if it had something to do with the man outside. Why would he tell her something like that? *Was it true?* Her stomach churned. She thought back to Griff and how he had been the night before and this morning; tender, loving, affectionate. She simply couldn't reconcile that he would have done what this man had said. She just didn't believe it. Her mind flitted to programmes she'd watched about serial killers and murderers. Was Griff like that? Surely not.

The door opened, a gust of wind slamming it against the wall with a bang, and she jumped.

'Sorry!' a man called. 'OK for coffee? There's seven of us?'

'No problem, come on in!' Tess said, plucking some menus from the pile and hurried over to seat them.

§ § §

Griff whistled tunelessly along to the radio as he drove back. He had a boot full of fresh turkeys that he had selected personally; he knew he wouldn't have got such a good selection if someone else had chosen them for him.

Sitting at some traffic lights his phone buzzed, so he quickly dragged it out of his pocket and opened the text. A familiar chill settled over his shoulders. He stared in horror at the picture of Tess standing outside the restaurant. The accompanying text read:

You kill something of mine, I'll kill something of yours. Then you will die.

A horn blasted from behind, making Griff lurch forwards in the car. He was desperate to get to a bit of road where he could pull over and call Ben. Finally, he saw a lay-by and stopped. He rang Ben's number which went to answerphone. He left him an urgent message and then racked his brains for the other guy's name.

Garland! That was it. He rang the main number Ben had given him and was told PC Garland was out, so Griff left a message for him to call back urgently. He pulled back out into traffic and drove back to the restaurant as quickly as he could.

Panicked, his imagination in overdrive, he ran into the restaurant, desperate to check Tess was OK. He stopped abruptly when he saw her busy in the restaurant with customers. He sagged with relief and then quickly unloaded the turkeys.

Griff had been desperate to find a moment alone with Tess all day. There was a slight lull in customers between five and six, so when she ducked out into the storeroom, he followed her. He shut the door behind him and leant against the shelving unit, watching her crouch down to get something off the lower shelves.

'Been trying to get you alone for hours,' he murmured. 'Come here.'

His mobile rang, loud in the small space. It was Ben.

'Hang on, I've gotta take this,' he said, ducking out to the rear small courtyard. He quickly relayed the text and the pictures of Tess, and Ben asked for them to be sent over.

'OK,' Ben said. 'I need to give you some direct numbers to call. In case I'm not around. Got a pen?'

'Hang on.'

Griff hurried back inside and tried to find a pen by the till, pulling open drawers to search. He stared at the letter that had been delivered earlier. He had forgotten all about it. He picked it out from the drawer, saw what it was, and a chill settled over him. He closed his eyes. It was happening again. Just when he was beginning to feel happy again.

He heard movement behind him and turned, the letter in one hand, his phone in the other. It was Tess. He looked at her questioningly, wondering why she had a face like thunder. Ben's tinny voice jolted him back to the call.

'Ben, I need to call you back in ten?'

'No problem. Everything OK?'

'Not sure. I'll call back.'

He ended the call and flicked a glance into the kitchen.

Linden and Beth were laying out starter plates together; the restaurant was empty.

'Tess, what's this?' he asked quietly. 'How come it's open?'

'Linden got it wet and gave it to me. It was already open. I didn't know what it was and I didn't want it ruined, so I tried to dry it for you.'

'You read it?'

'I did. What the hell is this about?'

She grabbed his arm and marched him over towards the window, away from the kitchen.

'Someone was looking for you today. Dark-haired bloke. Liverpudlian accent. Sound familiar?'

'Not particularly.'

'He asked me how long you've been working here.'

'What's your point?'

She glanced behind her and whispered angrily. 'He said that it was *nice* of me to give you a job, considering that you'd murdered a woman and had gone to prison for it. I mean, *Jesus*, Griff. Why would he make up stuff like that? I mean, that's bloody *slander* or something, isn't it? You can't go making things like that up, can you?'

Griff was silent for a beat. He stared at her.

Fuck.

'Tess… I told you,' he said sighing, running a hand through his hair. 'That night in the pub.'

'No, you didn't,' she said belligerently.

'I did. I sat there and told you everything about it and then you ran out.' He looked distraught. 'I figured you were shocked and then made peace with it, but didn't want to discuss it.'

'You didn't tell me,' she insisted, her hands on her hips, her face red.

'I swear, I did.'

'Fuck sake,' she snapped. 'I think I'd remember something as fucking horrendous as that.'

'What did he say exactly?'

She looked incredulous. 'What? Don't you think it's slightly more important we discuss the fact that you apparently fucking murdered someone and went to bloody prison for it? Talk about lying to me!'

'I haven't lied.'

'You've not been honest.'

'I told you, the night after we kissed. I'd been trying to tell you.'

Tess was fuming now. 'I would have remembered, don't you think? I certainly wouldn't have got myself involved with someone who's a bloody murder—' She stopped when she saw his face change. His expression moved from shocked to hurt.

'With a murderer?' he said quietly. 'Yeah. Thanks for the fair trial there, Tess.'

'Wait... I didn't mean—'

'Yes, you did. What do they say? First reaction is always the honest one.'

'Griff! Can you come and give me a hand, please?' Linden called.

'Two secs,' he called out loudly. He glared at Tess. 'Guess we know where we both stand now, don't we?' he said, brushing past her and heading for the kitchen.

CHAPTER 23

The rest of the day passed in a blur. Griff felt like he was on autopilot. He gave Tess a wide berth and she did the same. They managed to keep it professional. When service closed, Griff and Linden prepared for the forthcoming madness of Christmas Eve, and then Griff left quietly, via the back door, and went home.

He had called Ben back and kept the letter and envelope to give to him as evidence, but he didn't have any hope it would be processed before Christmas. Ben updated him on progress. He had found a record of Griff's late fiancée's brother being back in the country, but local police had interviewed him. He had alibis for the various times where Griff or his property had been harmed which they were checking. There was no news regarding the man that his fiancée had reported for stalking. The man's old neighbours reported thinking he had moved away from the area.

As Griff walked home, he considered how earlier, he'd felt like he had it all, and now he felt like a man who had lost it all. As he neared the front, he leant against the railing and watched the dark sea roll in, crashing against the rocks below him. He assumed this was the price he would always pay for taking a life. Never being allowed to be happy but being given glimpses of it to tease him so he lived in a near constant state of purgatory.

He cast his mind back to the conversation with Tess. He *had* told her. They'd sat in the pub and he'd told her, and she had bailed. He'd just assumed she didn't want to talk about it at all. In his experience, this was what people did. They accepted the big, awful thing, but then wanted to pretend it hadn't happened. They mostly did this by not discussing it or ever referring to it. Similar to how some people acted around the subject of death. Couldn't talk about it, or ever mention it.

The wind gusted and Griff shivered in the freezing air. Sighing heavily, he trudged home, ignoring the cheerful Christmas lights in the windows. He went to bed and tried to block out the memory of Tess in his bed only the night before.

Christmas Eve was grey, cold and overcast. The sky had a snowy look about it and wintry showers were forecast.

He arrived at the restaurant earlier than he needed to and tried to lift his mood by tuning in the radio to a Christmas station. Then he did what he always did when he had stuff on his mind. He cooked.

Hearing a knocking on the window, he peered through the chef's table opening to see Maggie at the window peering in. He went to let her in.

'Ooh, it's chilly out there!' Maggie said, as she stepped inside. 'Saw you coming by earlier.'

'How you doing?' Griff asked.

'Good, my love. You?'

He pulled a face. 'If you'd asked me yesterday morning, I would have said fantastic; not so much now. Coffee?'

'Absolutely.' Maggie settled herself at the chef's table. 'Come on. Spill.'

Griff started to make coffee. 'Me and Tess…'

Maggie clapped her hands delightedly.

'Hold your horses,' Griff warned.

'What?'

'Me and Tess spent the night together,' he began. 'Then…'

'Then what?' Magie said impatiently.

'Then some random bloke told her I'd killed someone and gone to prison and she swore blind I'd never told her.'

'But you had told her. Right?'

'Yes. I'd plucked up the courage. Told her. She went running out of the pub and we didn't discuss it again

Maggie frowned. 'Could she not have heard you?'

'Maggie, I sat in front of her and told her everything.'

'She ran out, did you say?'

'Uh huh. She said she saw her ex or something and had to leave.'

'Maybe she wasn't listening.'

'She said…' He stopped, glancing away, swallowing hard.

'She said what, darlin'?' Maggie pushed gently.

'She said she would never have got involved with a murderer if she'd known.'

Maggie gasped. 'I don't believe she'd say that.'

'Oh, she said it alright.'

Maggie sipped her coffee and shook her head as if she was disappointed.

'Anyway! Enough of my crap! It's nearly Christmas,' Griff said with false cheer. He set up a chopping board in front of the chef's table so he could face Maggie and carry on talking.

Mags watched him over the rim of her cup. 'I wanted to know what you were thinking of bringing to the party tomorrow and don't even think about bailing on me.'

He grinned. 'I wouldn't dare.'

'Good.'

'I was thinking nibbly stuff? Maybe a few quiches, some sausage rolls, with a twist obviously. Cheese straws, and a pasta salad? Picky stuff?'

'Good idea. Leave the pasta salad and the quiches unless they're tiny. Too much mess and hassle. Could you do me a tray of hot garlic roasties? People like to pick at those and my ovens will be full.'

'Yup. Anything else?'

'No, that sounds fine.'

A tapping on the window had them both looking over and Griff heard Frank barking. Tess was there, looking impatient.

'Shit. I left the keys in the lock,' he said.

'I'll let her in,' Maggie said, sliding off the stool. 'See you tomorrow, love,'

'See ya, Mags.'

Griff watched Mags let Tess in. They exchanged a few words and then Mags bustled off down the road towards the harbour.

'Morning,' Tess said, taking her coat off.

'Morning,' Griff replied, turning and walking into the cold store.

Griff glanced through the space at the chef's table and saw the restaurant was empty but for a couple of stragglers. The next round of customers was due within the hour. He needed to get on, but he had to make sure the staff had a meal first. He beckoned Beth into the kitchen and told her dinner was in five and asked her to check and see whether Tess wanted to eat. He passed Linden a plate and when Beth came back into the kitchen, he passed her a plate.

'Tess said she'd eat when they go,' she said, motioning to the restaurant.

'OK.'

Beth took hers and sat at the chef's table, while Linden and Griff stayed in the kitchen, standing to eat.

'Right,' Tess said, coming into the kitchen. 'They've gone.'

Griff set about dishing her up a plate and she met his eyes briefly to say thank you as she took it. For a while, everyone ate in silence.

'Everyone OK?' Tess asked. 'Just tonight and tomorrow, and then we can all relax.'

'I can't wait for a break,' Linden said. 'I'm literally gonna sleep for two days straight.'

Griff smiled. 'I think I might too.'

'I've got a houseful of family for days,' moaned Beth. 'My bedroom will be full of my cousins and I won't get a moment's peace.'

'What are you going to do, Tess? Go and see Lorraine?' Linden asked.

Tess finished chewing. 'I'm not sure yet. Way I feel, I just think I'll sleep through until we reopen in the new year.'

Griff finished his plate and carried it through to the pot wash area, stacking it neatly in the dishwasher. He gave a brief smile to Tess as he passed her on her way to do the same.

'Is this how it's going to be?' she demanded in a low voice to his retreating back.

'What?' he said.

'Ignoring each other. Being cripplingly polite.'

Linden appeared with his plate which Tess took off him. She grabbed Griff's arm and dragged him into the cold store, where she stood in front of him, her hands on her hips.

Griff remained quiet for a moment, unsure of what to say.

'I'm not ignoring you, Tess,' he said quietly. 'I just don't know what you want me to say.'

'How about fucking sorry? Sorry for lying to me. Sorry for getting involved and not being truthful about who you are and what you did?'

'I've never lied to you.'

'You never told me. You should have told me.'

'I *did* tell you. I sat opposite you and told you everything. For whatever reason, you have chosen to ignore the fact. Fuck me, talk about being considered guilty until proven innocent.'

'That's just it, isn't it? You *are* guilty,' she hissed.

'So you keep saying,' he said. 'But you don't seem remotely interested in hearing my side of the story. Now, are you done? I've got a restaurant full of people to get ready for.' He turned, wrenched open the door, and stormed back into the kitchen.

§ § §

Tess moved through the restaurant, delivering food and topping up drinks as she fumed. If she could have shut the restaurant and gone to bed for the rest of December, she would have. She was furious with Griff. She hadn't known. He hadn't told her. She had no recollection of him telling her anything that night in the pub; all she remembered was seeing Vincent and his pregnant wife.

She plastered on a smile for customers, but it slipped every time she went into the kitchen collecting full plates and returning dirty ones.

As she cleared the chef's table, she watched Griff subtly while he worked and shared a joke with Linden. She was angry with him. She hadn't known. She still maintained he hadn't told her. She had no recollection of him telling her anything as important as that. She sighed heavily. She just couldn't reconcile it. He seemed nice; he *was* nice. How could he have taken a life? Actually murdered someone. And more importantly, who?

She recalled Griff's saying that she didn't seem interested in hearing the truth. Should she try and hear him out or should she just quit and not get involved. She was so focused on dithering in her head that she didn't hear the drunken man lurching up behind her until he fell into her, causing her to drop the plate she was holding, which smashed on the floor.

'Oh God, oh God,' the man said. 'I'm so sorry.' He hiccupped. 'Sorry, sorry, let me help.' He swayed and then focused on the floor. 'I'll get that,' he said, almost falling over as he tried to bend down. 'Ugh, I feel a bit sick.'

'OK, buddy. Let us clear that up.' Griff appeared and swiftly took the man's arm, propelling him upwards and away from Tess, out towards the courtyard. 'Let's pop outside for some fresh air?'

Tess realised her heart was thumping and her hands were shaking. She hadn't had to deal with anyone like that since the man had attacked her, causing her to run out in front of Griff's car. She'd heard from Ben that her attacker had gone abroad, but Ben was still hopeful of tracking him down. As she shakily cleared up the broken crockery, she was relieved that Griff had taken care of it as soon as it happened. She quickly swept up and moved over to the table where the drunk man had been sitting.

'Everyone OK here?' she asked.

'Where's Jeff?' someone asked.

'Having some fresh air, I think. One of my colleagues is with him. Did he need anything?'

'We just wanted some more water, please. He realised he needed to sober up a little,' a young woman said. 'I warned him about mixing cocktails, but he said it was his night for sex on the beach and a Pornstar Martini.'

Tess winced. 'Always a bad idea to mix.'

'He's finding it out,' the woman said ruefully. 'Charge us for his breakages.'

'It's fine. I'll check on him and get the water.'

Tess hurried away and returned with two large jugs of iced water. Outside, she checked on Jeff.

Griff was standing with a pint glass of water, waiting while Jeff vomited loudly over the drain.

'Get it all out, buddy,' Griff said sympathetically.

'I'm never drinking cocktails again,' moaned Jeff.

'All OK out here?'

'Oh God. I'm so sorry,' Jeff moaned. He retched again and then grasped the water and rinsed his mouth out. He stood up, breathed deeply a few times, and took a big drink of water.

'I feel OK now.'

'I've put water on your table,' Tess said.

'I need to sober up. I'm asking my girlfriend to marry me tonight. She'll tell me to fuck off if I do it in this state.'

'Drink loads of water and you'll feel better after food,' Tess said.

'I need to get back,' Griff said.

Jeff held out a hand to shake. 'Mate. You are one in a million. Thank you.'

Griff shook his hand. 'No problem. No more booze and I hope the big question gets you the answer you want.'

'Me too, mate. Me too.'

'You going back in?' Tess asked.

'Yup.' Jeff went back inside. Tess followed, giving Griff a small smile and rolling her eyes.

'I'll sluice this down with some disinfectant. Just in case we have a repeat performance,' Griff said.

'Ask Linden to do it,' she said. 'Table 6 has just ordered.'

'No problem.'

'Service,' Griff called quietly, and Beth stepped in to take the last series of puddings to the table.

'These look amazing, Griff,' she said. 'Any spare?'

'Always a spare one for you, Beth.' He smiled. 'I'll plate it up now.'

'This is why you're my favourite,' she laughed.

Griff wiped down the last of the surfaces as Linden and Beth finished up in the pot wash.

'One more day to go,' Linden said. 'What time are we in tomorrow, Chef?'

'I'll be in for seven thirty,' Griff said. 'Get the birds in for a slow cook.'

'Cool.'

'Finish that off tomorrow,' he said, gesturing to the mound of clean pots which needed to be put away. 'They'll be dry then.'

'Thanks, Chef.'

'You're doing great, Linden,' Griff said, clapping him on the shoulder. 'Who knew bread was your thing?'

Linden smiled. 'Yeah. No idea. For what it's worth, I've never been so happy here.'

'Good to hear. Now go home,' Griff said.

Griff turned to Beth. 'Is your dad driving you home, Beth?'

She shook her head. 'No, he's out with the fam. It's fine, I'll walk.'

'I'll walk you,' Linden butted in, as he put his coat on.

'Oh, OK. Thanks,' she said, blushing.

Griff finished a few more things in readiness for the next day. He stepped into the storeroom and stripped off his chef's jacket and threw on a jumper and his coat.

Griff noticed Tess was chatting to the last table of customers who were all women. He was reassured he could leave and she would be safe. He watched as one of them poured her a glass of wine and gestured to a chair.

Buttoning up his coat, he opened his bag and pulled out her Christmas gift and card. He left it next to the till where she'd likely see it.

As Griff stepped outside, snow was falling lightly. Smiling, he turned his face towards the sky and watched as the tiny flakes danced around the air, reflected in the orange glow from the streetlight. He had always loved snow. There was something magical about it. Grinning to himself, he walked home through the town. He enjoyed seeing the snow settle on the cold ground and appreciated how it made the place look even more Christmassy.

CHAPTER 24

Griff awoke early on Christmas Day; he knew instantly the snow had settled overnight. Sound was muffled and there was a quietness over the town. He peered out of the window and was delighted to see a covering of about two inches of snow on the ground. Snowflakes were still whirling and gently settling. He wondered whether this would mean people wouldn't make it in for lunch, but then thought the majority of people might actually love a walk in the snow to Christmas lunch, and then home again afterwards.

In the bathroom, he searched for the spider and found him peering out of the extractor fan. Griff wished him a happy Christmas and stepped in the shower. As he figured it, he had a few days to decide what to do with himself once they shut later. He needed a break badly and wanted to sleep and relax properly. He was desperate for a few days where he didn't have to get up for anything.

Dressing warmly, he found some old hefty boots and set off, trudging along the beach in the snow. It was a slightly bizarre experience and fleetingly reminded him of snow he had once seen on a beautiful beach in Japan.

When he arrived at work, he saw Tess had cleared up and re-laid the tables. He figured that it probably would have been a late night for her. Switching on some jazzy Christmas music, he got started in the kitchen, noticing his gift to Tess had gone.

Griff was busy with some delicate piping when Tess arrived.

'Happy Christmas,' she said merrily.

'Merry Christmas,' Griff replied, giving her a half-smile but concentrating on what he was doing.

'That looks amazing. Is it for the starters?'

'Uh huh,' he said, trying to focus.

'Coffee?'

'Please.'

'Linden here?'

'In the back.'

Tess busied herself with coffee and carefully placed Griff's near him and took Linden's through. She increased the volume of the Christmas music in the restaurant and sang along as she lit candles and distributed small boxes of presents to each side plate.

'What are those?' Griff asked, snipping a few sprigs of holly off the big bunch in the window.

'Cool, aren't they? They're tiny bath bombs and Christmas soap. One of the local girls makes these so I thought we'd see how people like them.'

'Good idea,' Griff said. 'Nice, something different.'

'That's what I thought.'

She looked awkward for a moment. 'Look… I—'

Frank's barking interrupted her. Foxy was outside with Solo. Tess waved and went to open the door.

'Merry Christmas,' Foxy said cheerfully, bending to kiss Tess on the cheek. He extended his hand to shake Griff's as he stepped inside. 'Looks nice in here.'

'Merry Christmas to you too,' Griff said. 'Got time for a quick coffee?'

Foxy gave him a look that suggested it was a ridiculous question and perched on a stool.

'How are you?' Tess asked.

'Good. You busy today?'

'Full house.'

'You're coming to Maggie's later though?'

'Absolutely,' Tess said.

'Griff?'

'Yup. I've had my orders of things to bring.'

Foxy rubbed his hands. 'Tempt me.'

'Nope.'

Foxy's face fell. 'Come on.'

'Nope.'

'Where are you having lunch?' Tess asked.

'Me and Rudi are getting together. Mack is off with Gen at his folks' place. So it's us boys, then we'll help Maggie set up.'

'Nice.'

'How's Lorraine?' Foxy asked.

'Utterly besotted with a baker she's met. She wants to stay there and open a cafe next to his bakery. She's asked me to buy her out.'

Foxy raised an eyebrow. 'How do you feel about that?'

'Surprised.' Tess passed him a coffee.

'Thanks. What are you thinking?'

Tess blushed. 'Don't know to be honest. I can't really think straight at the moment. Just flat out trying to get Christmas over and done with. Then I'll give it some thought.'

Foxy threw back his espresso. 'Thanks. Let's talk later when food, alcohol and exhaustion have taken their toll.'

She laughed. 'Bagsy the corner to sleep in!'

Foxy stood, looking around thoughtfully. 'It's quite the opportunity, perhaps.'

'Perhaps,' she echoed. 'See you later.'

'Want me to take Frank? We're going for a walk on the beach, and I'll hang onto him until later.'

'He'll love that. Thanks, Foxy, see you.'

He called to Griff. 'Obviously, if you need any help tasting or carrying the food down to Mags's later, I'm your man.'

'Never doubted it for a minute.'

'Good to be on the same page. See you later.'

'See ya, buddy.'

Griff took a minute to stand in the kitchen doorway and listen to the happy sound of people enjoying the food, the clink of glasses, and the scrape of cutlery. To him, these were good sounds. People enjoying food; making each other try bits of what they were eating, exclaiming over new flavours, drinking wine and exchanging toasts. This is what made him happy.

He watched Tess and Beth interact with the customers, answering questions, taking empty dishes and topping up glasses. He loved the sound of what he called 'food happy'.

Tess caught his eye and gave him a wide smile and for a moment his heart lurched. Then he remembered what she had said and her face when she said it. She didn't want him; in her eyes, he was a murderer and always would be.

Sighing, he turned away and readied himself for the next round of meals. He was just about to head into the kitchen when the door was flung open and Jeff, the puker from the night before, stepped in with his girlfriend. He spotted Griff and shouted, 'SHE SAID YES!'

Looking highly embarrassed as everyone had turned to look at them, the girl held up her left hand and waggled her left finger.

'Congratulations!' Griff called and the whole restaurant clapped.

'Thanks for sobering me up, you guys! You'll get an invite to the wedding! We might even have the do here!' Jeff said loudly.

'Come on!' his fiancée said. 'Look, you're disturbing everyone.'

'Congratulations, guys, and happy Christmas,' Griff called, stepping back into the kitchen, smiling.

'What's going on?' Linden asked.

'Pissed bloke from last night popped the question to his girlfriend and she said yes. He came in to share.'

'Awww,' Linden said. 'Nice that, innit?'

'How are we doing for the next course?'

'Good to go.'

§ § §

When Tess had finally said goodbye to the table of women the night before, she had taken her time clearing the tables. She'd pondered on Lorraine's offer and the situation with Griff. She'd reflected that since Griff had been cooking, there hadn't been one complaint, and in her view, that was almost priceless.

She wasn't sure how she felt about him.

In fairness she *was* sure, but just didn't want to admit it to herself. She wondered if she had been fair to him. She knew her words had hurt him deeply; she had seen it written all over his face the second she had said it. Was that how she felt? It mattered to her what he had done. It mattered he hadn't told her. She couldn't believe that he would have told her and she wouldn't have heard it.

When the women had paid, leaving a generous tip, she had found the gift from Griff. She hadn't opened it immediately. Instead, she'd cleared up and taken it back to the flat. Sitting down with a small brandy, she opened it.

The card was a hand-drawn cartoon, on thick card, of a pug wearing a Santa hat. On closer inspection she realised it actually was Frank, as the small letters beneath the drawing said, 'Frank looking

Christmassy'. She assumed he'd got a local artist to do it. They had captured him perfectly. She unwrapped the gift and burst out laughing. It was a book. *Pugs – How to train them and get the best out of them.*

She had laughed and then been torn about whether to text him to say thank you or whether to wait and see how it was the next day. When she looked at the clock and saw that it was after midnight, she decided to wait and see how he behaved towards her the next day.

Tess was delighted. Christmas Day had gone brilliantly and takings were through the roof. Recently, she had taken the opportunity to increase the markup on alcoholic drinks and her decision was paying off this season. She had also increased the price of the set menu by a few pounds. By adding an extra course, which actually cost them very little to produce, it bought the kitchen a little more time before the main courses. All in all, she was happy with her choices.

Customers were now on desserts and people were delaying leaving, ordering cheese, port, cognacs and liqueurs. Many admitted to wanting to stay a while longer as they were enjoying themselves so much.

§ § §

With the main meals and desserts done, Griff was sorting the food to take to Maggie's. Desperate for a few minutes of fresh air, he popped outside the back door, into the courtyard.

He stood watching the snow falling; it was light but steady and was quite beautiful. He heard the strains of Christmas carols from the restaurant and he sighed happily. Snow and Christmas carols. He felt quite nostalgic.

He held out his hand and watched as snow fell into his palm, melting instantly. His phone buzzed in his pocket; it was a text from his old neighbour, Mark.

Happy Christmas, mate! Hope you're having a good one. Catch up soon. Miss you being next door! I've been remembering the Christmases we used to have!

He replied. *Same to you, mate! Let's get together in the new year!*

He laughed at the text from Tina, his friend in Pembroke, with the picture of a cooked turkey that she had affixed two goggly eyes to, and promised he'd be over for a drink soon.

He saw a few other texts from friends and replied to those too. Just as he was about to go back in, his phone buzzed again, this time from an unknown number.

Enjoy your last day. This will be the last Christmas you'll ever see. KILLER. Get ready to die.

Griff stared at the text, his stomach churning. He quickly activated the CCTV app and checked each camera. His house looked fine; no warnings had been sent.

'Chef.' Linden leant out the door. 'Got a sec?'

'Coming.' Griff stuffed the phone back into his pocket, and walked back inside trying to forget about it.

CHAPTER 25

Tess turned the sign to 'Closed' and locked the door. Just before the bulk of the customers left they had asked the kitchen staff to come out. Griff and Linden had stepped out to a massive round of applause from the majority of the restaurant. Embarrassed, they had both performed a quick bow and returned to the kitchen. Tess had finished up with everyone and then slumped with relief against the closed door.

'Well, that was an amazing day. Huge congrats to everyone. I'm so proud,' Tess said. 'I can't thank you all enough for sticking with it and making the last few days so special for everyone. Now, before everyone heads off, I want to have a toast. Beth? Can you do the honours?'

Beth produced a bottle of champagne and poured everyone a glass.

Tess held up her glass when the others all had theirs. 'Here's to a great Christmas and thank you very much, everyone. I'm so grateful to you all. You've all done brilliantly. Cheers!'

'Cheers' came the happy replies.

'Right. Before we clear up I have gifts for you all and bonuses too. Let's take five and have a mini-Christmas. Another glass anyone?'

Beth was delighted with the silver earrings and matching bangle that Tess had bought her. Linden was thrilled with his own knife roll complete with a small filleting knife to start him off on his collection. Griff opened his gift to find a book on Victorian house renovations and a cookbook on one-bowl salads.

He chuckled and met Tess's eyes. 'Touché,' he said, ridiculously pleased when she giggled.

'Now, if anyone wants me to keep their bonus in the safe until later, then it's fine. More fizz anyone?'

Tess cranked up the music and the team set about clearing up. Tess had arranged for their occasional pot washer (who didn't celebrate Christmas) to come in the next day and clear up and give the kitchen a deep clean. All they needed to do was stack neatly for him to sort out.

'Tess, my dad's here, I've gotta go,' Beth announced at seven. She grabbed her bag, hugged everyone and wished them a happy Christmas as she left.

'Linden, are you coming to Maggie's?' Tess asked.

'Wouldn't miss it.'

'OK. We can go now. I'm just switching off the lights.'

'OK to leave my gift here and pick it up another time?' Linden asked.

'Course. I'll put the bonus envelopes in the safe – you too, Griff?'

'Please'

Tess put the envelopes and the takings into the safe in the storeroom.

'Right, good to go?' she said, coming into the kitchen.

'So, take these and these. I've got to come back for the spuds as they need another ten, so I'll drop this down with you and pop back.'

'We could wait?'

'It's fine. Maggie will be impatient. Come on.'

Together, they packed up the food in various large plastic containers. Griff grabbed a heavy box of wine and followed them down to Maggie's.

§ § §

'Happy Christmas, darlings!' Maggie exclaimed as they walked in. Griff kissed her cheek.

'I'm dumping this and going back. Spuds are still in. Place looks amazing, Maggie.'

Griff looked around and had another flush of feeling Christmassy and nostalgic; the place was decorated with holly and Christmas bunting and the large tree was twinkling in the corner. There was a pleasant buzz, with lots of people chatting and Griff felt a warm glow. It felt like family.

'Right, back in a mo,' he said, squeezing past Maggie. Peter, his probation officer, tapped him on the back as he went past.

'Maggie said she was going to strong-arm you into coming,' Griff said, smiling. 'Good to see you. Merry Christmas.'

'Merry Christmas. She didn't have to strong-arm me at all.' Peter laughed. He lowered his voice. 'I don't see any sign of the boyfriend...' He looked at Griff expectantly.

'Maybe he's away,' Griff said diplomatically, not sure if he needed to have Maggie's back on this subject.

Peter grinned. 'I wouldn't have left her at Christmas.' He nudged Griff. 'But, while the cat's away...'

Griff chuckled and headed back to the restaurant.

§ § §

'Where do you want these, Mags?' Tess asked, gesturing to her container.

'Oh, I have a platter in the kitchen for those.'

Tess followed her in and put the Tupperware on the side.

'Everything OK with you?' Maggie asked.

Tess met her eyes. 'Yes. Why do you ask?'

'Maggie, do you have a cloth or something? Someone's just spilt a drink?' A man Tess vaguely recognised put his head around the kitchen door.

'Hang on, Peter. Oh, this is Tess by the way. Griff's working for her.'

'Hi, Tess,' Peter said, taking the cloth.

'Do you want me to—?' Maggie said, as if going to follow him.

He smiled. 'Stand down. I think I can cope. Nice to meet you, Tess.'

'Likewise.' She turned to Mags and whispered. 'Who is he?'

Then she remembered. He was the man she had seen Griff shaking hands with outside the cafe, who she thought had offered Griff a job.

Maggie folded her arms and eyed Tess.

'That's Peter. He's Griff's probation officer, or is it offender manager now? Who knows?' She waved a hand dismissively.

'He's what?'

'You heard me. Griff's on licence; he reports to Peter every month or so.'

'How do you know him?'

Maggie winked. 'Oh, I know him from way back. We had some fun back in the day.'

'Why's he here?'

'Because he's an old friend and he's been good to Griff with all his troubles.'

'Troubles?'

Maggie rolled her eyes. 'The death threats, the assault, the texts, the vandalism, the constant persecution. *Those* troubles.'

'What?'

Maggie shook her head. 'Someone has been threatening to kill Griff since he came back here. Trashing his house, starting a fire, beating him up, sending letters, vile texts and messages.'

'What? Somebody's specifically targeting him? I thought it was just vandals. Do the police know?' She suddenly remembered the funeral order of service that had been delivered for Griff. She wondered fleetingly if the letter she'd delivered to him at his house had been something awful.

'Of course they do.'

'Is it to do with who he killed?'

Maggie inhaled sharply and gave Tess a stern look. 'I won't have you using terms like that. Griff didn't kill anyone, well, not deliberately. It was a heartbreaking, tragic accident. Not his fault at all. I think he's suffered more than enough. Losing the person he loved the most hasn't been easy. And going to prison for it too.'

Tess's eyes were like saucers. *A tragic accident?* That wasn't what the man had said. He'd made out Griff had purposefully killed someone.

'Who was it? What happened?' she asked Maggie, her voice almost a whisper.

Maggie folded her arms and gave her a beady stare. 'Shame on you for not finding out. I expected better of you, particularly as you got close.'

Tess bowed her head. 'Tell me.'

'Poor Griff fell asleep at the wheel of a car. It wasn't his car, mind. His pregnant fiancée was with him. He was tired. He had just come off an overseas posting and was shattered, but he was worried about her, so he drove. Her brother had lent her a car, old thing by all accounts. No airbags, and what they didn't know was that there was a leak from the exhaust filtering into the car, so they didn't stand a chance. Griff fell asleep. They crashed and she died of a head injury. The brother denied all knowledge of the car and blamed Griff; said he was driving dangerously and had bought the car himself.'

Tess stared at Mags. 'Why didn't he tell me?' she whispered.

'He said he did. What you need to remember is that he didn't just lose his fiancée, he lost his baby too. It was too young to survive.'

'Jesus. I have to go and talk to him. The things I said—'

'He'll be here soon enough,' Maggie interrupted. 'Give you plenty of time to think about how you're going to say sorry to that poor broken lad and make it up to him.'

§ § §

Griff hummed the Christmas song that had been playing at Maggie's, as he stepped outside. He was looking forward to a few glasses of wine, catching up with some of the locals, and best of all, not having to get up for anything in the morning.

'Hey, bud,' Foxy said, as he came from around the back of the cafe with a large box. 'Did your mate find you?'

'What?' he said and then realised it had probably been Peter asking where he was. 'Oh, yeah,' he replied before Foxy could respond.

'You're not going are you?' Foxy said, looking disappointed.

'Just going to get the spuds.'

'I'll wait here then,' Foxy grinned. 'So I can get an early start.'

'You are *shameless*!' Griff laughed, shaking his head as he walked up the road.

Letting himself in the restaurant, he peered inside the oven and saw with satisfaction the potatoes were ready. Turning the oven off he found a container to transport the potatoes to Maggie's.

'Well, well, well, now this *is* a cosy set-up, isn't it?' The soft Liverpudlian accented voice at the chef's table made Griff jump.

Griff spun around, his heart thumping. He stared at the man who had spoken. He had to peer through the gloom as the main lights were off.

'*Mark*? JESUS! *Mark*? Is that you? What the hell are you doing here? Why didn't you text me?' Griff was confused for a minute. 'Wait. You did text me this morning!' He strode through the kitchen door approaching his old friend and gave him a hug.

'I wanted to surprise you,' Mark said. 'I'm here on business.'

'At Christmas? Well, you've certainly done that! It's so great to see you! How are you?' Griff stepped back, slightly confused at the lack of a warm response and the unkempt state of his friend.

Mark stayed sitting rigidly still on the stool. Saying nothing.

'Is everything OK?' Griff asked, with mounting concern.

Mark stared at him and sighed.

Mark looked terrible. A far cry from his usual fastidiously groomed self. Griff touched his shoulder.

'Mark, you're scaring me. What the hell's the matter? Come on, talk to me.'

Mark stared at Griff through red-rimmed bloodshot eyes. He made a noise like an animal in pain and dropped his head in his hands.

'I can't do it any more,' he said, his voice muffled.

'Do what, Mark? You're not making any sense.'

'I can't live with it any more.'

Griff frowned and sat on the stool next to him. 'Can't live with what? Come on, you're not making sense.'

Tears poured down Mark's cheeks. He raised his face and then looked at Griff with pure malevolence.

'I can't live with her not being around any more. I loved her so much. You took away the person that I loved the most.'

Griff leant backwards; he was struggling to comprehend what he was hearing. Suddenly he felt the need for more space. More air.

Something in his gut shifted, warning him of danger. He'd experienced this feeling in prison; just before he'd been set upon and stabbed.

'What are you talking about?' he asked quietly.

'Gabby.'

'*What?*' Griff pushed himself off the stool, stepping away from Mark. 'What the *fuck* are you talking about?' he asked harshly.

Mark stared at him; he was visibly shaking.

'I thought time might heal it. Heal the *gaping* void she left. But it's made it worse. I can't live without her any more.'

'*What?* Mark, NO! You were our *neighbour*. Our friend. You knew that. Nothing more.'

With a snarl, Mark leapt off the stool and grabbed Griff by the throat forcing him backwards against the counter. His grip was so tight Griff could feel his throat closing. Mark's face was red, his features contorted into a vicious scowl.

'She was THE WORLD to me. I WORSHIPPED her. I did *everything* for her,' he said, through gritted teeth. 'I loved her. I took care of her, while you were doing exactly what you wanted to do. Fuck knows why she loved you. It was me who picked her up when she was down. Me who took her out when she was missing you. Me who took her to the hospital when she needed to go. I loved her.'

Griff tried to wrestle Mark's hand off his throat. 'She was your friend. She only ever saw you as her friend.'

'DON'T SAY THAT TO ME,' Mark yelled. 'You weren't there. YOU were NEVER fucking there!'

'Mark.'

'DON'T. She DIED because of you. You KILLED her.' He abruptly let go of Griff and looked around wildly. He grabbed a knife from the counter.

Griff's heart was racing, his hands were shaking. The pressure on his throat had made him light-headed. He tried to think. He needed to calm Mark down.

'I know. It was my fault. I've got to live with the fact I was responsible for her death. She was the most precious thing in the world to me.'

'Yet here you are, shagging *her*.' He gesticulated around the restaurant with the knife. 'When Gabby's memory should live on. I should GUT YOU LIKE A PIG.' Mark's face was red, he was sweaty, and his pupils were huge.

'Gabby's memory does live on. Every day I think about her,' Griff said calmly.

'Bet you don't when you're SHAGGING her! I bet you don't think about Gabby then.'

'Mark.' Griff tried to move away from him. 'Come on now. Calm down.'

Mark smiled cruelly as he waved the knife in Griff's face. 'I'll bet you're not shagging her now I told her you went down for murder.'

'No, I'm not, no. Not any more.'

'You were being disrespectful to Gabby's memory.'

'Yes, I was.' Griff tried to think desperately how he was going to get away from him. He figured the best thing was to agree with him and not provoke him.

Mark nodded; his eyes bright, glassy. 'Fucking damn right. I told her. She needed to know who she was shagging.'

'Why are you here, Mark?' Griff asked quietly.

The expression on Mark's face wrapped a cold hand around Griff's heart.

He rubbed his head as if the thoughts inside were causing him pain. 'I need to feel better. I've thought about this. A lot. I've decided the best way for me to feel better is to kill you. So you pay for killing her, properly.'

He was almost panting. Griff saw the sheen of sweat on his face. He kept getting whiffs of ripe body odour from Mark.

'Mark. Listen to me. You need help. This isn't normal. I can tell you're not thinking straight.'

'DON'T FUCKING TELL ME WHAT'S NORMAL,' he screamed in Griff's face, brandishing the knife again. He looked at his hand in disbelief for a moment then threw the knife across the restaurant. He dug a hand into his jacket pocket and produced a gun, pointing it at Griff's forehead, his hand shaking.

Griff stared at him in horror, recoiling.

'JESUS!'

'Your fucking time has come. KILLER. You're gonna die and I'm going to enjoy it. I fucking hate you more than I have ever hated anything in my life. Now get in there,' he said, poking Griff in the chest with the gun and gesturing towards the kitchen. 'MOVE IT.'

§ § §

Tess felt terrible. Embarrassed. Guilty. Full of shame. Who was she to judge? She couldn't believe what Maggie had told her. She had never been more ashamed of herself than she was now. She desperately wanted to see Griff and say sorry. Beg his forgiveness for not listening. Not hearing his side. In her head, she needed to work out what to say and how to say it. She figured she'd only get the one chance. She gulped at a glass of wine, hoping it would help to get her thoughts in order.

'Tess, wasn't it?' The man who Tess now knew was Griff's probation officer, was standing in front of her, holding a large glass of red wine and a bottle. He offered to top up her glass. 'You own The Fat Gannet?'

She inclined her head. 'My sister does. In truth, she wants me to buy it off her.'

'Ahh.' He sipped his drink. 'Will you?'

'I'm not sure yet. Still pondering.'

'That young chap over there, Linden, was it? He was telling me he and Griffin had a round of applause from the customers today.'

Tess smiled. 'They did. They deserved it. Griff has completely turned the restaurant around. He's such an amazing chef. Such a great approach to everything. Flexible about things, calm. Done wonders for Linden.' She glanced at him, embarrassed. 'Sorry.'

'It's fine. Have you told him that? I imagine his self-confidence has probably been rock bottom for quite a while now.'

Tess gulped her drink. 'Do you know? What happened? With Griff?'

'I do. Yes. A terrible accident. Tragedy.'

'Was he right to go to prison?'

Peter sighed. 'Griff will tell you it's no more than he deserves. His penance if you like. My view? He should never have gone down for it. But that's well above my pay grade. All I can say is, the majority of the people I deal with are serial offenders. They spend their life in and out of the system. Griff isn't like that. I knew it from the first five minutes of meeting him. He wants to move on with his life.' He caught Maggie's eye as she moved past him and smiled. 'Perhaps your sister's offer to buy her out might be a fresh start for him? Maybe you too. Maggie said you were a trauma nurse. Covid must have been a living nightmare.'

'It was.' Tess found herself unable to form a full sentence; her throat had closed at the mention of Covid.

'You know, doing the job I do, I'm a strong believer that everything happens for a reason. Perhaps this is your time to do something different for yourself for a change. Merry Christmas to you, Tess.'

'Merry Christmas,' she echoed.

'Where's Griff?' Foxy moaned. 'He said he was coming back in ten minutes with the potatoes and I've been waiting outside for first dibs for ages.'

'Do you ever stop eating?' Tess asked, amused.

'Mainly when I sleep.'

He glanced out of the window. 'Maybe he's yapping to the—' Suddenly, Foxy's head snapped up.

'CHRIST!' He ran out of the door, leaving Tess with a confused look on her face.

CHAPTER 26

Mark waved the gun and Griff walked slowly towards the kitchen. Following, Mark dragged one of the stools behind him. As Griff walked, his foot knocked against something on the floor, and he looked down to see a petrol can. Fear blossomed anew in his belly.

'What's this?' Griff kicked it, the dull thud of a full can made his heart pound louder. His stomach roiled and he felt the sort of real raw fear he'd not experienced since his first night in prison.

'GET IN THE FUCKING KITCHEN!' Mark screamed as he swiped at his sweaty face. He looked mad; unhinged. Eyes too bright. Breathing too choppy.

Mark poked Griff in the back as he moved into the kitchen, following him, the stool screeching across the ceramic tiled floor.

'Where the hell did you get a gun from?' Griff muttered.

Mark snorted. 'Easy enough. Went back home for a few days. If you've got cash you can buy anything in Liverpool.'

'Jesus.'

'Turn around.'

'Mark, can we talk—'

'I DON'T WANNA TALK,' he yelled. 'I WANT YOU TO DIE!' Mark shook his head as if trying to clear it. He banged the side of his head with the flat of the gun. 'I don't wanna chew the fat. I don't wanna hear your excuses. It's too fucking late.' He breathed deeply as if trying to calm himself. 'Now, what I *want* to see, is you on the floor, writhing in pain when I set fire to you. Then I will know you died a painful death, just like Gabby. Then I'll feel better.'

'You don't have to do this.'

'I need to do it for Gabby.'

'She wouldn't want this.'

'Don't talk to me about her. You didn't know her like I did. SIT DOWN on there. Face the wall.'

Griff didn't move but a sharp jab in the kidneys with the gun made him. He sat on the stool. Mark dug around in his pockets and drew out some large cable ties.

'I've come prepared,' he said grimly.

He shoved the gun under his armpit while he grabbed Griff's hands and yanked them behind him. He slid the cable ties over his wrists, struggling to pull them tight.

Remembering his navy training, Griff forced his hands slightly apart, to try and give himself some wiggle room. Mark grabbed an oven cloth and tried to tie Griff's legs to the stool but it wasn't long enough, so he abandoned his efforts.

Griff watched Mark stuff the gun into his pocket and unscrew the lid of the petrol can. The smell hit him instantly and he wondered for a second if he'd turned the ovens off. He was sure he had. Then he realised how futile the thought was. He was going to die anyway. There was no escape from here. It was too far to the restaurant's main door. The door to the pot wash was propped open but there was no escape from there as the door to the outside was firmly locked. He closed his eyes as Mark started splashing the petrol all over the floor, up his legs and all around him.

The petrol can was finally empty. All Griff could do was close his eyes and think about something other than what was about to happen.

'Mark, you don't have to do this,' he said. 'Gabby wouldn't want it.'

'SHUT YOUR FUCKING MOUTH!' Placing the can down, Mark eyed him with satisfaction. 'Cold enough for a fire, I think. Any last words?'

§ § §

PC Ben Baker was most likely single again. His girlfriend had threatened to dump him because he was still at work even though his shift had finished three hours previously. He had been informed his Christmas dinner was in the bin. But Ben was a man on a mission. As he'd been trying to track down Griff's late fiancée's brother he had come across something in the system that had been missed previously, attached to Gabriela's name.

She had visited her local police station to discuss an issue with her neighbour. A man called Mark Mills. She was increasingly concerned he was overstepping the line with her and she had asked for an off-the-record conversation. She was seeking advice on how she could best deal with it, with him being her neighbour. This had been a few months before her death.

Because she hadn't made a complaint these were merely notes from the officer who had spoken to her. But the officer had been organised, and had made a record of this conversation, suspecting that potentially, the matter may become more serious.

Ben ran a check on Mark Mills. He wasn't happy with what he saw. Mark had quite the history as a younger man and a number of restraining orders were out against him. A few instances of assault and complaints of stalking. An issue of sexual assault with the complaint then withdrawn. After trying Griff repeatedly on his mobile, Ben logged off his computer and went to find an on-duty colleague to accompany him to find Griff. This man was dangerous by all accounts and Ben felt Griff needed to be warned. He climbed into a car with his colleague, PC Warren, and they set off for the restaurant.

§ § §

'I said, any last words?' Mark demanded. He'd retreated to the other side of the chef's table as he snapped and unsnapped his Zippo lighter.

Griff looked away.

'Come on. Say something. I want to hear your last words. Or shall we say, last rites?'

'JUST GET ON WITH IT!' Griff yelled. 'Put me out of my FUCKING MISERY.'

'YOU WANT IT?' Mark yelled. 'ROT IN HELL YOU MURDERING BASTARD.'

He leant forwards through the opening, and in one motion, flicked the wheel on the Zippo, throwing it into the kitchen. As the lighter left his hand, he turned and ran from the restaurant. There was a loud whoosh. He ran out the door and up the high street.

Mark left the restaurant door wide open. He figured the fresh air would feed the fire. He didn't need to hear the flames. Didn't need to hear Griff screaming. He decided in that split second he didn't want to see Griff burn. He thought he wanted to see it but he now realised the knowledge was good enough. He didn't *need* to see it.

He tried to calm himself. Now that was done he just wanted to get home and sit in his house and think about Gabby and pretend she was next door. Watch all the films he'd made of her. Remember her in *his* house. Having coffee, chatting, sharing a meal sometimes. Now he'd killed Griff he felt free. Reborn. Happy. Justice was done.

As he ran, he remembered the time they spent together and then he remembered how he felt when she stopped coming. He always wondered why. He missed her. When he hadn't see her as much, he'd started leaving little presents on her doorstep for her; to brighten up her day. She was always so grateful, but always so busy. He finally slowed to a walk, panting and feeling a stitch starting to form. He had often wondered why she was so busy so much of the time. As he stepped off the pavement to cross the road, he almost stepped in front of a police car.

§ § §

Ben Baker stared at the man in front of him who had almost stepped in front of the car.

'FUCK!' he shrieked. 'That's our man!' Leaping out, just before the car stopped fully, he slipped on the snow but managed to grab the man and thrust him up against the car, just as PC Warren brought it to a stop.

'I'm detaining you under suspicion—'

Ben staggered backwards, receiving a hard elbow to the face. His nose exploded and the man gave him a hard shove. Ben slipped again on the snow and fell backwards over the kerb.

Anticipating trouble, PC Warren had extended her cosh as she stepped out of the car. In a fluid movement, she swiped hard at the suspect's legs. He tripped and flailed, falling face down as he tried to get away.

PC Warren planted her knee firmly on the suspect's back while she cuffed him. All the time telling him calmly why she was detaining him. Once secure, with Ben's help, she dragged him upright. He stank of petrol. Ben patted him down and discovered a loaded handgun in his pocket.

As Ben was searching the rest of his pockets, he heard a shout and saw someone waving further down the high street. Smoke billowed out of a property, and he instantly made the connection between this man smelling of petrol and the restaurant where Griff worked. Ben told Warren to call for backup and a fire engine.

§ § §

Foxy had run up the road, in a panicked state, after realising Griff may be in danger. He had told the guy, who was asking after Griff, that he'd popped back to the restaurant and would be back in a minute but the guy had walked off up the road. For a moment Foxy had thought it was odd that he was holding a petrol can but had dismissed it immediately when Maggie called him.

As he approached the restaurant, Foxy was puzzled to see the door wide open. Stepping in the doorway, he almost collided with a figure who pushed roughly past him and ran off up the road. For a second, Foxy was torn – did he chase the man or see if Griff was OK?

In the split second it took him to decide, Foxy was forced back onto the street by an explosion from the restaurant.

Foxy rang for the police and fire brigade and stepped back into the restaurant. It was thick with smoke; he couldn't see much at all. He grabbed a tablecloth off the table and wrapped it around his head and neck, covering his nose and mouth. He crept forwards, trying to remember the route through the tables and chairs. He peered through the smoke and saw the flames were raging in the kitchen.

He wracked his brains for where he had seen a fire extinguisher. Then he remembered. Next to the till counter. He moved through the tables, avoiding spots of fire.

'GRIFF!' he yelled, frustrated his shout was muffled. 'GRIFF!'

He had a bad feeling. Part of him didn't want to think about it. He assumed Griff had been doused in something and he was terrified Griff had been burnt alive. He'd seen his fair share of it in the forces and didn't want this to be the end for his new friend.

He yelled again. Grabbing the fire extinguisher, he got it going, starting at the kitchen door where the flames were eagerly licking around. Pushing the door open, all he could see was smoke and a wall of flame. He moved to the opening where the chef's table was and directed the extinguisher into the burning mass, desperately trying to see if he could see anyone in there.

'GRIFF!,' he yelled hoarsely. 'GRIFF!'

The smoke forced itself into Foxy's lungs, making him cough, and his eyes were watering, but he didn't want to give up hope in case there was a chance Griff could have made it somewhere safe. He yelled again. 'GRIFF!'

Not hearing anything, he did his best to fight the fire. His fire extinguisher wasn't making a dent but he carried on. Determined. He hoped Griff had made it out somehow or to somewhere safe. Just as his fire extinguisher dribbled and died he heard the sirens of the fire engine. He ran through the restaurant to flag them down.

§ § §

Tess walked up the road, wondering where Foxy had run off to and where Griff was. She was desperate to talk to him. She had thought about what she wanted to say and how to say it. She was half expecting to meet Griff coming down the road but as she rounded the corner she saw smoke pouring out of a building. She stopped and stared, not quite believing what she saw.

She watched in disbelief as the fire brigade was flagged down by a smoke-covered Foxy. It took a moment for her brain to register what she was seeing. Then the horror clicked into place.

'NO!' she screamed, starting to run. 'NO! GRIFF!'

She ran up the road, her eyes wide, heart thumping, terrified something had happened to him. She looked around frantically for Griff, not seeing him anywhere.

'GRIFF?' she screamed, running towards the restaurant doorway where thick smoke was pouring out. 'GRIFF!'

Firm arms caught her around the waist and pulled her backwards.

'Tess.' Foxy held her against him, stopping her from running into the restaurant. 'It's too bad in there. Not safe.'

She looked at Foxy with panic in her eyes. 'Where's Griff?'

Foxy shook his head.

'WHERE'S GRIFF?' she screamed, struggling against him. 'Tell me he's not in there.'

'I think he is.'

'We need to get him,' she yelled, trying to wriggle out of Foxy's grip. 'GRIFF,' she screamed, sobbing.

'Keep back, please,' a passing fireman said. 'We're doing everything we can.'

Foxy pulled her back further from the door and she sagged against him.

'They're on it,' he said, wrapping his arms around her as she tried to break free. 'We're just gonna have to wait.'

They held each other tightly as they watched the firemen feed in hoses and heard them shouting to each other.

Tess jumped as another siren sounded; an ambulance had arrived.

'Oh God. Oh God,' she moaned. She heard a loud bang from inside and more shouting by the fire crew.

'GRIFF,' she shouted. Her heart pounded as fear tore through her at the prospect of Griff being hurt, or worse, not being around any more. She realised in a split second how she felt about him. She was terrified she was going to lose him.

'It'll be OK,' Foxy said. 'It has to be OK.'

A fireman stepped out; his face sooty. He removed his breathing apparatus. 'How many people did you think were in here?' he asked.

Foxy met the fireman's eyes. 'Just one, I think,' he said quietly.

Tess started sobbing. 'You need to find Griff. He's in there. You need to find him.'

§ § §

Griff had been fighting to get his hands free. He knew he had a split second. Everything seemed to happen in slow motion after Mark had flicked the lighter on. Griff had watched as Mark drew his arm back and hurled it into the kitchen. With a roar, Griff had thrown himself towards the pot wash and strained his arms to pull his hands free. Scrabbling for purchase on the slippery floor he'd launched himself towards the cold store, just managing to open the door as the fire ignited. He'd been thrown sideways by the force and he'd felt something hot hit his face and smelt his hair burning. Fighting to get in, he'd slammed the door and thrown himself on the floor. The door was thick and he'd hoped he'd be safe in there until at least either the fire reduced or the fire brigade came and put the fire out.

Shaking uncontrollably, he leant against the door, breathing heavily. How had he not *known* about Mark? How had he not *seen* it when he was at home? He assumed they were friends. That Mark was just being a mate and looking out for Gabby.

Closing his eyes, he tried to breathe deeply to try and calm his thumping heart. He could smell smoke. He rubbed his hands over his hair, feeling some of it singed. He touched his face and felt blood and a cut or burn of some sort. He felt pain on his leg and realised his trouser leg was on fire. Grabbing a tea towel covering a bowl, he patted his leg, putting the flames out, wincing as he touched scorched skin.

Part of him wanted to open the door to see if he could stop the fire but he knew he'd be instantly engulfed.

Instead, completely overcome with emotion, he sat on the floor and sobbed into his hands.

§ § §

The fire brigade got the fire under control; the loud bang had been a small gas canister for the catering blowtorch that had exploded in the heat. The fire brigade had dampened it down to safe levels and had finally opened the door to the cold room, finding Griff lying on his side coughing as the room filled with smoke.

The fire team looked at the state of the outside of the cold room door, at the melted seals, and concluded that Griff was a very lucky man to have escaped death.

Two firemen helped Griff to stand. They led him through the ruined kitchen and through the restaurant. Griff's face was blackened from smoke, he had blood on his face, hands and leg, and he was coughing relentlessly.

Snowflakes were still falling and mixing with the smoke, dancing crazily in the frigid night air against the lights from the emergency vehicles. Griff coughed again as he stepped out of the restaurant.

'GRIFF!' screamed Tess, wrestling free from Foxy. She ran over and flung herself at him, almost knocking him over. He coughed again and his knees almost gave out from relief to be free and to see Tess. Tess and the paramedics helped him get into the ambulance. He tried to hold her off with a weak smile.

'Watch out, I'm covered in petrol.'

Her face was sooty, with tear tracks down her cheeks.

'I don't care,' she said, stepping forwards, and bending to kiss him. 'Thank God. I thought I'd lost you.' She wrapped her arms around him and sobbed into his shoulder. 'I thought you'd gone.'

The paramedics cleaned up Griff's wounds and gave him oxygen. Once free of the smoke, he felt better and the coughing receded. After a while, Foxy helped him down to his flat so he could wash off the petrol.

The fire brigade spent time damping down to ensure no embers were present, and after a long wait, Tess was finally allowed to accompany the fire chief back into the restaurant.

'Seems largely superficial out here,' he said, gesturing to the restaurant. 'Apart from smoke damage. The bulk of the damage is in the kitchen. Some of the stainless-steel stuff might be just about salvageable. But I'm pretty sure it all needs gutting.'

'Jesus,' Tess said. 'Thank God we've got insurance.'

'We know it was arson. The police have him in custody.'

Tess swallowed back the tears that had been building since she had seen how close Griff had come to dying. 'It could have been so much worse,' she whispered.

The fire chief nodded. 'He's a lucky man. To have the idea to get in the cold room. Saved his life. I'm just pleased we got to him in time. Much longer and it would have been a different story.'

Tess exhaled heavily. The pressure of the last few weeks had mounted up. The fire chief escorted her back outside. He pulled a face. 'Do you want the rest of the bad news?'

'Oh. More? What is it?'

'I want a structural engineer to check out the corner of the kitchen and your flat above before I let you go back in there.'

She dropped her head and moaned.

'Have you got anywhere else you can stay?' he asked.

'No... I—'

'Yes, she has,' a voice beside Tess spoke.

She turned to see Griff, fresh from the shower. He was dressed in an Endure fleece and trousers that Foxy had donated. He had an angry red scorch on his forehead, and he had a large dressing on the lower part of one side of his face.

He placed an arm around her shoulders and rested his head against hers.

'She'll be staying with me.'

'You've got your work cut out rebuilding this place again,' the fire chief said. 'Mind you, some like a fresh start, don't they?' He rubbed his hands. 'Right. We're off. Try and enjoy the rest of your Christmas.'

They watched the team pack up and leave.

Tess turned to Griff. Tears poured down her face. 'Griff, I... I'm so sorry... I had no idea. I'm so ashamed. Maggie told me. I'm so s—'

Griff stroked a tear away from her cheek. 'Sshh.'

'No, I thought you'd... oh God, when I thought you'd been hurt... I couldn't...'

Griff stroked her face. 'Are you saying you might be warming to me?' he murmured.

She sniffed and stifled a laugh. She met his eyes.

'I think I might be, yes,' she whispered. 'Possibly a bit more than "warming".'

'Fire chief's orders are that you come and stay with me,' he said gently. 'Reckon you can handle it?'

She sniffed and gave him a watery mile. 'I'll give it a go, as long as Frank can come.'

'I can work with that.' He tucked a strand of her hair behind her ear gently. 'Don't forget, I've got phase two of my kitchen repertoire to put into action.'

She smiled and wrapped her arms around his neck, pulling him in for a kiss.

'I'm game if you are.' She stopped just before their lips met. 'One condition.'

'Anything,' he said, looking deep into her eyes.

'That spider in the bathroom has got to go.'

He laughed, pulling her close. 'What? No way! He's part of the family now.'

THREE MONTHS LATER

'I think it's pretty damn good,' Tess said, as she stood in the road and looked up at the sign on the restaurant. 'Don't you?'

Griff grinned, draping an arm across her shoulders, pulling her in close. He kissed her. 'I love it.'

'Scared that it's all ours now?'

'Absolutely terrified.'

She chuckled and turned to him. 'Really?'

'Good terrified though.'

She slipped her arms around his waist as they looked at the new signage for the refurbished restaurant. She sighed heavily.

'What's the sigh for?' Griff asked.

'It's happy. When I left nursing, I never for a million years thought that months later I'd be running a restaurant with the man I love.'

'Who's that then?' Griff quipped. 'Where is he? I'll kill him.'

'Stop it.' She nudged him. 'I'm serious.'

Griff kissed her gently. 'Never in a million years I thought I would get a second chance at life, doing what I love, with the woman I love.'

Tess smiled happily. 'Best you don't fuck it up then.'

'Absolutely.' He gave her a quick squeeze. 'You ready?'

'I am.'

Together, they walked into the refurbished restaurant which was packed full of friends and family to celebrate the relaunch of the renamed, The Gannet, now under new management. As they entered the restaurant, Tess's sister, Lorraine, clapped and cheered, and let off a handful of party poppers.

Smiling and greeting everyone, they walked past Maggie, who was standing with Foxy. She nudged him as she looked upon the couple fondly.

'I think I *might* need to buy a hat soon,' she whispered excitedly, as they walked past. 'We've not had a wedding here for ages!'

Overhearing, Griff turned and winked at Maggie. 'Heard that. You might wanna get cracking on that, Maggie. Between you and me, it might be a bit sooner than you think. I'm not wasting any more time.'

Many thanks for reading Christmas in Castleby and I hope you enjoyed it. If you'd like to read other books in the series, head over to Amazon or books can also be purchased through my website, www.jmsimpsonauthor.co.uk.

ACKNOWLEDGEMENTS

Right from the start I've jokingly called this book a 'novella' – but it is in fact the length of most normal novels, so it's not a novella in the slightest! For me though, it's certainly not the length of a normal Castleby book. I wanted to try a Christmas special to see how it did. If people like it, I may well do another one, perhaps picking up characters from the series and focusing more on them in a 'special.' So, we'll see how it goes! But! Never fear, there is more to come in the Castleby series and other books too. Now, onto the thanks bit.

Thanks as ever go to my first readers; I am always so very grateful for your comments and insight. I am genuinely touched that you are keen to read what I produce and I value all the feedback. Massive thanks also go to the wonderful Julie & Joanna for doing final read throughs!

Thanks to my editor, Heather Fitt. One of these days I WILL remember that people are who(s) and not that(s), which I think is the one thing you consistently pick me up on. Huge thanks go to Lorna

Hinde for her wonderful, sunny, helpful approach in proofreading this and all her efforts to put my many wrongs right.

Massive shout-out and thanks to Ken Dawson Design for a stunning cover. I gave you a very tight brief and you have done a superb job. I am very grateful for you indulging me with all the tiny tweaks too.

Endless love and thanks, as ever, go to the wonderful reviewers and bloggers who were so enthusiastic to be involved in reviewing this early on. I am so very grateful for the love you have for Castleby and how you champion the series as much as you do. For a struggling indie author like me, trying to get some traction, this makes the world of difference.

Thanks to my friends and my 'crew'. For doing what they always do. Supporting me, looking interested (when they're really not) and being there for me through the highs (really not that many) and the lows (plenty of these). I know I'm hammering away on a keyboard when I could be spending time with you all. So, I'm sorry if my head isn't always in the game. I just hope one day you'll be proud.

Finally, thanks to my amazing readers. The love for the Castleby series is something I never expected. I equally didn't expect quite so many of you to have SUCH a thing for Foxy either! Your love and support for the series is awesome and deeply moves me. I feel like I can't thank you enough for taking Castleby into your hearts and minds, but I guess the only thing to do is to keep it going and to also give you other communities to fall in love with. I'm hoping you'll all love The Whistlers Peak series which is out soon.

Thanks again for reading the book. I hope you enjoyed it. I'll stop whittering on now – there's important writing to do.

Printed in Great Britain
by Amazon